MW01135758

INSPIRED

BY

MURDER

AN EMERALD CITY THRILLER

AUDREY J.
COLE

ISBN: 1722043342
ISBN-13: 978-1722043346

For my neighbor, the drummer

CHAPTER ONE

Eric's blood pressure felt like it had doubled by the time he pulled into the parking lot of his psychiatry practice. He sped into his reserved parking spot before slamming on the brakes. His brake pedal pulsated under his foot from the activation of his anti-lock braking system atop the black ice. He swore as his six-month-old BMW slid into the metal sign post marked *RESERVED*. The one day a year Seattle had black ice he had to be late for work.

He got out and walked on literal thin ice to the main entrance of his office. His body tensed from the cold. Seeing his name, *Eric Leroy, M.D.*, etched across the glass depressed him lately. He knew it should be enough. It should be something to be proud of, but he wasn't. He was bored with psychiatry. What he cared about was murder. He wanted to be a writer. A good writer. A great writer. A gifted writer. One who wrote bestsellers and won Pulitzers.

He felt a rush of heat when he opened the door. *Crikey.* Patricia Watts, his eight o'clock appointment, was already seated in his newly-remodeled waiting room. He wasn't sure why this surprised him when it was after eight fifteen.

She tossed aside her magazine when he came through the door. From the look on her face, you'd think she'd been treading water instead of parking her ass in a comfy chair and catching up on celebrity gossip while she waited for him.

"Morning." Eric heard the voice of his twenty-two-year-old secretary. "Working on your novel again this morning?"

He turned to see her, bright-eyed as usual, waiting eagerly for his response. Telling her about his book was a mistake. She half-smiled at him from behind her desk while she chomped vigorously on a large piece of gum.

"Just a lot of traffic today," he said.

"Novel?" asked his eight o'clock, as though she were part of the conversation.

He pretended like he hadn't heard the question. Begrudgingly, Eric marched toward his office but turned back before he reached the door.

"Come on back, Patricia," he said in a professional tone, trying to rebuild the boundary in their relationship.

He closed the door behind her as she threw down her purse and plopped herself into one of his leather chairs as if she'd been on her feet for hours. The seat cushion let out a *whoosh* as it deflated. Eric took a seat in his chair across from her and tried his best to look interested in whatever she might have to say. He reached for his notebook and pen.

"How about you tell me how things have been going this last week." He tried to not stare at her cankle crease that became visible below her pant seam after she sat down.

"Well, I wish you hadn't been late because I have quite a lot I want to talk about."

So talk about it, he thought. "Right. Let's get started."

He leaned back in his chair and pretended to be engaged as Patricia rattled on about her latest woes. Judging solely by her looks, she was a hard woman to figure out. Her straight gray bob, cut to a blunt line above her jaw, suggested she was uptight. The lack of attention she gave to her figure, however, suggested something else.

For the last six months, he'd been listening to Patricia bitch about pretty much everyone she encountered. Her problems were always someone else's fault. As he'd had the pleasure of getting to know her, he'd observed Patricia was overindulged and completely absorbed with herself. At fifty-two, he surmised her personality bore no hope of improvement. At least, none that he could offer her. If it weren't at the cost of sounding too dramatic, he'd say listening to her had become beyond exhausting.

Eric doodled on his notebook as she talked. If he could only tell her the truth in less than clinical terms: *you're a whiner. You're a big, fat whiner.* Maybe then she'd be forced to look inward. But saying something to that effect would most likely lead to the loss of his practice. So, he allowed her to continue bitching about the newest pain in her ass, while he allowed his mind to drift back to his book. Where it belonged.

His mind also began to psychoanalyze itself after losing interest in the hopeless, self-obsessed Patricia. His mother was Australian and his father came from a long line of American patriarchs. They both had a love for the arts. Why he had decided to become a doctor he did not know. He realized now that he needed to create.

He was aware that Patricia had moved the focus of her bitching toward her husband. *Poor bastard.* Eric had been married once. She was nothing like Patricia. She was beautiful. Patricia was still complaining when he looked down at his wiry hand, startled by what he had drawn.

He had doodled Patricia lying in a puddle of her own blood with a dismembered arm laying off to the side. A ferocious beast looked ready to devour her, its jaw open wide, exposing ginormous fangs.

Interesting. Must've been his overactive subconscious.

Shockingly, Patricia said something intriguing enough to make him look up.

"I think this all started when I saw my brother die."

"How did he die?" he asked, genuinely curious.

"He was murdered."

Eric snapped forward in his chair. "Go on." He focused on Patricia for the first time that morning.

"I try not think about it."

"Do you think you can tell me what happened?"

He thought she would benefit from talking about it, especially after she brought it up. He also hoped it would be something he could use in his novel.

"I was twelve and he was eight. Charlie was his name." She paused, and he could see she was starting to tear up.

He handed her a box of tissues from the table beside him.

"Take your time," he said, hoping she'd get on with it.

She dabbed her eyes and seemed to compose herself. "It was a hot summer night. July. I had left my bedroom window open for a breeze. My mother's boyfriend was in a drunken rage."

Oh, drat. A domestic affair. But maybe he could use it. He listened closely as she continued.

"I closed the window so the noise wouldn't travel around the neighborhood. He was beating my mother, I could hear it all the way down the hall. I knew better than to interfere. But not Charlie."

She stopped to dab her eyes again.

"He finished with my mother but still needed someone to beat on. I heard his heavy footsteps come down the hall. I knew there was nothing I could do to stop him. He flung open my bedroom door and I braced myself for what was coming. He stumbled into my room and, at first, all I saw behind him was the poker stick. I didn't see Charlie until after he swung the poker into the back of my mother's boyfriend's head. But the blow didn't even faze him. He ripped the poker stick out of Charlie's hands before he took another swing...."

He waited in silence. After a minute, she went on.

"I'll never forget the look on Charlie's face after he died." Tears now freely ran down her face, and she made no effort to wipe them away.

Eric found it hard to feel sorry for her. He only felt for poor little Charlie. He wished it had been Patricia the boyfriend had killed. Charlie sounded nice.

When their time was up and she had collected herself, he offered his condolences and gave her his standard, *Well, I think you've got a lot to think about* response before pushing her out the door. He liked that last bit about the look on Charlie's face. He pictured Charlie, his soft brown eyes staring into nothingness and his hair matted with blood. *That* he could use in his book. At least their session hadn't been a complete waste.

Eric was eager to get home that evening and work on his book. Patricia's story had inspired him. He let himself into his small, modern apartment, poured a glass of wine, and sat down to write. He sat by his floor-to-ceiling window, enjoying the company of the city lights. The evening skyline was a mix of modern skyscrapers and smaller, historic buildings.

He could've easily bought a house in the suburbs with more space and a yard. But that felt like it was for someone with a wife, kids, and a dog. Not that he would've minded a dog.

So here he was, over forty, living in a small apartment, with his only heir to the world being his psychiatry practice full of self-obsessed, albeit well-paying clients. But that would all change when he published his bestseller.

The words flowed easily that night. But when he reread the pages, he knew it wasn't the edge he needed. The scenario wasn't quite right for his book. His writing felt more tangible and had improved after hearing Patricia's account. But he needed something more.

He shut down his laptop and had a terrifying thought. What if he died tomorrow, before he had written and published his brilliant novel? Before he accomplished his true purpose for being on this earth? It would mean he was no better than Patricia, just a waste of human life.

The week dragged on and he attended several more pity parties at his office for many different clients. The rush he'd felt from Patricia's account had already faded; he realized he still had a whole novel to write and was out of ideas. He wanted to craft at least three more murders but had no life experience to draw from.

He was down in the dumps again the next Monday morning when he met with Patricia. She looked the same as always, all her efforts going to her hairdo and none toward her physique. He crossed one of his lanky legs over the other and half-listened to her complain about her husband going out of town for the week on business. His mind drifted back to her account of Charlie's slaying. It dawned on him that he was jealous she had witnessed her brother's murder. That was exactly the sort of thing he needed for his book.

He wanted to write a masterpiece so bad he could kill for it. For reasons he couldn't explain, he examined Patricia from across the room, as a hunter would eye his game. She continued to grumble about her husband's business trip. This gave him an idea.

CHAPTER TWO

"We should do this more often," Adams said.

Stephenson glanced at his partner as he took the exit for the Auburn Airport. "More often? I don't know how often we can make an arrest by answering a Craigslist ad for items stolen during a home invasion turned double homicide."

"No, I mean go undercover. Even if it is my day off." Adams pulled his sweatshirt over his holstered firearm. "I'm good at this."

"You better be good at this. I'm planning to make a clean arrest and make it home in one piece."

"Don't worry, we will. What could go wrong when you're with me? I should be the one concerned; you're the rookie here."

Stephenson smirked. Although he'd been working homicide less than two years, he had proven he could handle himself in a life and death situation.

"Does it seem weird to you that these guys are storing their stolen goods in an airplane hangar? That can't be cheap rent," Adams said.

"They're not renting it. After Jason told me where to meet him, I checked and found the hangar is registered to Walter Perry, Jason and Bryce's father. He died in 2012."

"That makes more sense. How convenient for them to inherit such a large storage space when they make their living burglarizing homes."

Stephenson turned the unmarked vehicle into the airport and slowly headed in the direction of the hangars. As they got closer, he spotted the two brothers standing in front of a T-hangar halfway down the row.

Stephenson recognized Jason and Bryce Perry, both convicted felons who'd been the prime suspects in a series of home invasions over the last few months. When their latest robbery ended in the fatal stabbing of the two homeowners, he and Adams had taken over the investigation. Their deaths were two of the most brutal killings he'd ever seen. He stopped the car a few feet in front of them.

"Let's do this," Adams said before stepping out.

Jason approached Stephenson as he got out of the car. "I thought you said you couldn't bring anyone to help you? My brother could've stayed home."

"Tony said he could come last minute." Stephenson motioned to his partner. "I have a bad back, so I figured I could use the extra help. The TV looked pretty heavy."

"It's not *that* heavy, but whatever."

Jason looked back and forth between Adams and Stephenson before opening the door on the far side of the hangar. He and Bryce went in first. Bryce held the door open for Stephenson and Adams to follow.

Jason flicked on the overhead light. Although the hangar was only a third full, the two detectives could see it contained everything they were hoping for. Two large flat screens leaned against one wall. TV stands, a stereo, speakers, all kinds of electronics, home office equipment, and a few pieces of accent furniture were also stored in the large space. It was the final piece of evidence they needed to make their arrest.

"So here's the TV," Jason said, pointing to the larger of two flat screens.

Adams pulled out his badge when Bryce turned around to face them. Stephenson reached inside his jacket and placed his thumb on the release lever of his gun holster.

"Jason and Bryce Perry, you're under arrest for—"

Seeing Adams' badge, Jason shoved his brother into Stephenson and bolted toward the door. Stephenson pushed Bryce out of his arms. Adams drew his firearm and fixed it on Bryce while Stephenson turned and chased after Jason.

"Get down on the ground and put your hands on your head!" Adams ordered.

Bryce froze, staring at Adams in wide-eyed shock.

"Now!" Adams said.

Keeping his eyes on the detective, Bryce slowly got to his knees and complied.

Stephenson ran out of the hangar in time to see Jason disappear around the corner of the building. Stephenson sprinted after him. When he rounded the corner, he watched Jason turn left down another row of hangars. After turning down the same row, Stephenson picked up speed and started to close the gap.

A small, bright yellow aircraft was parked outside an open hangar and Stephenson realized Jason was headed straight for it. Stephenson watched the pilot manually spin the propeller before the engine roared to life.

Stephenson spotted the gun in Jason's hand as he neared the plane. The pilot threw up his hands when he saw the gun pointed at his head. Stephenson stopped twenty feet from the plane and drew his 9mm. He raised his weapon at Jason, but no longer had a clean shot.

Jason stood behind the pilot with his gun to his head, using him as a human shield.

"Drop the weapon!" Stephenson yelled over the rumble of the plane's engine.

Jason ignored the order and backed up to the door of the plane. With his arm around the pilot's neck and his gun pressed against the side of his head, Jason climbed into the small aircraft and pulled the pilot in after him.

Stephenson aimed his gun at the plane's windshield, but Jason sat behind the pilot who completely blocked his shot. The plane's engine grew louder and the aircraft came directly toward him. Stephenson jumped out of its path as the plane picked up speed.

The aircraft sped toward the taxiway as Stephenson holstered his gun and raced after it. He pushed himself as hard as he could. Despite the plane's increasing speed, Stephenson managed to come within arm's length of the tail.

The plane sped up and the distance between him and the tail widened. When the plane slowed to make the turn onto the taxiway, Stephenson knew this was his only chance to stop it. Already running as fast as he could, Stephenson threw himself forward and dove onto the tail. His hands slipped, but he managed to grab hold of the rudder cable. His feet dragged violently underneath him as the plane veered to the right.

His ankle folded underneath him against the pavement as the plane pulled him across the taxiway, but he was struggling too hard to hold on to the cable to notice. The plane bounced across the grass that separated the taxiway from the runway. Stephenson strained to maintain his grip as the plane swerved onto the adjoining runway.

Out the corner of his eye, he spotted Adams speeding across the taxiway in their unmarked vehicle. Adams drove over the grass and brought the car to a stop in front of the plane. The plane took a sharp turn to avoid colliding with the vehicle and Stephenson cried out as his legs scraped against the pavement.

One of his hands lost its grip as the plane bumped across the grass before continuing back onto the taxiway. The plane took a hard left, causing his other hand to slip off the cable. He rolled to a stop as the plane crashed into a parked four-seat Cessna.

The propeller broke in two upon impact. Half of it landed a few feet from where Stephenson lay on the taxiway. Oblivious to the pain in his ankle, he got to his feet and rushed toward the plane. Adams had gotten out of the car and followed right behind him.

"Are you nuts?" Stephenson heard his partner call out.

He ignored the question and kept running toward the plane.

"You okay?" Adams asked when they approached the back of the plane.

Stephenson drew his firearm before moving to the front of the aircraft. Adams did the same.

"I'm fine."

Stephenson stood at the door of the plane and aimed his gun at Jason. The pilot was visibly terrified but looked only mildly injured.

"Hands above your head!"

He kept his gun fixed while he waited for Jason to comply. Slowly, Jason raised both hands above his head. Stephenson used his left hand to open the door of the plane.

"Get out of the plane and get down on the ground. Keep your hands on your head."

Jason complied and Adams handcuffed his hands behind his back.

"Are you hurt?" Stephenson asked the pilot who was breathing heavily in the front seat.

He rubbed his temple. "I hit my head when we crashed, but I think I'm all right."

"Help is on the way," Adams said. "I've already called for backup and an ambulance. They should be here any minute."

Adams left Jason lying face down on the ground while he retrieved Jason's pistol from the back seat. Stephenson helped the pilot out of his light aircraft. After Stephenson made sure he had no visible injuries, the pilot took a seat on the ground away from Jason while they waited for more help to arrive.

Adams ran back to the car to radio their backup unit and let them know they were on the taxiway.

"Are you crazy?" Adams asked after he got back from making the call. "You almost gave me a heart attack."

"Sorry," Stephenson said, suddenly aware of the pain in his ankle. "I couldn't let him get away. Especially not with a hostage. Jason wouldn't have had any use for the pilot once they landed somewhere."

They heard the wail of their backup unit's siren as it pulled into the airport.

"How did you know the plane couldn't take off with you holding on to the tail?"

Stephenson glanced back at the plane before turning to his partner. "I didn't."

CHAPTER THREE

Stephenson's phone vibrated in his pocket as he stepped outside the boutique, family-owned jewelry store ten minutes east of downtown Seattle. He saw it was Adams and continued walking down the busy street to his car.

"Hey. How'd it go?"

"I just finished booking them. They'll have their first court date tomorrow. What did your x-rays show?"

"A couple bruised ribs and a sprained ankle."

"I'm surprised it wasn't worse. What did the sergeant say?"

"That he's glad I wasn't killed and to never do anything that dangerous again. But he understands my desperation to catch Jason and keep him from killing the pilot. He didn't say so, but I'm sure he would've done the same thing."

"You're lucky McKinnon is the only person in the department who's crazier than you when it comes to catching a killer. How long are you off for?"

"I'm hoping only a week. I'll see the doctor on Friday about coming back to work."

"Get some rest. I know you probably won't, but take more time off if you need to. Are you home now?"

Stephenson looked down at the small bag he carried from the jewelry store. "Actually, I had an errand to run."

"An errand? After you nearly died? Please tell me you're joking."

"I didn't nearly die. And no, I'm not joking."

"You're unbelievable."

Stephenson pictured his partner shaking his head on the other end of the call.

"Must've been an important errand," Adams added.

"It was."

"Well, I'm definitely not running any errands on my way home. I'm exhausted from watching you in action today."

Stephenson smiled. "Next time I'll let you chase the runner."

"There's just one problem with that."

"What?" Stephenson opened the door to his car.

"I don't like to run."

He let out a short laugh. "That's what I thought."

CHAPTER FOUR

Eric stayed up practically all night thinking of how he would kill Patricia. By the next evening, he had a plan. He'd done an incredible amount of research in the last twenty-four hours and felt certain he could pull off her murder without a hitch. Or a trace. Her husband's business trip was short, only two days. He'd be flying out of Sea-Tac on a red-eye to New York tomorrow night, and he planned to kill her right after he left.

He remembered Patricia telling him the conference her husband was speaking at paid for him to park at the airport, so she didn't have to drop him or pick him up. Eric would make sure her time of death was right after her husband left for the airport so he'd be the prime suspect. Or, at least, he would be after Eric sent the police Patricia's medical record that he'd doctored up to incriminate him.

He checked his mailbox first thing when he got to his apartment building and was ecstatic to find his lock-picking kit had arrived. How he loved living in a world with overnight shipping.

Once inside his apartment, he was filled with a nervous excitement. He gathered everything he would need for tomorrow night. He'd have to time it perfectly to ensure her husband went down for the crime. At least he would no longer have to live with Patricia. He was about to do the man a favor. This made him smile.

He made a neat little pile on his dining table with his leather gloves, lock-picking kit, and a black baseball cap. He couldn't risk forgetting something. A gun would have been easier. But, being from Australia, he had always despised Americans for their overuse of guns. He shivered at the thought. Guns just seemed so...violent.

He spent the rest of the evening going over every detail he'd preplanned in his head. Finally, he headed for bed, assured his plan was foolproof, if not ingenious. All this research and planning gave him a greater respect for murderers. At least, those who got away with it. Getting away with murder was no small accomplishment.

He climbed into bed with a book to calm his nerves. It was a romance, which wasn't his usual genre, but he needed something to relax him. It was also a *New York Times* bestseller, and he figured it wouldn't hurt to check out his competition.

The book was written by a bloke from the Pacific Northwest, the story taking place in Seattle. The author's name was familiar to him even though he'd never read any of his other novels. One of his patients must've mentioned him.

He snapped the book closed after only ten minutes upon reading the line: *Winter came and went.*

Winter never came and went in Seattle. It lingered and stayed way beyond its welcome until it seemed it would never end. By mid-February, the entire outside world looked to have turned a shade of gray. Life was sucked dry of color. Finally, when it felt like there was nothing left to live for, a tiny patch of sun would peek through the clouds just long enough to give one hope that spring was, although late, on its way.

No wonder he made so much money as a psychiatrist. Over the nearly twenty years he'd lived in Seattle, he'd heard several people say they didn't mind the weather. This never made any sense to him. Winter in Seattle was akin to watching a Renee Zellweger movie. The ending never came soon enough.

He turned out the lights, the book spoiling any further appetite for reading. He'd no sooner rested his head against his pillow when he felt a steady, rhythmic vibration in his head. He knew instantly what it was. The drumming. It was even louder than usual. He tried to ignore it, but he could feel it resonate in his bones. He needed to rest; he couldn't afford to be disturbed. He had a murder to pull off tomorrow. And not just pull off, but get away with. But only if he kept a clear head.

He'd tolerated the all-too-frequent noise coming from his neighboring apartment ever since the mediocre musician had moved in two months before. This was only because he was a night owl and the drumming always quit before he went to bed.

The drumming stopped. But who knew for how long, and he couldn't risk not being at his best tomorrow. He threw back his comforter, walked into the hall of his building, and knocked on the drummer's door. He waited for a minute and was about to knock again when the door opened.

There stood his twenty-something, good-for-nothing neighbor. His curly, shoulder-length hair looked its usual mess. He was dressed in sweats and a worn-out t-shirt.

The drummer seemed to be home at all hours of the day and he'd never seen him wear anything nicer than what he wore right now. He'd wondered on occasion how the drummer could afford to live in such an expensive building in the heart of downtown and had concluded his parents must be footing the bill.

"Hiya neighbor." He smiled. Eric didn't.

Who says that? he wondered. He realized the answer to his question was staring him in the face, grinning like an idiot while showing off his perfectly straight teeth.

He was glad he'd never had children. Imagine spending all that money on orthodontics only to have them grow up to be nothing more than an unemployed, semi-talented drummer who annoyed the other residents in his apartment building.

"Hi," he said. "I came to ask if you could stop drumming for the night, given the time and the fact that this is an apartment building."

His neighbor ran a hand through his hair. "Oh. Sure, man. No problem. Sorry."

He hadn't expected him to be so agreeable. He'd already planned on aggressively convincing him to be quiet. But apparently there was nothing more to be said.

"Thank you." He walked back to his room, perplexed by the obnoxious drummer having been so polite.

He lay his head back on his pillow and reveled in the quiet. Would he really be capable of murder tomorrow? It was a silly question to ask himself because he already knew the answer. He was, and had always been, capable. In retrospect, he'd always carried a grudge for the squeamish and weak because he had the ability to do whatever necessary to fulfill his destiny. No matter what. And killing Patricia was the only way to take his writing to the next level.

After tomorrow, he would never be the same. He could never take it back or erase it from his memory. He wondered how his life might have been different if he'd never come to America. There were some things he missed about Australia, like decent people. But he had grown accustomed to life in America, even preferred it. It was now his home.

When his excitement dissipated enough for him to fall asleep, he dreamt of Charlie.

CHAPTER FIVE

Eric couldn't stop daydreaming about killing Patricia the next day as he suffered through listening to all the pathetic problems of his patients. He envisioned her lying on her bathroom floor, her eyes bulging and her pale skin with a bluish hue. It grew harder to fake interest in his patients as the day went on. Fortunately, most of them were too consumed with themselves to notice.

Finally, his workday came to an end. The sun had already set when he pulled out of the parking lot right behind his last appointment and tailgated the slow-moving traffic back to his apartment. As soon as he let himself in, he went to his room and changed into running tights, athletic shorts, and a zip-up sweatshirt. This way, if anyone saw him in Patricia's neighborhood, they would just assume he was out for an evening jog.

He tied his running shoes and checked the time on his watch. He'd made better time than he thought getting home, and it was too early for him to go to Patricia's. Her husband's flight wouldn't leave for nearly another four hours.

He wondered how to fill the time until he went to her house and realized he was starving. He'd been so preoccupied with killing Patricia he'd forgotten to eat lunch. He surmised it would be best not to have low blood sugar when pulling off a murder and went into his kitchen to make a sandwich.

He sat down at his dining table next to his killing supplies. It surprised him how much he enjoyed his ham and cheese on whole wheat. No condiments. That was how people got fat. He was nervous, yes, but not too nervous to enjoy a good sandwich. The next half hour passed slowly, and he gathered the pile off the table. It would be better to be ahead of schedule than behind.

He used his free hand to wipe the crumbs off the table, take his plate into the kitchen, and load it into the dishwasher before leaving. He hated coming home to a mess.

Avoiding traffic cameras on the way to Patricia's Madison Park home took longer than he planned. He didn't put her address into his GPS in the unlikely event he became a suspect, but he'd found it on a map earlier and had a good idea of where he was headed.

He found McGilvra and turned onto it. He slowed when he saw 3890, counting aloud until the street number reached 3898. He made sure there were no other cars on the street and stopped in front of the two-story home.

Although it was dark, he could tell the front yard was immaculately landscaped. Much more than he would've expected, knowing Patricia. He couldn't imagine Patricia wearing gardening gloves in less-than-ideal weather pruning the bushes or weeding the lawn. Either her husband oversaw the yardwork, or they paid to have it maintained.

Blue lights flashed from inside a front room window. Just as expected, Patricia was home watching TV. He turned his car around at the end of her cul de sac and parked on an unlit part of the street a few blocks away. He checked the time on his phone before slipping it back into his pocket. Patricia's husband's flight would depart in just over two hours. It would take him about forty-five minutes to get to the airport, so Patricia should be all alone.

It dawned on him as he got out of his car that he should've come earlier and watched for Patricia's husband to leave the house. That way, he could've killed her almost immediately after his departure. *Oh well*, he thought, *by the time someone found her body, her time of death would be only an estimation anyway. An hour or so shouldn't make that big a difference.*

He felt his sweatshirt pocket for his lock-picking kit and gloves. Satisfied he had both, he got out of his car and zipped his keys into his shorts. He slipped on the gloves, assuring himself no one would find them odd in this weather.

His blood pumped with excitement as he jogged down the quiet street in the freezing cold. By the time he reached Patricia's, the ache in his ears and the burn in his throat from the cold reminded him of why he did indoor yoga to keep in shape. He stopped in her driveway, seeing his breath as it escaped his lungs.

The dimly-lit front yard made it easy to approach her fence. He reached over the wood structure and undid the gate latch. His pulse quickened as he trod softly along the gravel on the side of the house.

This was the first time, in all his preparation, that he stopped to wonder if she had a dog. He moved slowly, on his guard against a beast that might jump out and attack him.

But the yard remained quiet. Upon reaching her back door without having his plan ruined by some stupid mutt, he felt himself relax. He chided himself for worrying; Patricia was far too lazy to take care of a dog.

He tried the door and was glad to find it locked. It would've been a shame to not use his lock-picking kit when he'd come so prepared. He pulled out his tools and started to pick the lock. It wasn't quite as easy as the guy had made it look on YouTube. But after a minute, he heard the sweet click of the lock come free.

He entered a small, narrow room and quietly closed the door behind him. He listened for a security alarm, but the house was quiet except for the sound of the TV playing down the hall. He knew Patricia had an alarm system, but she'd told him in one of their sessions that she never set the alarm until she went to bed. So far, so good. The door at the end of the room was open to the hall. The hall was dark except for the flickering blue light from the TV.

He moved toward the door, his running shoes sticking to the linoleum floor. He could make out a washer and dryer against the wall and realized he was in the laundry room. Fortunately, the sound from the TV muffled his footsteps.

He peered out into the hall, making sure it was empty before he stepped out. The light from the TV illuminated the doorway at the end of the hall, which looked to open to a large living area. He paused in the hallway and listened. It sounded like a sitcom and when laughter from a studio audience sounded through the speakers, he heard Patricia let out a deep chuckle. Although he despised her, he was happy for her to have one last laugh. If she only knew what he had in store for her.

He turned and moved in the opposite direction down the hall. He needed to find her bedroom. The other end of the hall opened to an entryway and stairwell. A light shone from above the stairs, and he decided to try upstairs for her room.

He looked at the framed photos that lined the wall as he ascended the carpeted staircase. He was about halfway up when he realized Patricia wasn't in any of them. In fact, the two people who were pictured in most of the photos were a woman in her forties and her teenage daughter.

Patricia didn't have any children. It was the one thing he liked about her. His phone chimed to the sound of his reminder alarm. He scrambled for the phone in his pocket, cursing himself for not putting it on silent. He held up his phone and fumbled to silence it. The words, *Reminder: Kill Patricia* lit up his screen.

He cursed again at his phone when he caught movement at the top of the stairs out the corner of his eyes. He recognized the skinny teenage girl from the photographs standing at the top of the stairwell. Her curly brown hair came down to her waist, and, despite it being below freezing outside, she wore only a spaghetti-strap tank top and very short shorts.

Her eyes widened upon seeing him, and she let out a high-pitched scream as he turned and ran down the stairs. Obviously, somehow, he had gotten the wrong address. He immediately blamed Patricia. *Had she moved and not told him?*

The girl was still screaming when he reached the bottom of the stairwell. He ran toward the front door when he heard his phone skid across the tiled entry.

"Crikey."

When he stepped forward to pick it up he saw a woman running toward him from down the hall. He recognized her short, dark hair from the family photographs. He swiped his phone off the floor just as she grabbed a vase off the entry way table and threw it at his head. He dove to the side to avoid the vase. The porcelain shattered as it hit the floor next to him. The girl continued to scream at the top of the stairs.

The woman seemed to be looking for something else to throw at him as he stood. He put both hands in the air to try and calm her down.

"It's okay. I was just leaving," he said, moving toward the front door.

The woman seemed unassured and charged him. Fortunately, the woman was petite. He waited for her to get close and grabbed ahold of her forearm before shoving her onto the floor. The woman cried out in pain and struggled to get up while he made a move for the front door.

To his relief, the door was unlocked and swung open when he pulled. He ran across their front lawn. He could still hear the girl screaming when he reached the front sidewalk. He continued running until he reached his car. He waited to turn on his headlights until he had finally fled their neighborhood.

Eric caught his breath and tried to clear his head on the drive home. It was fortunate he'd been wearing the baseball cap. They shouldn't be able to give a very good description. But how had he gotten the wrong address?

"Dammit, Patricia!" he yelled.

His shout cut through the silence of his small sedan. He slammed his hand against the steering wheel, inadvertently honking the horn and making himself jump. "Dammit!"

CHAPTER SIX

Although last night had been a terrible blow to Eric's ego as a killer, he wasn't going to let one small slip keep him from carrying out his master plan. He just needed to regroup. He would count last night's mishap as a learning experience.

He also realized how he'd managed to show up at the wrong address. And it wasn't even Patricia's fault. In his excitement, he had turned onto McGilvra Boulevard East instead of East McGilvra Street. Who knew there could be two streets named McGilvra in the same neighborhood? It was an honest mistake.

He'd come home last night and had a meeting with himself over a large glass of red. He decided he could still kill Patricia in the exact way he'd planned, only he would have to do it tomorrow night, just before her husband came home. He realized it would be even better for him to discover her body and be at the scene when the police showed up. They would suspect him immediately.

He just needed to iron out a few more details before tomorrow night. He couldn't afford any more mistakes.

In the meantime, it was business as usual. He did his best to appear interested in his other self-centered, needy clients as the day went on while his mind focused on how to kill Patricia...and get away with it.

"My mother was an amazing woman. She won three Olympic gold medals for synchronized swimming before she went into politics. She served as the Ambassador to the United Nations for four years."

He looked up from his notepad to his teary client sitting across from him. Susan was in her late forties, and, if he remembered right, had just lost her mother to cancer. She paused from whatever she'd been saying for the last ten minutes and her eyes brimmed with tears. He handed her a tissue box, which she accepted.

"Take your time," he said. *I charge by the hour*, he thought.

Three more patients and many sob stories later, he was, at last, done for the day. His blonde, overly-bubbly secretary poked her head into Eric's office after his last appointment had left.

"I wanted to make sure it was still okay that I take Wednesday off next week?"

"For my birthday?" she added, seeing the blank expression on his face.

He vaguely remembered her asking him about it a while back. "Umm...sure. That should still be fine. You arranged for a temp to fill in for the day?"

"Yes. Did you need me to do anything else before I go?" she asked with a smile.

She was always smiling. Why, he could never be sure. She was what Australians would call *a few 'roos short in the top paddock*, but she was pleasant and always looked nice. In the eight months she'd worked for him, she'd always showed up on time and was competent enough to get the job done. He didn't need her to be a rocket scientist.

"Actually, yes. Would you mind smiling at me just a little bit less? You always act like there's so much to be happy about. It makes me feel like a rotten human being."

"Are you asking me out?" She beamed at him, as though he'd be thrilled by her discovery of his secret motives.

He was dumbfounded. She had to be kidding.

"No," he said.

She made no effort to hide her disappointment, and he realized she'd been totally serious. Hopeful even. She looked as though he had crushed her. He couldn't take the way she was looking at him.

"I mean, yes," he heard himself say. "I was."

Her depression quickly changed to giddy excitement. She smiled wide.

"I've been wondering how long it would take you to finally ask."

As if there had been anything between us? he wondered, perplexed.

"So, when?"

"When what?" he asked.

"When do you want to go out?"

"Oh. Right. Umm...." He wanted to say he was in the middle of planning a murder but figured that probably wasn't a good idea. Even though she would probably think he was being hilarious.

"How about tonight?" She looked gratified, like she'd done him a favor by offering to give him exactly what he wanted. Only he didn't want it at all.

"Umm...." He cursed himself for not being able to think of an excuse. He had nothing. "Sure."

She practically jumped in the air.

"Great! I'm starving, I'll just grab my purse. Do you mind driving? I know this amazing little sushi place downtown. You like sushi, right? You're going to love it. Their sake is the best. I'll just be two secs."

In a blur of movement, she turned to fetch her purse, sending her blonde curls swinging through the air. Apparently, both of her questions were rhetorical.

He sighed. This was not what he had planned for the evening. He wasn't even sure how he had gotten himself into this mess. He couldn't let himself be outsmarted by his twenty-two-year-old secretary and get behind in planning Patricia's murder. He was on a schedule. He would just have to tell her the sushi didn't agree with him and hurry home right after dinner.

No sooner had he gathered his thoughts when she reappeared in his doorway. She brushed her blonde fringe out of her eyes.

"Ready!" she announced with glee.

"Great."

CHAPTER SEVEN

Stephenson took a swig from his beer as he flipped the steaks one last time. It had taken longer than usual to barbecue them in the forty-degree weather, but they finally looked about perfect. Not wanting them to be overdone, he used his metal tongs to remove them from the grill. He turned off the barbecue before lifting the plate of meat and heading inside his townhouse through the sliding door.

Serena was already seated at his kitchen table but was too engrossed in her phone to look up when he came inside. Her shiny, dark hair framed her face as she looked down, fixated by her screen.

After making them each a plate with salad and a baked potato to go with their steaks, he joined her at the table.

"I hope you can put that down while we eat," he said.

She looked across at him through her long, false lashes.

"Of course I can."

She slid the phone away from her plate.

"You know you didn't have to cook for me. I could've met you somewhere for dinner."

Stephenson cut into his steak.

"I thought it would be nice since I had the day off. We always go out."

"You had the day off because you almost got yourself killed this weekend. I still can't believe you did that." She reached her hand across the table and grabbed hold of his. "But I'm glad you're okay. And thank you. This is nice."

He took another drink from his beer.

"You're welcome. I might not be in good enough shape to chase murderers around, but I'm not too beat up to cook you dinner."

"So, what'd you do today?"

"I had to give my medical leave form to Sergeant McKinnon. Then I met with a—"

Serena's ringtone blared atop the table. "Sorry," she said before picking it up. "Hi, can I call you back later?"

Stephenson took a bite of his steak.

"No, I just can't talk right now," Serena said. "I'm having dinner with Blake."

He looked across the table at her. She seemed to be looking anywhere but back at him.

"I told you about him," she continued. "Anyway, I have to go. I'll give you a call back later tonight."

"Who was that?" Stephenson asked after she placed the phone back down on the table.

She took a stab of her salad. "Oh, just another realtor from my firm. He wants to talk about doing a joint listing."

"You told him about me, huh?"

She looked up defensively, then saw he was smiling.

"So, what do you want to do for your birthday?" he asked.

"I've got a bunch of listings to show."

"On Saturday?"

"That's when most people are available to look. I've told you this."

"I was just hoping we could do something fun for your birthday."

Her phone went off again. She checked the screen.

"Sorry, it's a client. I have to take it."

She got up from the table to answer it. Stephenson finished his dinner alone while she took the call in his living room.

"They want me to do a showing tonight," she said, coming back into the kitchen as he rinsed his plate.

"What time?"

"I need to leave now."

"Seriously? You're not even going to eat?"

"I'm sorry. It's my first listing over a million. I need to show the firm I'm ready to sell high-end properties." She came toward him and wrapped her arms around his waist. "Thanks for cooking for me, I'm sure it's delicious." She lifted her head and kissed him softly. "I'll call you tomorrow."

She turned and grabbed her purse off the table. He leaned against the counter as she rushed out the door. He looked across at her untouched plate while he finished his beer.

CHAPTER EIGHT

They hit rush hour traffic on the way to the restaurant, and it took another twenty minutes to find a parking spot downtown. When they finally got to the modern sushi house, the place was packed. Eric held the door open for his secretary to enter first, which she appeared to take as a sign of his undying love. As soon as he stepped inside, he was accosted by potted bamboo plants slapping him in the face.

The few seats in the small entry area were already filled with people waiting for a table. The music that played reminded him of something from *Lost In Translation*. He put his name in for a table for two and was told by the hostess it would be at least a thirty-minute wait. *Thirty-minutes!* He didn't have thirty-minutes. He needed to get back to planning Patricia's murder so he could return to writing a bestseller. He couldn't believe he had agreed to this.

"You're welcome to wait at the bar if you like." She pointed behind her, where there were a few barstools still open.

"That sounds great," his secretary chimed in.

They walked together toward the bar. He realized he didn't even know her name. That could be awkward. He'd obviously known it at one point, like when he had hired her, but somewhere between then and the last eight months she'd worked for him, it must've slipped his mind. Probably because he didn't care.

"Do you like sake?" she asked after they'd taken seats at the white marble bar.

He did, but he needed to stay focused so he could continue with his planning and research after dinner. He couldn't afford to make any mistakes. Although, one drink probably wouldn't hurt.

"I do. You?"

"Love it."

His eyes followed the sound of the kitchen doors opening to the right of the bar. He watched a chef carry a huge tray of raw fish and veggies out to a table for a large group. He wore a Japanese-style chef hat, white with red trim and a flat top.

"What can I get for you two?"

He turned his attention to the bartender behind the counter. He looked like he was probably in college.

"We'll have two sakes, whatever's your best seller."

"You got it."

Eric looked over at his secretary. She stared at him while biting her lip and twirling a small piece of her hair. She was apparently enthralled with his ability to order nothing but the best. He noticed she had taken off the sweater she had worn all day at the office. Her low-cut, pink floral blouse showed off her large breasts.

She looked at him with her green eyes, and he appreciated her beauty for the first time. She had a slender nose, average-size lips, and baby-smooth skin that screamed of youth. She was a pretty girl but not his taste. Too dumb.

He came to terms with the fact he would not be able to think about Patricia's death until their dinner date was over. He forced himself to turn his attention toward his secretary, hoping to get through the dinner as quickly and as painlessly as possible.

"Have I ever told you I love your accent?"

He was about to reply when she continued. It seemed it was another rhetorical question.

"Where are you from again?"

She paused this time, and he assumed this one he was supposed to answer.

"Australia."

"That's right, I remember you saying that before. Isn't that where Arnold Schwarzawhatever is from?"

"I think that would be Austria."

"Oh." She looked confused. "So, anyways...."

She rambled on about how she couldn't believe it took him so long to ask her out when she'd known he'd had a thing for her since pretty much the beginning. She clearly had a wild imagination. She was still talking when they finished their sakes, and he wasn't sure how he could survive listening to her for the next hour. She changed the subject to her hair while he signaled the bartender for two more drinks. He felt himself relax after downing the second one.

A waitress called his name for their table and he practically jumped for joy out of his barstool.

His secretary giggled at his reaction. "You must be starving!"

Something like that. "Yes." He'd had enough sake that he smiled back at her as they followed the waitress to their table.

She seated them at a small table against the wall. The seat next to the wall was a cushioned booth and across from it was a chair. Eric extended his arm to offer his secretary the booth. She beamed at him before sitting down. His head had cleared a little from the sake by the time he took his seat. They needed to get the show on the road so he could get back to business.

"You like California rolls?" he asked his secretary before the waitress walked away.

"Love them."

Of course she did. "We'll start with some California rolls."

"Anything to drink?" the waitress asked.

His secretary looked eager for another drink, and he figured it would be just as easy to ditch her if she was drunk, even if he had to order an Uber to drive her home.

"We'll have a bottle of your best sake."

The waitress nodded and tried unsuccessfully to suppress her smile surfacing, presumably in hope of a big tip.

We'll see about that, he responded in silence. He looked over the menu as he inadvertently pictured himself standing behind Patricia with his hands around her throat.

"So...." His secretary said from across the table, apparently her best attempt at a conversation starter.

Oh, right. You again. "So." He set down his menu. "You know what you want for dinner?"

"You want to share something?"

Not really, but to speed things along, he agreed.

"How about the halibut?"

"Sure." *Whatever.*

He was staring at the pastel painting of over-fed tangerine and white coy swimming in a lily pad-infested pond that hung on the wall behind his date when the waitress came back with their sake and California rolls. Quick service. He liked it. He wasted no time in giving her their dinner order.

"Great. Won't be too long," she said.

Maybe she would get that big tip after all. He poured his secretary a large glass of sake and filled his only half full.

"Are you trying to get me drunk?" she asked hopefully.

"I'm driving."

"Oh, right." She laughed before taking a big swig of her sake.

She finished off her glass and had already halfway downed another when their food arrived. Thankfully it hadn't taken too long. His secretary's words started to slur as they ate.

She was in no shape to drive home from his office, where they had left her car. And this so-called date would be over right after dinner. He had work to do. Which reminded him, he was supposed to come down with food poisoning.

He waited until they had finished eating. Her sake glass was empty again, and he refilled it with what remained in the bottle.

"So, what made you decide to become a psychiatrist?"

He honestly didn't know and couldn't come up with one good reason. He wiped fake sweat from his brow. "Would you excuse me?"

"Sure, are you okay?"

"I think the sushi may have not agreed with me," he said while holding his stomach before scurrying away to the loo.

He took his time taking a leak and washed his hands for a full two minutes. He checked his over-bleached teeth for seaweed and splashed his face with water. He partially towel dried his face but made sure his hairline stayed wet when he left the bathroom. It was time to tell whats-her-face goodnight.

He was glad to see her sake glass was empty when he got back to their table. The drunker she was, the easier this should be.

"You don't look so good."

"I don't feel so good."

He caught the attention of the waitress as she walked by. "Can we get the check please?"

"Got it right here." She handed him a black leather booklet.

"Thank you."

Nothing like a waitress who already knows what you need. He slipped his Visa into the plastic cardholder and handed the booklet back to her.

"I'll be right back," she said.

His secretary looked either worried for him or depressed their evening was ending early. Maybe both.

"I'm probably going to be sick again and won't be able to drive you back to the office. Can I get you an Uber?"

"No. I—" She swallowed hard. She looked terrified, and he couldn't understand why.

"Are you feeling okay?" he asked.

"Um...it's just that I can't go home tonight."

"Why not?"

"I told my boyfriend I was spending the night at my sister's. And I can't go to my sister's because she's out of town and I don't have a key."

"You have a boyfriend?"

She reached across the table and put her hand on top of his, knocking over her empty sake glass in the process. "I know you're thinking I'm a horrible person, but it's not what it seems. I do have a boyfriend, but he's really controlling and I'm going to leave him. I've been planning to do it for a while, I just haven't found a way to tell him yet. Anyway, I didn't want to pass up the opportunity when you asked me out, so I told him I was spending the night at my sister's place."

"Maybe you should just tell him the truth." It seemed simple enough.

"You don't understand. He's—" she trailed off, looking frightened.

"Has he ever hurt you?"

"No, no, it's not like that." She shook her head in an overly eager effort to convince him. She squeezed his hand. "But please, let me stay with you. I can't go home tonight."

She pulled her hand away when their waitress came back but kept staring intently into his eyes.

"Have a great night you guys," the waitress said after handing him back his card.

He ignored her and stared back at his busty blonde secretary. He wasn't sure he believed her boyfriend had never hurt her. She looked genuinely scared. He'd seen enough cases of domestic abuse over his career to know, due to fear or denial, victims were often not forthcoming about their abusers. And, with how much she'd had to drink, he doubted this was an act. It wasn't like him to feel

49

compassion, but there was something about the way she looked at him with those big green eyes that he just couldn't tell her no.

"All right, you can sleep on my hide-a-bed."

"Thank you."

He could swear he saw her choke back tears as she leaned back against the booth and pulled her hand away from his. He stood from the table and held out his hand to help her up.

"Let's go."

CHAPTER NINE

"Your apartment's amazing."

Eric's secretary clutched her sweater to her chest as she turned to admire his living room.

As soon as he'd let her in, he quickly snatched his leather gloves and lock-picking kit off the table. He held them tightly in his hand just barely behind his back as to not look like he was hiding something.

"Can I get you something to drink?" He supposed even though his guest was a pain in his ass, keeping him from planning the murder that would shape his destiny by releasing his creative genius, he could still be a proper host. He also found her endearing despite her flaws.

"Yes, thank you."

She stepped forward to admire his expansive bookshelves.

"I've got water, wine, or vodka." He also had coffee, but he wanted her to go to sleep so he could get on with things.

She smiled at the options. "Wine would be great, but I can get it myself since you're not feeling well."

Oh, right. He was sick. "Yes, help yourself. The wine fridge is to the right of the sink."

"Thanks."

He went to the linen closet, pulled out a blanket and pillow for the hide-a-bed, and set them on the coffee table. "The couch folds out into a bed. You okay to do it yourself?"

"Sure, I'll be fine." She had already made her way into the kitchen.

This went easier than he had thought. He was free at last to plan Patricia's demise. He just needed his laptop.

"Well, I'm going to try and get some rest. You probably won't see me for the rest of the night."

"Thank you for letting me stay."

"It's no problem."

He grabbed his laptop off his desk and unplugged it from the wall. He noticed his secretary giving him a wondering look as he carried it into his room, but she didn't say anything. Probably because of his overreaching hospitality.

He waited until after two to sneak out of his room for a glass of water. His secretary was out cold on the couch. She hadn't even bothered unfolding it into the hide-a-bed. Her empty wine glass sat on the floor next to her. He picked up the glass and admired her for a moment, watching her sleep. Her chest moved up and down beneath the throw blanket with each of her even breaths. Her blonde hair lay sprawled out across the pillow.

He found himself wishing she were more of an intellectual. Maybe then, there could be something between them. Although, his true reason for not falling head over heels wasn't because of her IQ, but because no one would ever compare to his wife. Or rather, his ex-wife.

He pictured her as if their last day together was only yesterday. Her hair was neither brown nor blonde. It was a unique shade of honey somewhere in between. She was a natural beauty and Australian through and through. She shared many of the same magnificent qualities of her beloved country. He could never love another the way he loved her.

He sighed and continued to the kitchen to get his glass of water before returning to his room to iron out the final details of Patricia's death.

He awoke to the smell of coffee and nearly jumped out of bed at the sight of his secretary standing over him, holding a steaming mug in her hands.

"Crikey!"

She giggled. "I'm sorry, I didn't mean to scare you. I made coffee. Are you feeling better?"

He let out a breath and brought his hand to his forehead. There was no way it could be morning already. He had stayed up until after three going over every detail of his perfect plan for Patricia's murder, making sure he had thought of everything. There could be no room for error. He had fallen asleep after he'd finally assured himself his plan was foolproof.

His bedside clock read seven fifteen. He sat up and accepted the coffee. "A little."

She was wearing a gray Seattle Mariners t-shirt that he recognized as his own. His shirt came down to the top of her bare thighs. It was obvious from the shape of her nipples protruding through the thin cotton that she wasn't wearing a bra. Her normally smooth blonde hair had a kink on each side from where she had slept on it. She looked adorable. Beautiful, even.

She pulled at the bottom of the shirt. "I hope you don't mind; I got this from a pile of clean clothes in your laundry."

"How did you know they were clean?"

She smirked. "Because no one would fold their dirty clothes like that."

Except for him.

"You up for going to work today?" she asked.

"Yeah, I'm feeling much better."

"Good. Mind if I use your shower?"

"Not at all. Help yourself."

"Great." She turned and he took a sip from his mug.

"This is good. You know how to make a cup of coffee."

She flashed him a cheeky, American smile. "I know."

It was a normal day apart from the few times he caught his secretary eying him as if they'd had some top-secret love affair last night. But, instead of being annoyed, he found it endearing.

They walked out of the office together after his last patient of the day. A light, wet snow was falling when she turned to him before getting into her car.

The sun had just disappeared below the horizon, and he admired the way the street lamp highlighted the contour of her round cheekbones.

"I had fun last night. Thanks for letting me crash at your place."

"Me too," he said as she got in.

He'd wondered about her boyfriend a few times throughout the day. *What had he done to her that she was so afraid to go home last night?* He opened his mouth to ask her if she was sure it safe for her to go home, but he was too late.

She gave him a wave before pulling out of the office parking lot, and he assured himself she would be fine. He climbed into the heated seat of his BMW and suppressed a smile. There was no denying how he felt. Contrary to his best intentions, he liked her.

CHAPTER TEN

He counted his blessings for going to the wrong house on Wednesday night. He realized there was something he'd forgotten to consider. An alibi.

He knew there were security cameras in the building's parking garage, but whether they covered every parking space he wasn't sure. He had located two cameras in the parking area, but it seemed there were a few parking spots near the entrance that were not covered by the cameras.

Before work that morning, he called down to his building's apartment manager. A woman answered on the second ring.

"Yes, good morning," he said. "My car was parked in the underground parking last night and appears to have gotten scratched by another vehicle. I was wondering if there might be security footage that could show what happened?"

"I'm sorry to hear that. Yes, we do have security cameras that cover almost all the parking garage. Do you know what parking spot you were in?"

"42A."

"Okay, let me just double check if we would have footage of that area."

"Thank you." Eric waited on the line for a couple minutes before she came back on.

"You still there?"

"Yes."

"Unfortunately, our cameras don't reach to that parking spot. I'm so sorry. There are only about four spots outside of our cameras' view, and 42A happens to be one of them."

Just as he had thought. "What about at the entrance? Can you see what cars came and left overnight?"

"No, I'm sorry. Our only cameras are inside the parking garage; we don't have anything at the entrance."

"Well, that's disappointing."

"Sorry I couldn't be more helpful."

"Yeah, me too," he said before hanging up.

Perfect. That was all he needed to know before he carried out his plan. Luckily, 42A was open when he got home from work. Now all he had to do was create an alibi and he would be off to kill Patricia.

Dressed in his brightest-colored flannel pajamas, Eric knocked hard on his neighbor's door. He needed him to remember this.

When he didn't answer after about five seconds, Eric knocked even louder. He heard footsteps heading toward the door from inside the apartment. He knocked three more times before the door flew open.

"What's your problem, man? You didn't even give me a chance to come to the door."

His neighbor looked his usual self, like he'd just rolled out of bed. Eric wasn't sure, but it looked like his neighbor was wearing the same clothes as the last time he'd seen him.

"My problem is you."

To this, his eyes narrowed and a look of confusion washed over his face.

"I've got a busy day tomorrow, and I'll be turning in early. So, I just wanted to make sure you weren't planning on doing any obnoxious drumming this evening. I need a good night's sleep."

"I'm not gonna do any drumming. I realize it's getting a little late for that."

Eric couldn't leave until he made sure this conversation would stick in his neighbor's mind.

"Well, I'm not so sure. I remember a few times you seemed to go on a drumming rampage late at night without any regard for the rest of us in the building. I'm surprised no one's complained."

Eric knew no one else on their floor would complain. There were only four units on their level. One was currently unoccupied and the other was inhabited by ninety-year-old Betty Jensen. She couldn't hear a thing.

He opened his mouth to protest, but Eric cut him off. Eric raised the palm of his hand just below his neighbor's face.

"But I'm not here to argue with you. I just ask that you do me the courtesy of staying off the drums tonight so I can get a good night's sleep."

"No problem," he said. He frowned at him before slamming his door closed.

Brilliant. He had irritated him just enough to jog his memory if the cops ever questioned him about his alibi. Now he could go to Patricia's.

He went back to his apartment to change his clothes. When he walked by his neighbor's door on his way out, he heard him start to beat on the drums. He smiled at how easily he'd unnerved him. Bastard.

CHAPTER ELEVEN

Eric donned his baseball cap and gloves before getting out of his car at the end of Patricia's street. This time, he made sure to leave his phone behind.

With his lock-picking kit safely stowed in his pant pocket, he jogged down the neighborhood street with his head down. He expected his heart to be racing, but it was calm. Steady.

He paused when he reached the end of Patricia's driveway, feeling a sense of déjà vu from two nights earlier. Her front porch light was on, but, aside from that, the house was dark. He could tell her hedges needed trimming, and the plain front lawn could've used some landscaping. This was definitely Patricia's house.

He moved along a tall hedge on the edge of her property and stopped at a wooden fence. Just as he had done two nights previous, he reached his hand over the fence and undid the latch to open the door. He stepped into Patricia's backyard and softly closed the latch behind him.

Not surprisingly, there was no dog waiting to attack him on the other side. Her backyard was even darker than the front of the house. He moved slowly along the house's exterior, careful not to trip on any crap she might've left laying out on the lawn. He made it to the French doors off the back patio and felt into his pocket for his lock-picking kit. His hand slipped in the darkness just as he was about to insert his tool into the lock. He felt the metal instrument scrape against the door handle before he inadvertently jabbed it into the wood door.

He took a deep breath and tried again. This time the tool slid easily into the lock, only the lock didn't budge as easily as it had when he broke into the wrong house. He pulled it out and tried another time, wiggling the tool back and forth. The lock still didn't give, and he worried he might have to devise another way to get inside. He hadn't seen any other doors on the home's main level other than the front, which he hoped to avoid using if possible.

The lock pick finally glided farther into the lock and he heard a click. He tried the handle and felt relief when it turned inside his hand. He pulled on the lock pick to remove it, but it was stuck. He tugged harder to no avail before he wrenched it back and forth with enough force that it came loose.

He tucked the pick back into his pocket. When he twisted the handle again, he realized he had all but dislodged the lock in his effort to remove the pick. Loose bits from the lock rattled inside the doorknob as he slowly opened the door and stepped inside the house.

Eric had intended to break in without a trace, but now he wondered if the cops would be able to deduce that the back-door's lock had been picked. It wasn't as bad as breaking into the wrong house, but it wasn't according to plan.

His eyes had adjusted well to the dark, and he could see that he stood in a breakfast nook off the kitchen. He heard a TV going in the other room. That was good, it would cover the noise of his footsteps. He crept toward the sound of the TV while he kept an eye out for Patricia. As he moved closer to the open doorway, he could see a blue, flashing light shining out into the hall. He paused before leaning his head just enough to see into the room.

He realized he risked exposing his presence much too early by poking his head inside the doorway, but it was too late. He was already exposed. His heartrate increased. He took an inward sigh of relief when he recognized the back of Patricia's gray bob on the sofa.

He judged her for being such a slug that she wasted her life away sitting on the couch, staring at a screen until her mind went numb. Although, he should have been grateful. This was exactly how he had hoped to find her.

He turned to look for her bedroom, where he would wait for her to come to bed. He saw a staircase at the end of the hall and figured it would be a good place to start. He caught himself stopping to look at her wall of family photos when he was halfway up and quickly reproached himself. *What do I care?* he thought.

He entered the room closest to the top of the stairs and could tell, even in the dark, it was the master bedroom. He felt repulsed but not surprised by the unmade bed and pile of dirty clothes on the floor. What an animal.

He found her walk-in closet and stepped inside in search of one of her husband's ties. He felt around in the dark, but with his gloves on it was impossible to find what he needed. *Oh, screw it*, he thought. He flicked on the light to the closet. Patricia was immersed in her TV anyway; she wouldn't notice the light. He just needed to be quick. Her husband's clothes occupied the right side of the closet, and, fortunately, he was much more organized than Patricia.

Unlike her chaotic hodgepodge of clothes on the left, her husband's shirts were hung according to color and shirt type. His shirts went from white to black, t-shirts on one side and dress shirts on the other. Pants were folded neatly on the shelves below. His neckties hung on hangers next to his dress shirts, and he grabbed one before flicking off the light.

He looked around for a better place to hide as his eyes readjusted to the dark and saw she had an en suite bathroom. *Perfect.* He checked his watch. Now for the hard part: he had to wait. From what Patricia had told him in their sessions, she always went to bed by ten. She complained about her husband being a night owl and disturbing her when he finally came to bed after midnight.

He waited behind Patricia's bathroom door with a rush of nervous tension. The minutes passed by about as slowly as Patricia moved toward anything, other than the fridge. He used the time to remind himself to take detailed mental notes on everything about Patricia's murder. Even the way it felt to kill. He had decided to write his novel from the point of view of the serial killer he had crafted in his mind. They say all a writer's characters are a part of themselves, which, he supposed, was probably true.

He suddenly felt the urge not to kill, but to pee. He laid the necktie down on the bathroom counter and untied the drawstring of his joggers. He could see well enough now in the dark that he had no problem aiming into the toilet bowl. He had just released a stream when light flooded the bathroom and Patricia waltzed in. Upon seeing him, she let out a scream. His body involuntarily jerked in her direction before he was able to stop the urine flow, and he trickled piss onto the floor. In a panicked attempt to pull up his pants, his waistband slipped out of his hand. His sweats fell to the floor from the weight of the lock-picking kit in his pocket.

Patricia wore a grandmotherish nightgown, and, after the initial shock of finding him taking a wiz in her en suite bathroom, she looked relieved when she recognized him.

Truly, she couldn't think this was a social call. He supposed his baseball cap didn't exactly say *I'm here to kill you*. But she would be beyond delusional to think he came over to keep her company while her husband was away. He was a good ten years too young for her, in addition to being out of her league. Plus, he couldn't stand her.

He took as big a step toward her as he could with his pants down at his feet and watched her face change to suspicion and then to fear. She screamed again, louder this time, and took a step out of the bathroom. He had planned to strangle her from behind, but, knowing he wouldn't be able to catch her with his pants down, he had to improvise.

He swiped the tie off the counter and used both hands to loop it over the back of her head. Her eyes filled with terror as he pulled it taut across the front of her neck. She scratched and clawed at the tie as her face turned the color of beetroot. He felt a tinge of nostalgia for his homeland. He would never understand why Americans didn't put pickled beets on their sandwiches.

He hadn't intended on strangling her head-on and didn't like the awkwardness of watching the capillaries burst in her bulging eyeballs as he squeezed the life out of her. He forgot about the details he needed for his book and closed his eyes until she stopped resisting and he felt her weight start to sink to the ground. He loosened his hold on her neck and opened his eyes.

He expected her to fall to the floor but was taken aback to see she was still alive. Patricia's face was now an ugly purple. She gasped for air and placed the back of her hands against the counter to stay on her feet. She looked at him in shock and horror of what he had done before she swung her fist toward his face. It was as if she saw him for who he really was for the first time.

He grabbed hold of her hand before she made contact and twisted it behind her back, forcing her to turn toward the bathroom counter. She let out a weak cry of protest. He grabbed her by the back of her hair and threw her forehead into her bathroom mirror. Patricia groaned. When he pulled her head away, he saw the mirror had cracked as though a baseball had hit it. Before she could react, he flung the tie around her neck once again, only this time he tightened it from the back.

She groped at the necktie and threw her legs back one at a time in an unsuccessful effort to kick him. It didn't take long for him to realize this was no different from strangling her from the front since her asphyxiated face stared back at him in the shattered mirror. He didn't like it any more than he had the first time. He closed his eyes, promising himself that if he ever killed again, he would keep them open.

He pulled the tie as tight as he could and felt the weight of her body as it went limp. He leaned forward, pressing his body against hers to help take some of the weight from his arms. He continued to hold the noose tight around her neck for what felt like an eternity.

Once he was sure she was dead, he opened his eyes. Out of breath, he let her go. He thought her fat corpse would slump forward onto the counter. But, before he could stop it, he watched her body heave to the side. Her skull smacked against the side of the toilet on the way down.

She lay on the tile floor, her swollen face littered with burst capillaries. Blood seeped out from a gash in her forehead where it had collided with the mirror. His breathing slowed. He looked down at the mess of his yellow piss and her dark blood on the pale tile, reminding him of ketchup and mustard on a hot dog. This had not gone at all to plan. And, judging from the color of his urine, he needed to drink more water.

This led him to wonder, *was there DNA in urine?* The fact that he was uncertain made him question his abilities as a doctor. But it had been a long time since medical school and, thank goodness, he didn't ever have to deal with his patients' piss. After a moment's consideration, he decided there probably was. *Drat.* He was going to have to clean this mess up.

He should've been a medical examiner. Then he could've written a crime thriller without needing to kill one of his own patients. He realized his pants were still around his ankles. He pulled up his joggers and cringed as the urine-soaked fabric rubbed against his legs.

"Crikey."

Keeping his gloves on, he checked under her bathroom cabinet for cleaning supplies. There were none. Of course not. He was about to go in search of some, and, when he thought there was no way this night could've gone more wrong, he heard the sound of the front door close. A man's voice echoed through the house.

"Patricia, I'm home."

CHAPTER TWELVE

Eric considered his options as he assessed the mess around him. Either he needed to make a quick escape or kill her husband too and make it look like a murder-suicide. He opted for the quick escape. He pulled a few sheets of toilet paper off the roll and wiped his urine spill as best he could, careful not to smear Patricia's blood.

He tossed the paper into the toilet bowl and automatically flushed. He realized the noise this would create as soon as he pulled the lever. Footsteps sounded up the stairs.

The man's voice called out again, but this time it was louder. "Patricia?"

There was no window in the bathroom, so his only route of escape would be out the window beside her bed. Patricia's husband would no doubt see him before he could get away. He would have to kill him.

He pulled at the tie that was still tight around Patricia's neck. He struggled to get his finger in between the tie and her neck since he had looped it through itself to get a better cinch on her neck. Her neck fat sagged over the tie, making it impossible to grip with his gloved hands.

He didn't have time for this. Patricia's husband was probably already at the top of the stairs. He swung open the door to the bathroom cabinet and pulled out her curling iron. He turned off the bathroom lights, ran across the dark room, and dove under Patricia's bed.

No sooner had he tucked under it than the bedroom lights came on. His heart pounded against the carpet as he watched the man's patent leather dress shoes stop in the doorway.

"Patricia?"

Eric gripped each end of the curling iron's electric cord and wrapped them once around the back of his hands. He waited for the feet to move. He thought maybe the man was going to turn back downstairs when they started toward the bed. They didn't slow as they moved past him, and Eric knew he was headed for the bathroom. For this to pass as a murder-suicide, he needed to minimize any signs of a struggle with Patricia's husband. That would probably be easier if he killed him before he saw Patricia.

His feet had almost reached the edge of the bed when Eric stretched out and grasped his ankle just as he started to take a step. Eric yanked it backwards as hard as he could from his awkward angle. He felt the floor shake when the man fell to the ground.

Eric moved fast, crawling over the husband's back until he was within arm's reach of his neck. The man started to flip onto his back, but Eric used his weight to keep him face down to the floor. With one of his knees pressing into the middle of his back, he looped the electrical cord around the front of his neck, crossed his arms, and pulled it taut.

The husband yelled out. Eric pulled harder. His yell turned into a wheeze as Eric compressed his vocal cords.

Just like Patricia, he brought his hands to his neck and frantically scratched against his noose. Eric estimated the man had about fifty pounds on him. He was concentrating so hard on strangling him that he was knocked off balance by the sudden roll of the man's body.

Next thing he knew, he was staring at the ceiling with the heavy weight of Patricia's husband on top of him. Eric had slightly loosened his grip on the cord when Patricia's husband knocked him onto his back, but quickly regained his hold when he heard him gasp. The man rolled back and forth on top of him, his weight crushing the air from Eric's lungs. Eric wrapped his legs around the man's middle as best he could to keep him from rolling away. It took all his strength to maintain a tight pull on the cord. His hands shook from the strain on his muscles as he noticed the man's movements become weaker. He exhaled and forced himself to hold tight for a little longer.

Eric was overwhelmed by the powerful scent of the man's cologne. It was about five times too strong for what was socially acceptable. There was something wrong with a man who wore that much. For a moment, he pitied Patricia. Her husband's body finally went limp, but he didn't let go. He wasn't about to make the same mistake that he did with the man's wife. He counted backward from thirty in his head to distract himself from the burn in his arms and hands. It felt like an eternity until he reached zero. Satisfied Patricia's husband was dead, Eric pushed his fat corpse off him. He moved onto his hands and knees to catch his breath.

He lowered himself onto his elbows and examined the man he had just killed. He had a thick build, in addition to the medium-sized potbelly that was obvious underneath his dark suit. His balding hair was overly-slicked back. He was clean-shaven and wore a large class ring on his right hand. He had even more neck fat than Patricia.

Eric wondered if maybe he had judged Patricia a little too harshly.

The man's face was now the color of merlot, and he decided to have a glass when he got home. Eric wiped the sweat from his brow and looked around the room for a way to rectify the situation. He needed to hang him from something, but the room only had recessed lighting on the ceiling.

He left him on his bedroom floor and stepped out into the hall. He crossed his arms at the top of the staircase and looked at the nineties chandelier that hung over the stairwell. A chain helped support its weight on the electrical socket. *Perfect.*

He went back and grabbed the fat man's lifeless hands to pull him out to the stairwell. He was surprised by the effort it took to drag him. He had a new appreciation for the term *dead weight*. He thought he was in shape from his regular yoga practice but now wondered if he needed to incorporate something more into his daily workout routine. He released him when they reached the top of the stairs and took a deep breath.

Eric looked again at the chandelier and then at the length of the curling iron's electrical cord. He surmised it would be possible to hang him from the chandelier. Possible, but not easy. He was glad he had worn active gear.

He reached down and linked his forearms under the husband's armpits. Eric stood, pulling the dead man with him. He leaned the man's top half over the railing, careful not to let him fall. Once Eric had him propped in a stable position, he looped the electrical cord inside itself around the man's neck and pulled tight against the power inlet.

After checking if it would hold, he grabbed the end of the curling iron and climbed on top of the wood stairwell railing. He stood up slowly, stopping a few times midway to find his balance with his arms held out at his sides. He held tight to the curling iron attached to the man's neck and used the weight of his corpse to help him stay upright.

He realized the cord was a little short to reach the chandelier unless he pulled the corpse forward. Eric carefully pulled on his neck so that his feet were barely touching the floor. If he pulled any farther, he was afraid his body might topple over the staircase.

Now for the tricky part. He now had enough cord, but he couldn't reach the chandelier without falling. He would have to lob it over the top and hope the curling iron caught on the gaudy crystals.

He threw it over the chandelier, but, when he did, he inadvertently jerked the corpse's neck. The curling iron had almost crossed over top the chandelier when the weight of Patricia's husband pulled it down, before it had a chance to snag on anything. Eric watched as the man's body pivoted over the railing and crashed to the hardwood floor near the front door below.

Eric felt himself fall forward and reacted by throwing himself backward. His back landed hard on cheaply padded carpet. He rushed to his feet and leaned over the railing. Patricia's husband lay face down on the floor in his pinstripe suit with the curling iron wrapped around his neck.

That wasn't good. Eric had read enough true crime to know a medical examiner could tell if a body had been moved postmortem, so he couldn't just drag him up the stairs and have another go at hanging him by the chandelier. He'd probably also sustained injuries from the fall. Eric figured he only had one choice.

He climbed back on top of the railing and launched himself toward the chandelier. He only managed to grab it with one hand. The light fixture swayed to the side while he reached for it with his other arm. He had no sooner gotten hold of it with both hands when it detached from the ceiling, bringing Eric and its surrounding drywall down with it.

He felt the air leave his lungs when his back hit the floor. He decided to leave this part out of his novel.

He stayed there for a moment while he regained his breath and waited for a sign that he had broken his back. He wiggled his toes and, once certain he hadn't broken a bone, sat up slowly. He pushed the chandelier off him and onto Patricia's husband. He wound the curling iron securely around it before standing.

He shook himself off from the fall and assessed his work. He moved some of the drywall pieces on top of the dead man and wiped his hands together over his body to rid his gloves of the white powder. He looked up at the hole in the ceiling then down at the dead man again. *This could pass as a suicide.*

He had one more look around before concluding his work here was done. He let himself out the back, the same way he had come. He broke into a jog when he reached the sidewalk in front of the house. The cold night air felt good as he headed back to his car and reflected on the evening.

Although there were a few hang-ups, he thought he pulled off the two murders swimmingly. Especially when he had only planned the one. Not too bad for someone who'd never killed before. He couldn't wait to translate them into his novel.

He got to his car and opened the driver's side. Before getting in, he took one last look in the direction of Patricia's house. He was completely alone on the quiet street. *Sayonara Patricia.*

CHAPTER THIRTEEN

"Can I get a name for the coffee?" the gothic barista asked from behind the counter.

"Blake."

Stephenson checked his watch and backed away from the register to wait for his drink. He had plenty of time. His girlfriend wouldn't be leaving for work for another hour. He'd already bought flowers to go with her skinny vanilla latte.

Counting Crows played throughout the coffee shop as he looked over at the small, empty table where he and Serena had spent their first date over a year before. She'd picked the coffee shop—an artsy, locally-owned cafe where most of the customers stayed to drink their coffee out of bright-colored pottery while they lounged on a couch or in an overstuffed chair. They'd had an instant connection and ended up talking for hours. He'd never met another woman like her.

His hand brushed against the small, square jewelry box he'd safely zipped into his jacket pocket. He wanted to surprise her with something thoughtful without being too over-the-top. Serena hated any sort of grand gestures, especially in public. So, he would propose on her front doorstep on the morning of her birthday. It would be private, which she would appreciate, but Stephenson hoped it would be romantic enough.

It was Saturday, and he was planning to take her out to dinner when she got off work. He would've preferred to propose to her then, but he was on call over the weekend and next up for a homicide case, so the chances he might have to cancel were high.

"Blake!" the barista called out before moving on to make the next coffee.

He grabbed the latte off the bar and walked out of the busy coffeehouse to his car. He seemed to hit every light on the way to Serena's house. He drummed his hands nervously against the steering wheel as he waited for light after light to turn green. He didn't want her latte to get cold; he wanted everything to be perfect. His heart was pounding by the time he pulled in front of her house. He checked to make sure the ring was still in his pocket before getting out of his car.

He was surprised to see a Land Rover in the driveway. It was early, but maybe one of her friends had also stopped by to wish her happy birthday.

With Serena's latte in one hand and flowers in the other, Stephenson strolled up her drive and rang the doorbell. He waited a minute for her to come to the door and was about to ring again when he heard Serena's footsteps come through the entry way. Only it wasn't Serena who answered the door.

A shirtless, muscular man a few years older than Stephenson stood inside Serena's doorway squinting from the morning sun.

"It's a little early to be ringing people's doorbells, don't you think?" The man ran his hand through his bedhead of dark hair.

Serena appeared behind him, wrapped in a towel with wet hair dripping down her shoulders. Her eyes widened when she saw who was at the door. She nearly dropped her towel but managed to recover it before it fell to the floor.

"Blake! What are you doing here?" She saw the flowers and latte in his hands. "I mean...um...look, I'm sorry. I meant to tell you." She pushed herself in between her male guest and Stephenson. "Shawn and I met through work. I never meant for any of this to happen, but one thing just led to another. We've been seeing each other for the last few weeks."

"Few *weeks*?" Stephenson was in shock. He thought they were in love, that they'd spend the rest of their lives together.

"I was just trying to find the right time to tell you."

She laid her hand on Stephenson's arm, but he shook it off.

Shawn remained in the doorway behind Serena, as if he were part of the conversation.

"That would've been before you decided to start cheating on me."

Stephenson's cell rang from inside his pocket. He tossed Serena's bouquet of flowers onto her front lawn before he answered. His fingers rubbed against the leather jewelry box inside his pocket when he pulled out his phone and he fought the urge to throw it out alongside the flowers.

"This is Stephenson." He stayed on Serena's front porch as he took the call.

"Hey, it's Adams. We're up. A jogger found the body of a young woman just off one of the trails at Discovery Park this morning. So, looks like you and I get to spend some quality time together this weekend. I'm already on my way to the scene."

"I'll be right there."

Stephenson hung up and put his phone back in his pocket.

"Happy birthday," he said before taking a drink from her latte and turning back toward his car.

"Blake, wait!" Serena ran out onto the porch in her bath towel.

He ignored her and took another swig from the artificially-sweetened coffee. He needed a shot or two of whiskey, but it would have to do for the moment.

Serena continued to holler at him from her front lawn as he peeled out and headed for the crime scene.

CHAPTER FOURTEEN

The next morning, Eric stared out his apartment window while he breathed through chair pose. In the distance, he watched a sailboat glide across the sound. He took a deep breath and could almost smell the fresh sea air.

He wore an almost identical outfit to what he had worn to kill Patricia. Since he practiced yoga seven days a week, nearly half his closet was active wear. He had already laundered everything he wore last night, including his running shoes, just in case they had picked up anything that could link him to the crime scene.

He decided not to do any novel writing last night when he got home from killing Patricia and her husband. He thought it would be best to let the night's events sink in. He jotted down some notes and made a few sketches while he enjoyed a glass of merlot before going to bed. He wished he could've taken pictures of their dead bodies, but he couldn't afford to have that kind of evidence on his phone.

He surprised himself by sleeping like a baby. He had thought he might have trouble sleeping after committing murder, but he was totally at peace. When his alarm woke him at seven that morning, he felt refreshed and ready to dive into his soon-to-be bestseller.

The sailboat disappeared behind a skyscraper and he moved into humble warrior. He wondered how long it would be before Patricia and her husband's bodies were found.

He liked to do yoga before he started writing. It helped clear his head and get the juices flowing. He focused on his breath entering and leaving his lungs.

He was three breaths into bird of paradise when there was a hard knock at his door. He took one more deep breath before going to answer it. He opened the door to find a man with pale blond hair and gray-blue eyes dressed in business casual. He was clearly of Nordic descent. He flashed his police badge at chest level.

Eric hadn't expected to be questioned so soon. Patricia's murder investigation seemed to be moving much faster than he had anticipated.

The detective was young. That was good. Probably hadn't been solving murders for too long. Eric smiled inwardly, thinking to himself that these were two he wouldn't solve.

A shorter, brown-haired man stood behind him. He looked to be closer to Eric's own age, probably in his forties. He reminded him of Mark Wahlberg, only more muscled. The buttons of his shirt barely contained his pectoral muscles, and his biceps protruded out of his leather jacket. *No one was naturally built like that,* Eric thought. It was a clear sign of a man who was trying too hard. Surely, he spent hours in the gym every week trying to boost his self-esteem.

"I'm Detective Stephenson, and this is Detective Adams," the blond one said. "Are you Dr. Eric Leroy?"

Eric felt a tinge of nervous tension run through his bowels. He knew this was probably just routine to ask if he knew what kind of relationship Patricia had with her husband, but he suddenly feared they somehow knew what he had done.

"I am," he said, hoping to sound as if he had no idea why the police would be knocking on his door on a Saturday morning.

"We need to ask you a few questions. Just routine. Do you mind if we come in?"

"Not at all." He opened the door wide.

"Thank you."

He led them into his living room and motioned toward the couch. "Would you like to have a seat?"

They followed in single file. "Thanks," Blondie said before they both took a seat.

Eric moved his yoga mat out of the way and sat down across from them. He decided to let them speak first. It was utterly important he not seem as though he knew why they had come knocking on his door. He crossed his legs and felt himself relax. He had planned his reaction to Patricia's murder to the tee. They didn't know what he had done, he reminded himself. The ball was in his court.

The Marky Mark lookalike cleared his throat before speaking. "I'm afraid we have some bad news."

Eric relaxed his mouth and opened his eyes wider as if to say *Oh, no*.

"The body of your front office assistant, Daisy Colbert, was found early this morning in Discovery Park. She appears to have been murdered," Blondie said.

My secretary? They must be confused. He refused to accept what they were telling him. They had come to question him about Patricia's murder, not his secretary's. There had to be some mistake.

"I just saw her at work yesterday. She was fine. Are you sure you have the right person?"

"Yes, her body has already been identified by a next-of-kin. We know this news is a shock, but we wouldn't have come before she'd been positively identified."

"I just saw her yesterday," Eric repeated, in disbelief of what he had heard. It couldn't be true. Not his beautiful, sweet secretary.

"Do you have any idea of who might have wanted to hurt her?"

It took him a moment before he realized the blond one had asked him a question. It was the boyfriend. He knew it was the boyfriend.

"From what she said, it sounded like her boyfriend could be pretty controlling. In fact, I think she was afraid of him."

Both detectives wore flat expressions, giving Eric no idea whether they believed him or not.

"And, just for our records, where were you last night between ten p.m. and two a.m.?"

Eric was in shock but fortunately had already prepared a response to this very question. "I was in bed, asleep."

"Can anyone verify that?"

"Not really. But I did knock on my neighbor's door around eight to ask him to keep his drums down."

The bodybuilder pulled out his cellphone. "Which neighbor?" he asked.

"915."

He appeared to type this into his phone. Or maybe he was just texting his girlfriend.

"Is there anyone else you can think of who may have wanted to hurt Daisy?" Stephenson asked.

Daisy. Her name was Daisy. "Like I said, from what she'd told me, her boyfriend was very controlling. Jealous too. If I were you, I'd be looking at him."

"Was he ever jealous of the two of you?" the brown-haired detective asked.

Eric thought quickly about his response before he answered. "No."

Marky Mark put his phone back in his pocket, and the two of them exchanged glances before getting up from the couch. "I think that'll be all, Dr. Leroy. Thanks for your time." Stephenson reached out his hand to shake Eric's, and he returned the handshake.

Eric followed behind them as the two men walked toward his door.

"Do you have a suspect? I mean, have you arrested her boyfriend?" he asked.

"Everyone is a suspect at this point in the investigation. We haven't made any arrests yet."

"I'm sure it was her boyfriend."

"We'll look into that."

From Blondie's expression, Eric couldn't tell if he took him seriously.

They reached his front door and Adams let himself out first.

"How did she die?" Eric asked before Stephenson went through his doorway.

Stephenson turned and looked him in the eyes, examining him for his reaction. "She was strangled." Stephenson stared at him for a moment before closing the door behind him.

CHAPTER FIFTEEN

"Play it again." Stephenson stood over Adams' shoulder and looked down at his partner's computer screen.

Adams played the video from the beginning. Sweat shone against Dwayne's forehead as he sat across the metal table from Stephenson and Adams earlier that morning. His hands fidgeted on his lap.

"We know this isn't the first time you've hurt Daisy," Adams said. "We've seen the reports from police responding to your residence for domestic disputes—three different times. The police were called twice by your neighbor…and once by Daisy."

"Is that what happened last night? Did things get out of control?" Stephenson asked.

"That was different. I didn't kill her."

Stephenson and Adams waited in silence to see if he would continue.

"We've had our fights, but I would never kill her." Dwayne chewed his lip and looked back and forth at the two detectives. "All couples fight."

"It seems a little one-sided to call it a fight when you're the only one throwing the punches. We also know your ex-girlfriend, Kristi Tilman, filed a restraining order two years ago claiming you knocked her around," Stephenson said.

"She's a liar."

"What happened to your hand?"

Dwayne glanced at his red knuckles on his right hand.

"Did you hit Daisy last night?"

"Yeah. But only once. We'd both been drinking. She told me she was gonna move out, and I lost my temper. I hit her on the side of her face. Then she told me to get out, so I did. She was alive when I left."

"Was it an accident? Now's your chance to tell us your side of the story," Adams said.

"I didn't kill her!" He pounded his fists onto the table, spilling his paper cup of water.

Stephenson held out his hands. "Calm down."

"Your neighbors heard shouting and doors slamming in your apartment right before the time Daisy was killed," Adams said.

"We had a fight, okay? I stormed out around ten and drove around the city to try and cool down. I ended up crashing at a friend's place in West Seattle."

"Where exactly did you drive around for an hour?" Adams asked.

"Downtown."

"Downtown Seattle?"

"Yeah."

"That's a thirty-minute drive from your apartment. What made you go there?"

"I don't know."

"We'll need the name and address of your friend who let you spend the night."

Stephenson looked away from the screen at the sight of their stickler superior, Lieutenant Greyson, marching through the Homicide Unit on a Saturday afternoon.

"What brings you here on a Saturday?" Stephenson asked as they made eye contact.

Adams stopped the video.

Greyson paused a few feet from their desks. "I have to lead a press release later today," he said. "Two people were found dead in their Madison Park home this morning, and one of them was Martin Watts."

CHAPTER SIXTEEN

Eric stared blankly at his computer screen. He'd been trying to write his novel for over an hour, but all he could think about was his secretary. And her son of a bitch boyfriend who had killed her. He was so upset he nearly cried for her.

He Googled to see if they'd arrested him yet, but there weren't any new articles since the initial one saying her body had been found. He skimmed the article again. It ended by stating no arrests had been made. He balled up his fist before releasing it to slam his laptop closed.

He wasn't sure how long he'd been sitting there plotting her boyfriend's demise when he heard another knock at his door. Happy for the distraction, he got up and answered it.

He was surprised to see the same two detectives standing in his hall. Their expressions were just as unreadable as the last time they came.

"I'm afraid we've had an unexpected development," Blondie said.

What could be more unexpected than his beloved secretary being murdered?

"We'd like you to come downtown and help us straighten a few things out."

Eric wanted to appear helpful and like he had nothing to hide. Plus, getting an inside tour of Seattle's Homicide Unit would be great for his story.

"Sure," he said. "Although, I don't know if I'll be of much more help. You really should be talking to her boyfriend."

"This isn't about your front office assistant. It's about one of your patients," Marky Mark said.

Oh, yeah. Patricia. They must've found her. He tried to look confused. He'd been so sad about his secretary's death that Patricia's had escaped him.

"Oh, no. I hope it's nothing serious. I don't think I can take much more bad news today."

Both detectives eyed him suspiciously. "We'll explain at the precinct," Blondie said.

"Okay, I'll just grab my coat."

The Homicide Unit was different than Eric had imagined. He realized he'd pictured it looking like the ones he'd seen on TV. It was smaller, more open, more cluttered, noisier, and much less glamorous than he had anticipated. Walking through the depressing hallway to the tiny shoebox of an interview room made him feel like he should pay more taxes. He would never understand why Americans fought socialism so hard.

The detectives let him enter the room first and motioned for him to have a seat. He obliged and hoped he wouldn't have to sit in the ass-numbing, unpadded chair for too long. Beavis and Butthead took their seats across from him in what looked to be equally uncomfortable chairs. They stared at him in silence, sizing him up. Eric stared back, his face revealing nothing.

Marky Mark finally broke the silence. "Do you have a patient by the name of Patricia Watts?"

"Yes."

"We're sorry to inform you that she was killed last night." The two detectives exchanged a look. "Probably not long before Daisy."

Eric dropped his jaw. "What?"

"We're sure this must be a shock, especially after the death of your front office assistant."

He tried to appear dumbfounded. "Yes, it is." He brought his hands to his face and wondered why he never pursued a career in acting. There were plenty of Australian actors who had made it in America.

"Patricia's husband, Martin, was also found dead this morning. At this point, we're treating both deaths as suspicious. Did Patricia ever say she was afraid of her husband? Or that he had ever hurt her?"

Eric slowly took his hands away from his face, as if he were still taking in the news about Patricia's husband. He hoped he looked as though he was struggling to focus.

"Well, um...she never said he had physically hurt her. If she had, I would be obligated to report it. But, I wouldn't be surprised if he ever was. From what she'd said, he was extremely controlling. Oftentimes, that type of behavior is a precursor to abuse."

"What do you mean by extremely controlling?" Blondie asked.

"I would have to look over my notes to give you all the details, but he didn't like her having any friends and tried to keep her away from her own family. Many abusers use isolation as a way of controlling their victims."

Fortunately, he had already doctored up her medical record to match what he had just said.

The detectives looked unimpressed by this information. So, he gave them more.

"He was always telling her she was fat, always lowering her self-esteem. I remember a specific instance when he wouldn't let her buy any new clothes until she lost weight."

He was annoyed he hadn't come up with anything better. He tried again. He figured he could always alter her medical records to substantiate his statement.

"He had also threatened to kill himself on several occasions if she didn't do what he wanted. He sounded incredibly unstable, but, according to Patricia, he refused to get any help. He always blamed everything on her."

To this, they raised their eyebrows. Eric withheld a smile to their reaction.

"And Patricia? Was she unstable?"

"Patricia? No. Most of her problems were because of her husband, she even said so. I encouraged her to leave him if she ever felt unsafe, but she insisted he would never physically hurt her. I wish I could've done something to prevent this, but, unfortunately, my hands were tied unless I knew he had hurt her physically."

"We've got a warrant for Patricia's psychiatric records. We'll need you to send those over ASAP."

"Of course. I'll go by the office on my way home and send them to you. All our records are electronic."

"Where were you last night between eight p.m. and midnight?" Marky Mark asked.

Eric scoffed. "I already told you, I was at home. In bed. Asleep."

"Actually, I only asked you earlier where you were between ten p.m. and two a.m. Did you leave your apartment at all last night?"

"No."

"Well, that'll be all. Thanks for coming down, and we'll need those medical records as soon as you can get them to us," Stephenson said as he and his partner stood up from the interview table.

They pushed in their chairs and moved toward the door.

"Oh, and just one more thing," Stephenson said, turning around to face him. "We haven't been able to locate the cell phone of your front office assistant, Daisy. Are you aware of her leaving it at the office or have any idea where we might find it?"

"No."

"All right. We may need to search your practice if we don't find it soon."

Eric nodded and followed them to the door. "Have you arrested Daisy's boyfriend yet?" he asked as Stephenson held the door open for him to exit first.

"No. But don't worry, we'll make sure her killer doesn't get away with it."

Then he remembered the question he had planned but had forgotten to ask. "How did Patricia and her husband die?"

"They both died by asphyxiation due to strangulation."

"Could it have been a murder-suicide?" Eric asked.

"We haven't ruled out that possibility." Stephenson answered.

"Strange that two people you know are murdered on the same night, in the same way, at almost the same time. Almost seems like too much of a coincidence to be a coincidence," Marky Mark said.

Eric decided in that moment that Blondie was his favorite of the two. "I hope you're not insinuating that I killed anyone. You know, sometimes coincidences are just that. Coincidences." Like Daisy's boyfriend killing her the same night he killed Patricia. How he hated him.

"You okay to walk yourself out?" Blondie asked.

"Sure." *You good-for-nothing cops.*

CHAPTER SEVENTEEN

Adams took a sip from his cold coffee when they got back to their desks.

"I can't believe you volunteered us for the Martin Watts case after we just got the girl in the park. Now we'll definitely be working all weekend."

"Their deaths could all be related. You don't think it's strange that three people who all know Dr. Leroy die by strangulation on the same night?" Stephenson asked, annoyed his partner cared more about being home on the weekend than solving their case.

"Stranger things have happened. The guy's a psychiatrist. I'm sure she's not the first of his patients to die of unnatural causes. I just don't like the idea of taking on an extra caseload when we don't even know if they're connected. The husband and wife are probably going to be ruled a murder-suicide by the ME anyway. And the media is going to go crazy when they learn a famous romance writer offed his wife before hanging himself."

"We don't know that yet."

"Not officially, but I'll be shocked if that's not what happened. Plus, the girl was killed by manual strangulation on the other side of town from where the husband and wife were strangled using a necktie and an electrical cord from a curling iron."

Stephenson normally got along fine with Adams, but after catching Serena cheating on him that morning, his partner was getting under his skin. He looked down at the framed picture on his desk of his late partner, Detective Christina Rodriguez. She had been only thirty-three when she was murdered. There wasn't a day that went by he didn't think about her; sometimes he still couldn't believe she was gone.

"The ME isn't going to be able to explain why their back-door lock had been picked. And Pete thought Martin's ligature marks were more suggestive of homicide than suicide when we were at the house. If he'd hanged himself, the ligature line would've moved upward on the back of his neck. And the ligature marks were straight all the way around. My gut says it'll be ruled a double homicide, or at least undetermined pending our investigation.

There is no way that chandelier would've held the weight of a man that size long enough for him to suffocate. It would've been practically impossible to even ensure the curling iron would catch on the light fixture anyway. He would've had to jump off the railing at the top of the stairs. I don't see how he could've done it."

"Well, I guess we'll just have to wait for the autopsy results. At this point though, it looks like Dwayne killed Daisy."

Stephenson couldn't disagree. Since Daisy's body had been outside on a near-freezing January night, determining her time of death at the crime scene had been difficult for the ME. For now, they were relying largely on other environmental factors to pin down the precise time of her death. A light snow covered the top of her body when the jogger had found her that morning. When the medical examiner checked underneath her body at the scene, it was dry. The snow had started around midnight the night before, so they were working with an approximate time of death between ten p.m. and midnight.

Daisy had bruising on her left temple. It looked consistent with her being punched in the side of her face, as Dwayne had admitted. She'd also sustained bruising to both of her arms, probably from being restrained by her killer while he strangled her. Both these injuries helped explain her lack of defensive wounds.

Stephenson and Adams had found ten empty beer bottles scattered around the main living area of Dwayne and Daisy's apartment, which matched Dwayne's story that they'd been drinking.

Dwayne gave them the names of the two friends that let him stay the night but told them they'd left early that morning on a week-long snowboarding trip to Canada. Being out of the country, they didn't have cell service, leaving no one to confirm his alibi. Dwayne stated he hadn't returned to his and Daisy's apartment until that morning. Both Dwayne and Daisy's cars had been parked outside their residence when the detectives visited him earlier that day.

Dwayne had willingly answered all their questions and gave them permission to search his car. CSI was processing it now along with Daisy's.

Stephenson wasn't ready to admit that his partner may be right, but it was shaping up to look like there was no connection between Daisy's death and Martin and Patricia's.

Although, there was something not right about Patricia and Martin's deaths. It was a bizarre scene, and Stephenson didn't buy the murder-suicide theory. Why would the husband leave the front door unlocked and pick the lock on the back door only to hang himself? It made more sense to Stephenson that he'd come home and walked in on his wife's killer.

When Stephenson learned earlier that day that Patricia was a patient of Daisy's boss, he'd insisted they take the case. He couldn't pinpoint exactly why, but Dr. Leroy had given him a bad feeling. And to have three people he knew all strangled on the same night seemed like more than a coincidence.

The doctor had looked genuinely shocked when they informed him of his front office assistant's death, but his reaction to the deaths of Martin and Patricia had felt rehearsed to Stephenson. Adams hadn't seemed to notice.

"They were an odd couple, you know?" Adams mused. "Daisy was a beautiful girl from a seemingly normal family. What was she doing with an overweight sleazeball who probably liked to beat on her?"

Stephenson let his question linger in the air while he continued going through Dwayne's cell phone records. His gaze drifted to the sleeves of his navy sweater that Serena had bought him for Christmas. He wished he would've worn something different. He didn't need the sweater serving as a constant reminder of her. The wool was beginning to feel like sandpaper against his skin. He tugged at the neckline and tried to focus on the stack of papers in front of him.

Adams studied his partner from across their desks. "You seem agitated today."

Stephenson shot Adams a look of annoyance before going back to looking through Dwayne's phone records. "I'm not."

"You piss off your girlfriend or something?"

Stephenson ignored the question.

Adams let out a snort. "All right, whatever you say."

"Dwayne made several calls to Daisy's cell after she died. Makes me wonder if he didn't know she was dead."

"He could've done that just to try and look innocent. Or maybe he was calling it to try and find it. That could be why we haven't been able to locate it," Adams said.

"Maybe. Two of the calls did ping a cell tower in vicinity of Discovery Park just before midnight, which places him at the scene of where Daisy's body was dumped but could also confirm his story about driving around the city for an hour before crashing with friends."

"I doubt his story is true."

"Found anything yet on the traffic camera footage in that area?"

"Not yet. I'm still looking."

Stephenson's desk phone rang.

"Stephenson."

"Hey, we've finished processing the cars of both your victim and her boyfriend."

Stephenson recognized Matt's voice from CSI.

"I've sent you an email with our preliminary report. We found Dwayne's fingerprints inside Daisy's car on both the driver and passenger side. His prints were also on both front doors. No prints inside the trunk and no blood anywhere. Daisy's fingerprints were all over the inside of Dwayne's car. We also found a few strands of hair that look to be a likely match to hers in the front and backseat. Nothing inside the trunk. And no blood."

"Thanks, Matt."

"No problem."

Stephenson hung up and briefed Adams on what Matt had said. Afterwards, Adams went back to looking through the traffic cam footage.

"Looks like you're no longer the only rookie on the squad," he said a few minutes later.

Stephenson turned to see an attractive, blonde woman in her mid-twenties being shown her desk across the room by another detective.

"I'd like to be her partner," Adams said.

"Thank you."

"No offense."

"None taken," Stephenson went back to looking through the phone records.

"I'm gonna ask her out."

Stephenson looked up to see if Adams was serious. It appeared he was. Adams looked back at him with a straight face. Stephenson didn't know how to respond. Adams was a great detective, but when it came to women, he was a total screwball. Apparently, it hadn't occurred to Adams that the beautiful, young detective might not be interested in an overly-muscled, forty-something divorcee such as himself.

"I don't think that's such a good idea. Plus, she just got here. You don't even know her."

Stephenson watched Adams check out the new detective as her partner showed her around the Homicide Unit.

"I'll give it a few days first."

Stephenson rolled his eyes.

Detective Suarez came over to their desk to introduce them to his new partner.

"Stephenson, Adams, this is Detective Tess Richards." He motioned toward the blonde rookie at his side. "She's just joined the squad."

Adams leapt from his chair and shook her hand. Stephenson subtly shook his head when he saw Adams lay his left hand on top of hers, sandwiching her hand between both of his during the handshake.

"Great to meet you. It's about time we had another female on the squad," Adams said, finally letting go of her hand.

Only so you can hit on her, Stephenson thought.

"Thanks," she said. She pulled her hand back to her side as he let go.

Stephenson stayed seated. "Welcome to the squad," he said with a friendly smile.

She returned his smile. "It's great to be here."

The two detectives stepped away from their desk as Suarez continued showing her around.

"I think she likes me," Adams said after they walked away.

"You're an idiot."

CHAPTER EIGHTEEN

Eric got a call from the homicide detectives later that afternoon. They hadn't found Daisy's phone and wanted to search his office building. They said they'd get a warrant if they needed to but asked if he'd instead drive over and let them in. Eric obliged. He didn't have anything to hide. At least, not at his practice and not about Daisy.

He hung around while they searched his entire medical suite. They started with his office, and Eric followed them inside while they searched. He took a seat in the chair normally reserved for his patients, hoping to make them uncomfortable enough to hurry up. Not that he had to worry what they would find; there was no way they could know he altered Patricia's medical records. He just didn't like them going through his stuff.

"It's not here," Marky Mark said after rifling through every drawer of his desk.

"I could've told you that," Eric said before following them out into the hall.

Eric reclined in the waiting room while they went through the front desk area where Daisy spent most of her time. He longed to see her again, sitting behind the desk, too bubbly and bright for a psychiatry practice. An hour later, he wished he'd brought his laptop to work on his book. Although, everything in the office reminded him of Daisy and he probably wouldn't have been able to concentrate anyway.

Soon after that, the two of Seattle's finest announced they were done with their search.

"Did you find it?" Eric asked.

"No," Blondie said. "Thanks for letting us in."

"No problem. If there's anything else I can do to help, let me know."

"We will," Marky Mark said with a flat expression.

CHAPTER NINETEEN

Stephenson pulled into the darkened driveway of his Northgate townhouse late Saturday night. He killed the engine but didn't get out of the car. Daisy's preliminary autopsy results had come back just before he'd left the precinct. The bruising on her left temple was consistent with her being punched in the head, as Dwayne had said in his interview. Pete believed the contusions on both her arms were caused from her killer restraining her during her strangulation. He guessed the killer straddled her, using a knee on each of her arms to hold her down. They'd have to wait and see if any DNA could be obtained from under her fingernails, but, without any defensive wounds, it seemed unlikely.

Her boyfriend was still their prime suspect in her death. Adams had found Dwayne's car on a traffic camera less than a mile away from Discovery Park around ten thirty the night before. The park was a twenty-minute drive away from downtown where he said he'd driven around. It was also in the opposite direction from West Seattle where Dwayne claimed to have spent the night. It didn't make sense for him to have gone there apart from dumping his girlfriend's body. They were close to being able to arrest him, but they needed a little more evidence.

Pete wouldn't have the preliminary autopsy results back for them on Patricia and Martin until tomorrow morning. With not much more they could do that night, he and Adams had called it a day nearly sixteen hours after they'd arrived at Daisy's crime scene.

He reached into his pocket for his phone and was surprised when his fingers rubbed against the smooth leather case that housed Serena's ring. In his rush to get to the crime scene that morning, he'd forgotten to take it out of his coat.

He pulled the small jewelry box out of his pocket and opened it. He wanted to get her something unique, so he'd gotten the ring specially designed. He'd made sure there wasn't another one exactly like it.

After taking the emerald-cut diamond ring out of its case, he held it up. The diamond gleamed in the faint light coming from his neighbor's front porch. He placed the ring back in the box before slipping it back into his pocket.

He took out his phone and tapped on her photo that was still on his home screen. A shortcut came up with an option to *Call Mobile*. His finger hovered over the screen as he struggled against the desire to call her. *Where is your pride?* he thought before finally shoving his phone back inside his coat. He wiped away the tear that managed to escape down his cheek before he got out of his car and went inside.

CHAPTER TWENTY

Stephenson pressed his palm against the cool tile of his shower wall while he closed his eyes and let the hot water beat against his face. He pictured Serena from yesterday morning wearing nothing but a towel with her hair dripping wet, standing next to her newfound love. Or whatever. Maybe he'd just been replaced by some casual fling.

He forced the image out of his mind and tried to focus on his new case. He heard his phone ring over the sound of the water and turned off the nozzle before stepping out of the shower. He grabbed his towel off the wall and quickly dried his hands before picking his phone up from the bathroom counter.

"Hey, Pete."

"Morning. I just wanted to let you know I've sent over the preliminary autopsy results for Martin and Patricia."

"Great. I'll have a look now." Stephenson wrapped the towel around his waist and walked into his bedroom. He placed Pete on speaker and set the phone on his bed while he logged onto his work laptop. "What's the manner of death?"

"For Patricia, homicide, as we'd already surmised. She suffered a nonfatal injury to her forehead prior to death when she collided with the bathroom mirror. The injury was significant enough that she would've been shoved with significant force against the mirror. She also has scratch marks around the ligature mark on the front of her neck and what looks to be her own tissue present under her fingernails. We'll have to wait for the DNA testing to be sure it's only her tissue and not her attacker's. And you know, these defensive wounds would be consistent with her trying to free herself from the necktie when she was strangled. At the scene, you saw the ligature mark around her neck was straight. The lack of blood pooling above the ligature mark and the way her body was found are also inconsistent with hanging."

Stephenson had begun to skim the report as Pete spoke. "And what about her husband, Martin?"

"His autopsy, I'm afraid, was not as straightforward. His ligature mark does angle upwards slightly on the back of his neck, which could be consistent with hanging. However, like Patricia, the lack of blood pooling above his ligature mark suggests the pressure around his neck was released shortly after death, which would be inconsistent with him hanging himself. Although, being that we found him on the floor, it's possible he fell from the chandelier not long after he asphyxiated. I suppose it will be up to you to determine if that chandelier could've held his weight long enough for that to have happened.

"Also like Patricia, he has scratches around the ligature on his neck. This could be consistent with defensive wounds in a homicidal strangulation, or he could've panicked at the last minute and tried to free himself from the cord around his neck.

"He sustained some bruising across his torso which appears to have occurred just prior to his death. But I'm unable to determine if this was a defensive wound he incurred in the process of killing his wife or if he was held down during a homicidal strangulation. There's more details in my report, but, for the time being, I've ruled Martin's manner of death as undetermined."

Stephenson looked at the photo of Martin's body lying atop the metal autopsy table, the bruising across his middle exposed.

"Could his killer have pinned him down by wrapping his legs around Martin's chest while he strangled him from behind? If the killer was positioned slightly higher than Martin when he killed him, that could also account for why his ligature marks come up on the back of his neck."

"I suppose that would be one plausible scenario," Pete said. "I've finished the evidence collection process from both of the deceased, so they are ready for you to pick up and submit to the crime lab."

Stephenson had investigated enough cases by now to know that this evidence collected by the ME would include clothes, hair samples, swabs, blood, nail clippings, and a DNA card from each of the victims.

"Great. I'll be right over."

"Oh, good. I'm ready to get out of this place. I'd like to think I've done enough work for one weekend."

"Wish I could say the same, but I've got a lot more still to be done." This wasn't exactly true, but he wanted to sound normal. Truth was, he was grateful for the distraction his work had provided that weekend. "See you soon."

He ended the call and dialed Adams.

"Is it morning already?" he asked, sounding groggy.

"Yes, and we've got an undetermined manner of death for Martin. Patricia's been ruled a homicide, but no surprise there."

"Huh. Well, maybe you were right after all. I take it we're treating Martin's death as suspicious, then?"

"Sure are. I'll meet you at the station in half an hour. We've got some work to do."

"Can't wait."

Adams got to the Homicide Unit five minutes after Stephenson. He slapped the Sunday edition of *The Seattle Times* on Stephenson's desk and waited for his partner to read the headline.

"This is thanks to our press release last night." Adams sighed. "It's all over the national news too. I told you the media was going to be in a frenzy over this case."

"We had to do a press release. He's a world-famous author."

"I know. I just don't like the added pressure."

Stephenson scanned the news story before handing the paper back to Adams. "It doesn't matter whether he's famous or not. We were right to take the case, and we'll treat it no different than any other."

"I just hope we can solve it soon."

They sat across from Daisy's sister, Emily, three hours later in what the detectives called the "soft room". It was similar in size to their two interview rooms, but instead of stark white walls, a one-way mirror, and chairs that were bolted to the ground, the soft room provided neutral colors with painted walls, a carpeted floor, and multiple chairs that could be moved around.

Emily had come to the Homicide Unit on her own accord, tearfully asking to speak with them when she arrived. Stephenson set a cup of water on the table in front of her before taking his seat.

"Thank you," she said.

She wore no makeup and looked about five years older than Daisy. Her eyes and nose were red from crying, and she dabbed her eyes with a tissue.

"So, you wanted to talk with us about Dwayne?" Stephenson asked.

She nodded. "He left a voicemail on my phone Thursday night threatening to kill Daisy."

Stephenson and Adams exchanged a look.

"Do you still have the voicemail?" Adams asked.

"Yes." She pulled her phone out of her purse. "He called me three times that night looking for Daisy, but I didn't answer. I was out of town. She must've told him that she was staying with me, but I had no idea where she was and didn't want to get in the middle of it. She would stay with me sometimes when she wanted to get away from him. I don't know where she was that night..." her voice broke into sobs. "Maybe if I'd answered and told him she was staying with me she'd still be alive."

"This isn't your fault," Stephenson said.

She wiped her face with her tissue after she placed her phone on the table and played the voicemail for them to hear.

Dwayne's voice came through the phone's speaker: Where's Daisy? I know she's not with you, that lying bitch! Tell me where she is. I'll kill her if she's with another guy. You tell her to call me—or she's dead.

"I didn't think he was serious. He and Daisy fought all the time. It was their normal. Don't get me wrong, I hated him. But I didn't think for a second that he'd actually kill her."

Stephenson watched the color drain from her face. He recognized the look that washed over her as one he'd seen before on other victims' family members. He pulled the garbage can beside her chair moments before she threw up. Most of her vomit made it into the can, but some splattered onto the beige carpet.

"I'm so sorry." She covered her hand with her mouth as she looked down at the mess on the floor.

"Don't be," Stephenson said. "We know this is really difficult. And you're doing great."

"I just can't believe she's dead!" Emily burst into fresh tears and buried her face in her hands.

"Don't blame yourself." Stephenson placed his hand on her arm. "You did the right thing by coming in. May we borrow your phone?"

With her hands still covering her face, she nodded.

"Is this the only voicemail Dwayne left you that night?"

"Yeah."

"All right. We're just going to make a copy of it for evidence. Are you okay to wait here?"

She pulled her hands away from her face, exposing her red, tear-streaked cheeks. "Yes, that's fine."

"We won't be too long."

Stephenson picked up her phone and followed Adams out of the interview room.

Adams turned to Stephenson after they stepped out into the hall. "Well, it looks like we need to bring Dwayne in to have another chat. Maybe we won't be spending the entire weekend here after all."

They went back to Dwayne's apartment and he agreed to ride back to the station with them to answer more questions. They brought him into Interview Room One. If he was aware that they were close to arresting him for murder, he didn't show it. It seemed that asking for a lawyer hadn't even entered his mind.

"We've confirmed your friends' address in West Seattle where you say you stayed last night," Adams began. "We also tried calling both of their cells, but they were turned off. Based on their social media pages, it looks like they did in fact head to Canada for a week-long snowboarding trip like you said."

"Okay. So why did I need to come in then?"

Adams cleared his throat. "Well, here's the thing Dwayne. Daisy probably died between the time you say you left your apartment and when you arrived at your friends' place. So, even if you did stay at their house, you still could've killed Daisy and dropped her body at Discovery Park before you went to their place."

"We also know that your cell phone pinged a cell tower near Discovery Park around Daisy's time of death, which places you close to where her body was dumped. And we have your car on a traffic camera a mile away from the park at 10:37 p.m.," Stephenson added.

"I didn't kill her," Dwayne said matter-of-factly.

They played him a recording of the voicemail he'd left on Emily's phone Thursday night.

"Did you leave this voicemail on Daisy's sister's phone the other night?" Adams asked as the recording played.

"Yeah, but I didn't actually mean it! I was pissed, okay? She didn't come home that night, and I was worried she might've been with another guy. I just wanted her to come home. I swear."

"Maybe you didn't mean to," Stephenson said. "Like you said, you were pissed. If you explain it to us, we might be able to help you."

"I didn't kill her!"

Dwayne stood up from the table.

"All right, calm down." Adams put up his hands. "We're going to give you a little time to think and make sure there's nothing more you want to tell us. We'll be back in fifteen minutes, okay?"

"I've already told you everything."

Dwayne paced back and forth in the small space.

The two detectives got up and started for the door. "We'll be back," Stephenson said before leaving Dwayne alone in the interview room.

"I think we can get a confession out of him," Adams said after Stephenson closed the door behind him. "He already admitted to striking Daisy and he hasn't asked for a lawyer. Hopefully, he'll open up when we go back in there."

They walked back to their desks where they sat down across from each other.

"I'm thinking Dwayne probably strangled her at home and then dumped her body at the park," Adams said.

Stephenson leaned back in his chair. "So, we have the neighbors hearing an argument between Dwayne and Daisy right before her time of death, a history of domestic disputes, Dwayne's admission to hitting her, his threatening voicemail to Daisy's sister, traffic camera footage and a cell tower placing Dwayne near the location of where Daisy's body was dumped right around the time of her death, and her fingerprints and strands of hair inside his car. And he's got no alibi."

"You still think there's a connection between Daisy's death and that couple in Madison Park?"

Stephenson sighed. "No. I think Daisy's killer is sitting in Interview One," Stephenson said.

"I'll fill out the affidavit if you call the judge to get the arrest warrant. Then let's go back in there and see if we can make him crack."

Dwayne hadn't exactly cracked, but they'd had enough on him to arrest him even without his confession.

"How about I take you out for a congratulatory beer since we closed our case?" Adams asked as they walked side by side through the parking garage.

"Thanks, but I'm pretty tired. I think I'll just head home."

"Yeah, me too. But I plan on enjoying what's left of my Sunday. You should too. There's even still time for you to see your girlfriend."

Stephenson didn't respond, and they walked in silence the rest of the way to their cars.

Adams stopped when he reached his car, parked across from Stephenson's. He pulled his keys from his pocket and looked up at his partner.

"You've been acting different this weekend. You sure you're okay?"

"Yeah. I'm fine, thanks."

Adams stood still for a moment and looked like he was trying to read him. "Okay. I'll see you tomorrow."

"See ya," Stephenson said.

Adams watched his partner get into his car before he climbed into his own and followed Stephenson out of the parking garage.

CHAPTER TWENTY-ONE

Eric got up early Sunday morning and decided to go to his favorite café, The Streamliner, on Bainbridge Island for breakfast. He hoped that its organic coffee and buttermilk biscuits might help take his mind off Daisy. Maybe even clear his head enough to work on his book.

With his laptop bag slung over his shoulder, Eric made his way down the steep, city street to the ferry. A light mist was falling, but he didn't mind. He needed to get out of his apartment.

The ferry ride was uneventful. He sat inside and stared out the window at the calm water that shone a cobalt blue in the winter morning light.

Only a short walk from the ferry, The Streamliner was busy as usual when he stepped inside.

It was more American diner than Australian café, but there was a quaintness about it that reminded him of his home country. Although, it had grown busier in recent years. Its notoriety for good food and local feel had caused it to become a tourist destination.

He took a seat at the counter and ordered the breakfast special. He sipped his steaming coffee and was about to open his laptop when he realized he was in no state to write. Or, for that matter, to eat. His grief was just too strong.

His eyes wandered to *The Seattle Times* on the counter to his left.

"Care to read it?" his fellow diner patron asked, motioning toward the paper. "I'm all done."

"Thanks," he said.

He slid the paper toward him as the man stood from his seat. He held up the front page.

NEW YORK TIMES BESTSELLING AUTHOR MARTIN WATTS AND WIFE FOUND DEAD IN SEATTLE HOME

They must be mistaken. *How had I not known this? Why hadn't Patricia ever told me?* He racked his brain through all their sessions. Strangely, he couldn't recall much of anything other than the murder of her brother and her never-ending complaints about her husband. So, maybe she *had* mentioned it. His mind might've just been elsewhere.

He moved his attention back to the paper and read through the entire article. The police hadn't yet released their cause of death. But, according to the article, they were treating both deaths as suspicious. Eric wondered what that meant exactly. Hopefully, they were just waiting on official autopsy results to announce it as a murder-suicide.

Apparently, Martin was a famous man. Not only were most of his books *New York Times* bestsellers, but many of them had also been made into high-earning film adaptations. None that Eric had seen, however, being that they were all romance.

He looked for an article on Daisy's death and was saddened to find it all the way back on page 8. His breakfast arrived and he set down the paper, still blown away that he had killed a bestselling author without even knowing it. He supposed it was one way to get rid of some competition. The scandal of Martin's death would undoubtedly boost his book sales for the short term, but Eric hoped people would've forgotten about him by the time his own book was released.

Despite having no appetite since he'd heard of Daisy's death, his poached eggs and buttermilk biscuits looked incredibly delicious. Before he knew it, his plate was empty. Eric set down his fork and looked again at Martin's headline. He sighed, wondering how many million copies Martin Watts would sell today.

If only he could be on the front page of *The Seattle Times*. In a way, he was famous already. The man who killed Martin Watts. Too bad the world would never know.

Seeing the media craze over Martin's death had helped take his mind off Daisy, but by the time he got back to his apartment she had crept back into his mind. Eric spent the rest of Sunday moping around his apartment, trying to get her out of his head so he could make progress on his manuscript. He needed to write while Patricia and Martin's murders were fresh in his mind. After finishing his hour of yoga, he went to work on the novel.

His thoughts drifted between his book and his secretary for the rest of the day. In his grief over Daisy, he kept thinking back to his ex-wife, Stella. *Gorgeous Stella.*

They married young. She had been nineteen and he had been twenty. They had some pressure from their families, he supposed, because Stella had gotten pregnant. But that wasn't the only reason they got married. In fact, it only made them happier. They were madly in love, and he had been planning on marrying her one day anyway.

She was a professional surfer, which made her a local celebrity in their hometown. She'd even won some international competitions by the time they got married, and her name was becoming well-known in more than just Australia.

Stella's family despised him for getting her pregnant, as if he'd ruined her life. Although they hated him, they thought them getting married was *the right thing to do.*

They were married on the beach in Nelson Bay, the small coastal town in Eastern Australia where both Stella and he had lived their entire lives. He replayed the day in his mind like a scene from a movie. It was January, in the middle of a heat wave. How he missed January in Australia. Stella looked radiant. He remembered sweating through his suit, looking at her and thinking he was the luckiest man alive.

Poor Stella must have been sweltering in the heat, being pregnant, but she didn't complain. She had never looked happier. The ceremony was small, private, and low-budget, with just their families and a few close friends. The minister finally pronounced them man and wife, which they sealed with a tender kiss.

Afterward, Stella grabbed his hand with a twinkle in her eye and pulled him toward the turquoise water. She kicked off her heels when they reached the waves. She waded into the water, pulling him along behind her. Before he knew it, they were swimming side by side in the refreshing sea, he in his suit and she in her wedding gown. Dolphins surfaced not far from where they swam. Thinking back on that day still made him smile.

When Stella lost the baby only a couple weeks later, they were devastated. This made her family hate him even more. Eric was sure that her sister or parents tried to talk her into divorcing him at that point. But he knew that he didn't have to worry. The love they shared was real. They tried to get pregnant again over the next few years, but never did. Even though they weren't without their problems, they were very much in love. Or, so he had thought. Their life together was as close to perfect as one could get. Until the day she left and never came back.

Eric woke the next morning before his alarm. When he saw the book on his nightstand, it suddenly dawned on him why Martin's name had sounded familiar. It was the book he'd tossed aside after reading that stupid line about winter in Seattle. He picked up the novel and opened it to the last page, already knowing who he would see.

There he was. Martin Watts, *New York Times* Bestselling Author. Martin looked better in his photo than he had in person, even before he killed him. His photo had no doubt been photoshopped to make him look more attractive. You couldn't even tell how fat he was.

Eric set the book back on his nightstand and got out of bed. He supposed readers preferred books written by attractive people. Fortunately, for him, that wouldn't be a problem.

When he walked past the drummer's apartment door on his way to work, Eric wondered if he'd played his drums at all the day before. If he had, Eric hadn't even noticed.

CHAPTER TWENTY-TWO

It was Monday night when he saw the news. Eric had taken a break from writing his book to check if there were any breakthroughs in Daisy's case. And, lo and behold, there was. Dwayne Morrison, Daisy's live-in boyfriend, had been arrested for her murder.

When Eric had opened his internet browser to his national news homepage, he was annoyed to see that Patricia and her overrated husband were once again the center of attention. Although, Eric did feel a little prideful that his handiwork had resulted in the biggest news story in the country. For today at least. Bold, red letters filled the top of the page.

MANNER OF MARTIN WATTS' DEATH STILL UNDETERMINED; WIFE'S DEATH RULED HOMICIDE

He wondered what exactly they meant by undetermined. The article said Martin was found at the base of his staircase lying under a fallen chandelier with an electrical cord around his neck. Everything Eric read implied suicide. It made him wonder why they hadn't made a ruling on his cause of death. He clicked out of the article and searched for news related to Daisy's murder.

Eric set down his glass of wine and read through the article on his laptop more than once. It didn't give many details, like what evidence had led to Dwayne's arrest. Just that his bail had been set for $300,000. Eric scowled at Dwayne's picture at the top of the article, his hatred for him growing the longer he stared.

The picture showed Dwayne being led out of an apartment building by Marky Mark and Blondie. Dwayne was overweight and there was little distinction between his chin and his neck. He had dark brown hair and his polo shirt was too tight for his gut. Eric wondered what beautiful Daisy could've possibly seen in him. Aside from his looks, Daisy deserved to be with someone who appreciated her, who loved her. Someone like himself.

He got up and paced around the living room before refilling his glass of wine and sitting back down to work on his book. Daisy would get justice, and he needed to focus on finishing his manuscript. The world needed his novel.

He'd only written half a page when he realized that Dwayne getting arrested wasn't justice at all. What if he gets some unconscionable attorney to make a jury find him not guilty? Or what if he strikes some sort of deal for a lighter sentence? He could be a free man in less than ten years. The thought made Eric nauseous. Even on the minute chance that Dwayne got the death penalty, he'd probably die of old age on death row. And that was much, much more than he deserved. He should've killed him before the cops could get to him. That would've been justice.

He stared at the picture of Dwayne on his screen. The more Eric thought about him, the madder he became. He should've never allowed his fate to be determined by the so called "justice system" of the United States. He deserved to die just like Daisy.

Eric fantasized about winding an electrical cord around his neck, hearing the pathetic sound of him wheeze as he slowly tightened his grip. Dwayne would try to disarm him by swinging his arms behind him, but it would be to no use. Eric would only pull tighter and soon his attempts to pull the cord away from his neck would stop. Eric would relish in taking the last breath from his body.

When he looked at the clock he realized he'd been daydreaming about revenging Daisy's death for over an hour. How could he have been so careless? He got up to pour another glass of wine, hoping the distraction would help take his mind off Dwayne so he could concentrate on the matter at hand: becoming the greatest author in the world.

But it didn't help. As he walked past his couch, he remembered the way Daisy had looked in her sleep. So lovely.

He sighed, thinking of the temp he had hired to replace Daisy for the time being. She was twenty years older than he had hoped, hard on the eyes, and had an extremely unlovable personality.

She seemed to snub her nose at him every chance she got. Whenever he asked her to do something, she pursed her lips before mumbling an unenthusiastic *all right*. As though he was being completely unreasonable for asking her to do her job. As if he was working for her. Just thinking about her frumpy brown hair and sensible flats made him cringe.

It reminded him that he needed to hire a permanent replacement for Daisy. Preferably a bubbly, young blonde who liked to wear spiked heels. But he'd have to worry about that later. He had a book to finish.

He took a sip from his wine after sitting back down to write. He closed out of the article about Dwayne and forced himself to recall everything about Patricia's murder. He opened a new document, ready to reconstruct every detail about that night for his book. He would change the victims' names, of course, but everything else would be the same.

No sooner had he started typing when he heard the familiar sound of his neighbor's drums pulsating through the wall. He tried to tune it out, but the beat grew louder, faster. He couldn't think straight.

He needed total silence when he wrote. He found any noise, even classical music, a total distraction that blocked his creative pathways. While he would've loved to get lost in his favorite AC/DC album while he crafted his novel, that is exactly what his novel would be if he did: lost.

In his book, *On Writing*, Stephen King tells how he cranks head-banging hard metal while he pens his manuscripts. Eric was in awe of this. For him, that would be utterly impossible. His genius was best unleashed in the quiet.

His neighbor never drummed this late. At least, he never did until Eric asked him not too. The throb of the drums felt like it was coming from inside Eric's head. He couldn't take it anymore. He jumped out of his chair and marched down the hall to his door. He banged twice. Then again. But the drums didn't stop. He banged again, but his neighbor probably couldn't hear it over his obnoxious drumming.

Eric took a deep breath and tried to calm down. But his anger about Daisy's death, Dwayne's arrest, his new dud of a secretary, and his neighbor's relentless drumming was an overwhelming force he could no longer contain.

He had tried to be nice. If his neighbor had answered the door, he would've politely asked him to stop. But now he had forced his hand. There was only one thing left to do. Eric turned back for his apartment to retrieve his gloves, lock-picking kit, and something he could use to strangle the drummer.

Eric ended up grabbing one of his ties out of his closet. He figured it worked well enough on Patricia, it would do the job for his neighbor—who was still hammering away on the drums.

Eric went out into the hall and double-checked that he was alone before using his gloved hand to try his neighbor's door. Lucky for him, the dimwit had left it unlocked.

Eric slid his lock-picking kit into his pocket before he let himself inside and closed the door behind him. His neighbor's apartment was a mirror image to his own. Eric spotted him as soon as he stepped inside.

The drum set sat smack in the middle of the living room. Fortunately, his neighbor faced away from him toward the window. Eric wrapped each end of the tie around his gloved hands as he crept toward him.

Eric could see his reflection in the window in front of his neighbor. But he was oblivious to Eric's presence, his head bobbing up and down with each beat. Eric almost felt sorry for the insensitive little prick. Almost.

A large, painted canvas stood on an easel to the left of the drum set. Eric couldn't help but admire the oil painting as he snuck closer. Painting supplies were scattered on the floor under the painting. Although it looked to be a work in progress, it was an exceptionally beautiful work of art. Maybe the drummer should've spent a little more time creating masterpieces and a little less time perturbing his neighbors with his late-night, so-so drumming.

He was directly behind him when his neighbor finally noticed his reflection. He jumped and started to turn around, but it was too late.

Eric wrapped the noose around his neck and pulled with all his strength. The young man's drumsticks fell to the floor as he stood. He grasped at the necktie and spun around to face Eric. Eric moved quickly to stay behind him and keep a tight hold on the noose, but his neighbor kept spinning. Eric jumped onto his back so he wouldn't lose hold of the necktie. The drummer stumbled forward, knocking Eric into the side of easel. The intricate painting fell to the floor. Eric cringed as his neighbor stepped on it as he struggled to free the tie from his neck. They moved across the living room until Eric's weight finally pulled the drummer backward. Eric grunted as his neighbor slammed him against the wall that divided their apartments. Eric's back slid down the wall and they dropped to the floor.

His neighbor thrashed about in a wild motion until finally his movements slowed. Eric held tight until he went limp like an overcooked vegetable. A couple minutes later, he knew it would be safe to let go. His neighbor fell to the side. Eric pushed the rest of his body off his lap before getting up. He didn't look down. He had no desire to see his bloated, discolored face. After all, he did have a heart.

Standing next to the drum set, Eric suddenly wanted to play. It seemed a shame to kill the people that irritated him most if he couldn't enjoy it a little. He had drummed in a band in his early years in Australia, before medical school. They were called Great White. He smiled at their choice of name. They weren't half bad—but never picked up much of a following. They toured around New South Wales the summer after they graduated from year twelve but were too broke to tour any longer.

He bent over and picked up the drumsticks from the floor. When he did, Eric inadvertently got a close look at the whites of the drummer's bulging eyes. They were now pink with pops of bright red from the broken blood vessels. He knew the neighborly thing to do would be to close them, but he didn't do it. Instead, he stepped over his body and took a seat on the stool in front of the drums.

He tapped softly at first, timid that he wouldn't be any good after so many years of not playing. It didn't feel right with his gloves on. If he was going to play, he wanted to put his heart and soul into it. He slipped off his gloves and dropped them on the floor next to him. He made a mental note to wipe the drumsticks off before he left. He closed his eyes and started again.

Gradually, the beat took over him, and his rhythm grew louder and louder. He was amazed by how good he was, like he had never stopped playing. He and the rhythm were one, and, for a while, he lost track of time. It was magical. Like he was high on drugs though he was completely sober. He felt as though he could stay until his neighbor's body decayed.

Eric finally came to his senses. He needed to get back to his book. He let out a sigh and let the drumsticks rest atop his thigh. He knew he shouldn't have taken off his gloves. That was a rookie mistake. But the temptation had been too sweet. He looked around the apartment, wondering what he could use to wipe away his fingerprints. He spotted the small can of paint thinner lying next to the fallen easel. That would work.

He picked up his gloves and went into the kitchen in search of paper towels. He retrieved a nearly full roll from the pantry. He turned the can on its side, soaking a few paper towels and spilling the solution onto the floor. He vigorously wiped the drumsticks until he was certain no trace of his fingerprints remained. Like a good neighbor, Eric disposed of the paper towels in the kitchen garbage before he pulled his tie away from his neighbor's neck and headed for the door.

He felt elated as he meandered back to his apartment. Not only would he never have to hear the sound of those drums come through his apartment walls again, but this killing would make a wonderful addition to his story.

CHAPTER TWENTY-THREE

Eric was a page into recreating his neighbor's death when he remembered that his car was parked in a spot visible by the building's security cameras. He would likely be the prime suspect in his neighbor's murder once his body was found. Having his car parked in the parking garage all night wouldn't do him any favors.

He checked the time and did a quick Google search for local movie showtimes. A movie he hadn't heard of was starting in ten minutes at the theater closest to his apartment. He grabbed his wallet and keys and dashed out of his unit.

He fought the urge to take the stairs and waited impatiently for the elevator to take its thirty seconds to come to his floor. He looked away from his neighbor's door as he stood in the hall. He didn't want to succumb to feelings of guilt and ruin his night at the movies. Two minutes later, he drove out of the parking garage into the dark, rainy night.

He couldn't remember the last time he'd seen a movie at the theater. Although his outing was a forced necessity to create an alibi, he was actually looking forward to it. The only downside was it meant he would lose two hours that he could've been writing. And he would never get that time back.

Playing his neighbor's drums had made him nostalgic for his old rock band. He remembered as he drove that he had one of their old hits downloaded onto his phone. He connected it to Bluetooth and rocked his head back and forth to the beat. As time had gone by, he'd forgotten how good they were. He wondered if they would've stuck together if they could have made it big. He replayed the song for the rest of the drive. By the time he got to the movie theater, he was in a fantastic mood.

"One for *Fifty Shades Freed*, please," he said to the teenage girl behind the ticket counter. *Freed from what?* he wondered. He guessed he'd find out soon enough.

She smiled awkwardly as if she were trying to suppress a giggle. "That'll be twelve fifty."

Eric reached into his wallet and pulled out his credit card so the detectives could verify his purchase.

"Unless you have a senior's discount," she added.

His jaw dropped open. Her smile was gone.

"Are you kidding? I'm forty-five."

Her face flushed as she took his card. "Sorry, we're told to ask if..." she paused, as if realizing what she was about to say.

"If what? Do I look like a senior?"

She avoided eye contact as she passed him back his card and movie ticket. "Enjoy your movie," she said, ignoring his question.

"Unbelievable," Eric said, stepping away from the counter.

The previews had just finished when he walked into the theater. It was empty aside for a middle-aged woman seated in the middle of the back row. He sat down on the end of her row, pretending not to see her smile as he sat down.

The movie was not exactly what he was expecting, although he wasn't sure what he'd expected. It was horrible, all the way to the end, when he read *Based on the Bestselling Novel by E L James*.

Bestselling novel? If that was what it took to write a bestseller then his book would be winning him a Nobel Prize.

The story wasn't even as entertaining as his co-inhabitant of the theater, who he caught making pathetic eyes at him more than once during the film. *Women*. He hurried out to the men's room while the credits played, sparing her the embarrassment of trying to pick him up.

He checked his watch on his way out of the theater and saw it was just after ten thirty. If his neighbor wasn't found for a few days, he wondered how precisely the police would be able to pinpoint his time of death. He might need a longer alibi.

He went back to the ticket counter where the teenage girl was still working. She looked less than thrilled to see him.

"I'd like to see another movie. What do you have playing?"

"Um, *Fifty Shades Freed* starts again in five minutes. That'll be our last showing of the night."

"I don't mind being a little late. Have any other movies started in the last half hour?"

"No, sorry. Everything else is just getting out."

Right. "Then it'll be one adult for your next showing of *Fifty Shades Freed*," he said, passing her his credit card.

"Oh. Okay." She ran his card before handing it back to him with another movie ticket and a dumbfounded expression. "Enjoy the show. Again."

"Thanks."

He walked back into the theater and was glad to see that his ex-movie patron from the eight fifteen showing was gone. He just wished he'd brought a book.

Eric was startled awake by a sharp poke in his arm. He swatted at the hand that jabbed him, disoriented by his unfamiliar surroundings. The young girl from the ticket counter slowly came into focus. She backed away, putting him at arm's length.

"Excuse me, sir. The credits have been finished for over ten minutes, and we're closed. We need you to leave now."

He rubbed his eyes and got up from his seat. He could remember watching the opening scene of the movie for the second time but realized he must've dozed off soon after. The girl followed him out of the theater and into the main lobby.

He pushed open the glass door and walked through the parking garage to his car. He started his engine and saw that it was after midnight. But since he napped through the second showing, he knew he wouldn't be able to fall back asleep. At least not for a while.

He stopped in front of the first bar he saw and went inside for a drink. Or two. He figured he might as well extend his alibi until he was tired enough to go home to bed.

The bar was surprisingly not as sleazy as it looked from the outside. The black and white interior appeared recently renovated and had a modern, industrial feel. The lights that hung from the ceiling were turned down low and pop music blared through the speakers. The seating was a mixture of booths and tables with a long row of barstools set against the bar's concrete counter. A giant mirror covered the wall behind the bar.

The place seemed busy for a Monday night. He took one of the last two empty seats at the bar, next to a twenty-something blonde who was involved in a heavily animated conversation with the two women on the other side of her.

"What can I get you?" the bartender asked.

"Scotch and soda. Make it a double," he said.

The bartender placed a short glass tumbler in front of him a minute later. It was filled to the brim. A single round ice cube floated in the pale brown liquid. Eric emptied the glass after only a few swigs and signaled the bartender for another. He replaced Eric's empty glass with another filled just as full as the first.

Eric started to take a drink as the blonde to his right turned in his direction. After quickly looking him over, she smiled.

"Hi," she said.

He swallowed his mouthful of Scotch. "Hi."

"I'm Laci."

"I'm Eric."

"Do you come here often?" she asked.

"No. This is my first time here. You?"

"Every once in a while, with my friends."

Although not nearly as beautiful, her facial features and blonde hair shared many similarities to Daisy's. As they continued to engage in small talk, he couldn't help but think about sitting at the sushi bar with Daisy while they waited for their table a few nights before.

"What are you drinking?" he asked when his glass was empty.

She glanced at her half-full martini glass, still half full. "A lemon drop."

He flagged the bartender who made his way toward them at a tortoise's pace.

"We'll have two lemon drops," Eric said when he finally came within earshot. "And make mine a double."

He nodded and turned to make their drinks.

A comfortable silence passed between them, and Eric continued to feel nostalgic for his lovely secretary.

"You remind me of someone," he finally said.

She playfully rolled her eyes. "Like who? You're ex-girlfriend?"

"Not quite. Her name was Daisy."

"Was? Like you don't know her anymore?"

Their lemon drops appeared in front of them and he wasted no time in taking a drink. "Mmm. This is good."

She grinned. "Yes, they are. You said her name *was* Daisy?"

He took another drink. "Yeah." He looked down at the lemon rind floating in his martini glass. "She's dead."

"Oh. I'm so sorry."

He noticed this made her uncomfortable and watched her take a sip of her drink. She looked straight ahead as if trying to think of what to say. Or maybe she was debating whether to keep talking to him. He finished his delicious lemon drop and pointed to hers that she'd left untouched while she finished her other martini.

"You mind?" he asked.

"Oh. Umm, no. Go ahead," she said. "You bought it."

She turned back toward her girlfriends as he downed half the lemon drop in one swig.

"I'll have another," he said to the bartender as he walked past. "And make it a double."

Eric watched him unenthusiastically make him another martini. He finished off what was left in his glass and pushed it in the bartender's direction when he set down his newly-made drink. Sometime between his first sip and the bottom of the glass he sobbed for his beloved secretary, overcome by the tragedy of her death. His glass had not long been empty when Laci stood to leave.

"It was nice meeting you." She placed her hand on his shoulder. "I'm really sorry about your friend."

She turned to follow her friends out of the bar. Seeing her long blonde curls bounce against her back as she moved struck a chord inside him. He jumped from his barstool, nearly losing his balance on the unsteady floor. His eyes were blurred with tears as he chased after her.

"Wait! Daisy, don't go!"

He grabbed her by the arm, but she pulled away and hurried toward her friends at the door.

A male patron stepped away from the bar and pressed his palm against Eric's chest when he started to go after her.

"I think you better just let her go, dude."

Eric wanted to punch him in the face but knew he was in no condition to put up a fight. The room was spinning despite his standing still. Instead, he put up his hands as a sign of surrender.

"Okay. I'll let her go."

The man slowly pulled his hand away from Eric's chest. Satisfied when Eric didn't make a run for the door, the man walked back to the bar. As soon as he was out of reach, Eric bolted outside.

He scanned the cars parked along the street before jogging to the parking lot adjacent to the bar. Eric saw her climb behind the wheel of a red Honda with her two friends in tow. He raced to the car as she started the engine.

"Hey!" a male voice shouted from behind him.

It was probably the tough guy again, but it didn't deter him. He needed to get to her. Her eyes widened when Eric reached the car and he heard its doors lock.

"I'm calling the cops!" the man yelled from the sidewalk.

Eric rapped frantically on her window.

"Daisy! You can't do this. You can't leave!"

He tried to open her handle with no success. Her friend shrieked in the backseat.

The car pulled forward and Eric dove onto the hood in a desperate attempt to make her stay. She screamed from behind the wheel and the car jolted to a stop. Eric rolled off the front of the car onto the wet pavement. He stood up, staggered to the side, and shook himself off before climbing back on top of the hood toward the windshield. All three of the women made terrified noises from inside the car.

He pressed his face against the glass in front of the driver's seat. "Please, don't go. I beg you. I can't bear to lose you again." He sobbed with his hands and face still against the windshield. "Daisy!" he cried.

The women's shrieking eventually quieted, and Eric rolled over onto his back. He continued to cry for his secretary while he looked at the unexpectedly clear sky. He hardly noticed the flashing red and blue lights from the squad car that pulled up beside him. Two uniformed officers stood over him with stone cold expressions. They were completely unsympathetic to his state.

"Sir, we're going to need you to get off the car and place your hands on top of your head."

Eric did as he was told and was shocked to feel the cold metal of a handcuff lock around his wrist in exchange for his cooperation.

"You're under arrest for disorderly conduct," the officer said while he secured the cuffs to his other wrist.

The other officer read him his Miranda Rights as they led him into the back seat of their car. Eric watched through the window as they questioned the three women. The officers walked back to the squad car when they were finished and Eric saw the red Honda pull out into the street.

"Daisy," he muttered under his breath as the car disappeared into the night.

CHAPTER TWENTY-FOUR

Stephenson watched Adams stifle a yawn from across their desks Tuesday morning. The city was wet and gray out the window behind him. He and Adams had spent the day before interviewing Martin and Patricia's neighbors, family members, and Martin's publicist. They also revisited the crime scene and went through Patricia's medical file from Dr. Leroy.

The neighbors neither saw nor heard anything the night of the murders. The victims' family and friends had no idea who would do this to them. And revisiting the crime scene had given them no new information.

Nothing appeared to be missing from the home. Both victims' wallets were left in the house full of credit cards and cash. Expensive electronics and Patricia's jewelry had also been left untouched.

They had no clear motive for the crimes. According to Patricia's file from the psychiatrist, her husband was a controlling narcissist who often inflicted emotional abuse on his wife. However, everyone they interviewed loved Martin and had nothing but glowing things to say about him. But, if there was one thing Stephenson had learned during his time as a detective it was that no one ever really knew what went on behind closed doors. In this case, either way, it seemed to be irrelevant. Martin didn't kill Patricia. The husband and wife appeared to be victims of the same crime.

Although they'd arrested Dwayne for Daisy's murder, it was bothering him that three people connected to Dr. Leroy were murdered on the same night by strangulation. The doctor's neighbor had confirmed his statement that he'd knocked on his door and asked him to keep the noise down for the evening, but that was about two hours before Daisy's time of death and approximately an hour before Patricia and Martin's. Because the building's security footage in their parking garage only covered part of the parking area, they couldn't tell if his car had been parked in the garage or whether he came or went anywhere that night.

The doctor seemed to have no motive to kill Daisy, or Patricia and Martin for that matter. And all the evidence pointed to Dwayne as Daisy's killer. Nothing so far had linked the doctor to Martin and Patricia's deaths, but there was something he didn't trust about Dr. Leroy.

Despite all their efforts yesterday, they'd gotten nowhere in the investigation. When they'd finally decided to go home and get some rest late last night, it had felt like a waste of a day.

Adams' face lit up when he saw Detective Richards walk past their desks. *Here we go*, Stephenson thought.

"Got your first case yet?" Adams asked, raising his voice just enough to get her attention.

She turned to face the detective. "Yep. Suarez just got the call. We'll be heading to the crime scene in the next few minutes."

"Enjoy," Adams said with a wry smile.

"Thanks." Her eyes traveled to Stephenson and lingered for a moment before she smiled.

"Morning," he said casually.

"Morning." She looked down at the framed photo of Detective Rodriguez on his desk. "Your girlfriend's a cop too?" She motioned toward the photo.

"My late partner, actually. She was killed just over a year ago."

Her expression turned somber; she obviously had no idea. "I'm so sorry. That's horrible."

Stephenson was about to respond when Adams interjected. "He does *have* a girlfriend though. Getting pretty serious, right Stephenson?"

"Actually, we broke up."

Adams' eyebrows shot to the top of his forehead. "What? When?"

"Saturday morning."

"What happened?"

Richards glanced at her desk before turning back to Stephenson. "Looks like Suarez is ready to go. I'll see you guys later."

"Sure," Stephenson said, grateful she'd excused herself from their conversation that had just turned personal.

"So?" Adams pressed.

Stephenson took a deep breath. He might as well tell him the truth. He knew it would probably do him good to talk about it. "I went over to her house to propose on her birthday and found another guy had spent the night. Apparently, they'd been seeing each other for a few weeks."

Adams' jaw dropped. "Why didn't you tell me?"

"I didn't want to talk about it."

"Wow. I'm sorry, man. I really am. That's rough."

Stephenson nodded.

"Well, at least you didn't marry her," Adams said.

"I guess."

Stephenson's cell phone rang half an hour later. "Stephenson."

"Hey, it's Richards. We just got to the crime scene and I wanted to make sure our homicide isn't related to those cases you're already working on. Our victim is a twenty-three-year-old male who was strangled in his apartment. I know you picked up other strangulation cases over the weekend."

"Yeah, we made an arrest for one of them, but we're still working the other two."

"You guys want to come have a look at the scene? See if it might be connected?"

"Sure, what's the address?" He scribbled it down on a notepad as Richards rattled off the downtown location. "Could you say that again?" He looked in disbelief at the address he'd jotted down.

She repeated the address.

"Thanks, we'll be right there."

"Be right where?" Adams asked as Stephenson hung up.

"You're not going to believe this. Dr. Leroy's neighbor has been murdered. And guess how he died?"

"Our victim is twenty-three-year-old Robert Benson," Richards said.

The apartment looked the part of a bachelor pad. A drum set took up much of the space in the small living room. A pair of drumsticks sat neatly atop the stool. Next to the drums, a large painting and easel lay on the floor of the small living space, surrounded by a mess of painting supplies. Presumably, it had gotten knocked over in the struggle that led to Robert's death.

In the kitchen, Detective Suarez spoke with a member of the CSI team. The team was already working away at processing the scene. Stephenson and Adams stood over the body of Dr. Leroy's neighbor. He lay face-up on the hardwood floor. He was barefoot, wearing a faded black t-shirt and baggy jeans. Even though his face was now mottled with a purplish-gray hue, Stephenson recognized him as the young man he and Adams had confirmed the doctor's alibi with a few days before.

"We spoke to him over the weekend to confirm his neighbor's alibi for our other strangulation cases."

Richards raised her eyebrows. "Really? That's interesting. Well, looks like you two might need to have another chat with that neighbor."

"What's that smell?" Stephenson asked. "Acetone?"

"Paint thinner." Richards pointed to an open can on the floor with clear liquid surrounding it. It lay next to a fallen easel and painting. "We found paper towels in the kitchen garbage that appear to be soaked with it."

Stephenson looked at the mess of liquid on the floor. "If Robert was cleaning up a spill, he didn't do a very good job."

"Maybe it got knocked over during the struggle, and the killer tried to wipe up the mess," Adams said.

It seemed too sloppy for Dr. Leroy. And Stephenson doubted anyone else was responsible for his neighbor's death.

Richards pointed down at the victim. "His friend found him just like this earlier this morning. Robert here was supposed to pick the friend up from the airport last night at eleven thirty but didn't show. His friend called him several times without an answer and ended up taking a taxi home. He came by this morning to make sure Robert was all right. He's pretty shaken up."

"How'd the friend get in?"

"The door was unlocked. There's no sign of forced entry."

"No indication the lock been picked?"

"Not that we could tell."

Stephenson looked over at Adams. "So maybe he knew his killer and let him in."

"Or he felt safe enough to leave his door unlocked," Adams said.

"His friend has already given us his statement, but I asked him to stay in case you two had any questions for him. We haven't been able to find what was used to strangle him. It looks like the killer may have taken it with them."

Stephenson bent down to get a closer look at the victim. "His ligature mark is very similar to Patricia's. I'm guessing it was a necktie." He lifted one of Robert's hands to his nose with a gloved hand. "I can't smell any paint thinner."

"Doing my work for me, detective?"

Stephenson looked up to see Pete heading toward them from a few feet away. His coat was wet from the rain and his normally neat short curls were in disarray atop his head. Despite the ME's slightly disheveled appearance,

Stephenson could tell he was in a good mood. He placed his black canvas bag of supplies that he brought to every crime scene down next to Robert's body.

"As best I can, doctor," Stephenson said, stepping back from the body and allowing Pete to start his examination.

Pete knelt over the victim. "I agree, it does look very similar to Patricia's ligature mark." He carefully turned Robert onto his side and inspected the back of his neck. "Do you have reason to believe his death is related to Martin and Patricia's?"

Stephenson looked at Adams before he answered. "Yes."

Pete continued to inspect the body while Stephenson turned back to Richards. "Have you requested the building's surveillance footage?"

"We've placed a call to the building's manager. She should be here any minute and can show us what they have. There are no cameras on this floor or in the elevator, but there are a couple in the building's parking garage."

"Yeah, we learned that when we requested footage over the weekend to check the doctor's alibi. Problem is, the cameras in the parking garage don't cover the exit or the parking spaces close to it. But we'll see what they show. We should talk to the building manager about getting a camera on the exit. You said the friend who found Robert is still here?"

"Yeah, he's waiting out in the hall. His name is Travis. He confirmed the address for Robert's parents. They live in Kirkland." She handed him a small piece of paper with their handwritten address.

"Thanks. We'll take over from here. Sorry to take your first case away from you."

"That's all right. You owe me one," she said, nudging him with her elbow.

"Okay," Stephenson said before turning to Adams. "Let's go talk to the friend."

Adams nodded and turned to Richards before following Stephenson out of the apartment. "See ya later."

They reached the front door of the apartment and Stephenson bent down to examine the lock for himself. Like Richards had said, the lock looked perfectly intact.

"Richards was totally flirting with you back there," Adams said in a lowered voice.

"Really? I didn't notice."

"It was obvious." Adams shot him a sideways glance. "I hope you're not planning to ask her out before I do."

Stephenson grinned at the overly-concerned look on his partner's face. "Relax. I'm not planning on asking anyone out. I've got other things on my mind."

He stepped out into the hall and Adams followed behind. It was easy to spot Robert's friend. The young man had taken a seat in the hallway with his back resting against the wall. His knees were pulled to his chest. As Stephenson approached him, he saw that his eyes were red from crying.

"Hi, I'm Detective Stephenson and this is Detective Adams. You're the one who found Robert this morning?"

He nodded. "Yeah. I already gave the other detectives my statement, but they asked me to hang around in case there were any more questions." He stared at the wall opposite him as he spoke, avoiding eye contact with the detectives.

"When was the last time you talked to Robert?" Stephenson asked.

"Um...I texted Rob before my flight left from Boston yesterday and he texted me back saying he'd be there to pick me up when I got to Seattle."

"And what time was that?"

"Around nine p.m. in Boston, so I guess around six o'clock here."

"Did he ever mention any problems with any of his neighbors?"

"No. Why?" Travis looked up and made eye contact with the detectives for the first time. "Do you think one of his neighbors killed him?"

"How did you get into Robert's apartment this morning?" Adams asked.

"I knocked a bunch of times and he didn't answer. I called his phone and could hear it ringing inside his apartment. When I tried the door, it was unlocked. I went inside and that's when—" his voice broke. Travis cleared his throat. "That's when I found him."

Stephenson watched Travis' eyes brim with fresh tears.

"Thank you for staying. We're very sorry about Robert."

"Are you going to catch whoever did this?"

Stephenson made a point not to make promises he couldn't keep to friends and family of homicide victims. But, in this case, he felt strangely confident he would bring Robert's killer to justice.

"Yes we are."

Stephenson could feel Adams' eyes on him as they walked back down the hall to Robert's apartment. But if he felt Stephenson was wrong for promising to catch Robert's killer, he didn't say so.

Pete turned Robert's body onto its side and pulled his t-shirt up to his arm pits as the detectives reentered the apartment. Richards knelt beside him, listening intently, as the medical examiner took advantage of the teachable moment with the young detective.

"This is the lividity I'm talking about." Pete pointed to the purplish discoloration of Robert's back as Stephenson and Adams approached. "When the heart stops, blood pools in the dependent parts of the body. Since there is no lividity present on the victim's abdomen, it would seem he died in this position. The discoloration doesn't shift when I turn the victim, which means the lividity is fixed. This tells me the victim has been dead for at least eight hours." Pete looked up at the two detectives standing over him. "The victim's liver temperature is seventy-eight degrees; he's in full rigor, and, as I was just showing Detective Richards, his lividity is fixed. Right now, I'm estimating he's been dead for approximately eleven to thirteen hours."

Adams checked his watch and turned to Stephenson. "That puts our time of death between seven thirty and nine thirty last night."

"I'll notify Robert's parents if you want to chase up that security footage," Stephenson said.

"You sure?"

Stephenson nodded.

"Okay. Call me when you're on your way back. I'll probably still be here. I want to see what else CSI finds in Robert's apartment before I go back to the homicide unit."

"Will do."

"I'll call you when I get done with the autopsy," Pete said.

"Thanks." Stephenson took a deep breath as he moved toward the elevator and prepared to do the hardest part of his job.

Stephenson checked his phone before pulling out onto the street as he left the home of Robert's parents. He'd placed it on silent before doing the notification.

He looked out his window at the landscaped lawns that lined the steep street as he drove to the end of the block. The Benson's large water-view home was like all the others in its Kirkland neighborhood. Overlooking Lake Washington, the newly-built, two-story house left little space between them and their neighbors. Like many homes in the area, the lot was developed for a much smaller structure in the sixties or seventies, which would've been demolished and replaced with their current dwelling. The upscale neighborhood was just up the hill from the lake and offered a mixture of both mature trees and new homes.

He felt drained after informing the Bensons of their son's death. It didn't matter how many death notifications he'd done before, it never got easier. He doubted it ever would. The Bensons were obviously well-off, but Stephenson didn't envy them. No amount of money could ever replace their loss.

He reflected on his conversation with Robert's parents as he drove across the floating bridge over Lake Washington back to the city. On a bright summer day, the view of the lake with Mount Rainier in the backdrop made for a spectacular sight. But on this dreary day in January, the visibility from the bridge was poor. Stephenson could only make out the water close to the bridge, which rippled on the surface from the wind and rain.

He called Adams when he got to the other side of the bridge.

"How did it go?" Adams asked.

"They were in shock. Grief stricken, as expected. I wish I could unsee the look on their faces when I told them. I hate that part of the job."

Adams exhaled into the phone. "I know. Me too."

"Are you still at the scene?"

"Yeah, CSI is still processing it. After you left, I noticed Robert's drumsticks reeked of acetone. We dusted them for prints but there were none. It seems they were wiped clean with the paint thinner that had spilled on the floor. I'll have them sent to the lab to be tested for mineral spirits and acetone."

Stephenson wasn't surprised by the finding but still found it disturbing. It left only two possible scenarios in Stephenson's mind. Either the doctor had played his neighbor's drums prior to killing him or he'd played them after strangling Robert and while his dead body lay at Dr. Leroy's feet. He thought the second scenario more likely, which meant they were dealing with a psychopath.

"I'm still going over the building's security footage so I'll be here a little longer. You coming back?"

Stephenson passed the exit that would take him to Robert's apartment, deciding to make another stop first. "No, I'm going to pay Leroy a visit. I'll meet you back at homicide this afternoon." The only positive thing that had come from his visit with the Bensons was it made him even more determined to catch their son's killer.

"Okay, see you then."

A few minutes later, Stephenson pulled into the parking lot of Dr. Leroy's psychiatry practice. He was all but convinced the doctor had murdered his neighbor. And he sure as hell wasn't going to let him get away with it.

CHAPTER TWENTY-FIVE

Eric was half asleep listening to a typical whiny millennial complain about the stresses of her day job when his drab new secretary rudely interrupted them. She threw open his office door and butted into the middle of his client's private session. He noticed she didn't even have the good grace to look sorry. He felt his left eye begin to twitch.

After sleeping off his few too many drinks in a jail cell, he'd been released early that morning. Slapped with a thousand-dollar fine, Eric was told he would receive a subpoena in the mail with an upcoming court date for his misdemeanor charge. His head throbbed despite the aspirin and half a pot of coffee he'd consumed before coming to the office. He tried not to feel down on himself for the absurdity of his actions after he'd left the theater.

"There's a police officer here to see you. He says it's urgent," she blabbed.

"Police officer?" His client sat forward in her chair.

He really needed to get a new secretary.

"Well, tell him that he has to wait. As you can see, I'm with a client."

"I don't think he's going to take no for an answer."

It seems like the one who's having a hard time taking no for an answer is you, he wanted to say. He checked his watch. There was only fifteen minutes left in his client's session, and he had lost interest in anything she said nearly an hour ago. He looked down at her chart to find her name.

"I'm sorry, Bridgett. But it looks like we will have to pick this up again next week. My apologies for the interruption."

Bridgett looked at his secretary and then back at him.

"Okay."

She sheepishly stood from her chair and followed his secretary out of the room. It was moments like these when he missed Daisy almost more than he could bear.

The door hadn't yet fully closed behind them when Blondie pushed it back open. He did not look happy to see him.

"Good afternoon, doctor."

Eric crossed his leg and set down his notepad.

"Good afternoon, detective."

He shut the door but remained standing just inside of it. Eric looked from him to the chair and then back to him again, as if daring him to sit down. He didn't. Probably afraid Eric would start reading his mind if he did. And then he would know they had nothing on him.

"What were you doing last night between seven p.m. and midnight?"

Well, fair dinkum. They'd found his body already. That was quick for a bloke who never seemed to leave the apartment. Eric thought it might be weeks before his body was discovered, after someone finally complained of the smell or a relative came to check on him.

"Um...let me think."

He picked up his pen and tapped it against his notebook.

"I went to the movies. I think I have my ticket stubs in my wallet if you'd like to see." He reached into his back pocket.

"I would. What time was the movie?"

"I actually saw two movies, back to back. Well, the same movie. Twice. The first showing was around eight thirty." Eric pulled out the movie tickets and held them up. "Eight fifteen to be exact," he read aloud before handing it off to the detective. He had made sure to also have the receipts handy. He pulled them out next and held them out. "Here's my receipt with my credit card information."

Blondie took it from him, looking unimpressed. His expression changed, and Eric realized he must've seen the movie title.

"Fifty Shades Freed, huh?"

"Yes."

"You go by yourself?"

"I did."

"Interesting. And it was good enough that you had to see it twice?"

"What can I say? I liked it. So kill me." He smiled. Blondie frowned. "No pun intended."

"You were late," he said, ignoring Eric's joke. "This receipt is timed eight twenty-one."

"Only a few minutes. They were still playing previews for a while after I took my seat."

"What did you do from seven p.m. until the time you got to the movies?"

"Let me think." Eric motioned toward the chair across from him that was usually occupied by his patients. "Are you sure you wouldn't like to have a seat?"

"I'm sure."

The detective shifted his weight from one foot to another and Eric could tell he'd made him uncomfortable.

"Suit yourself. Anyway, I got home about six. I made dinner and then watched TV until I decided to go to the movies." That last part was a lie. He never watched TV that early in the evening. But there was no way he was going to tell him about his book. Or murdering his neighbor. "Why do you ask?"

The cop looked like he was trying to read him before he answered.

"I'm afraid that yet another person that you know has been murdered."

Eric portrayed a look of surprised concern. "I hope you're joking."

"I never joke about murder."

His stone-cold expression and unmoving form reminded him of a statue, and something about this struck Eric as funny. He did his best to suppress the laugh that rose to the surface but was unable to control the smile that escaped his lips.

"Something funny?"

He relaxed his mouth.

"No. It just doesn't seem like that could be possible."

"You're not going to ask who it is?"

"I assume you're going to tell me."

"Your neighbor, Robert Benson. The one you asked to stop drumming the night of Patricia, Martin, and Daisy's murders."

"That's awful. He was so young."

"Yes. I've just come from notifying his parents of their twenty-three-year-old son's death. Their lives will never be the same."

If he was trying to make him feel guilty about killing the drummer, he was wasting his breath. Eric had heard the TV going in his neighbor's apartment during the day and all throughout the weekends. He shuddered at the thought. *What kind of lowlife watched TV during the day?* His neighbor, apparently.

Eric had always been revolted by people who watched TV during the daylight hours. It seemed a little more civilized when it was at least dark out. But people who sat on their ass wasting the daylight hours by numbing their brains with mindless television and having no ambition whatsoever never ceased to disgust him. Eric reminded himself of this whenever he started to feel sorry for killing him.

"Did you go straight home after the movies?"

"Well, no. But that's a long story."

"I have time," he said.

Eric sighed. Of course he did. "I stopped at a bar on the way home."

"You have a receipt to show for that too?"

"No. I got arrested before I was able to pay my tab."

His face perked up. "Arrested? For what?"

"Disorderly conduct. I had a few too many. I slept it off in a jail cell and they released me this morning. I'm sure you'll be able to verify that without a problem."

"I will."

Eric could see the detective was intrigued by his arrest. More so than he thought he should be.

"Was something bothering you that caused you to drink so much?"

Eric scoffed at his lousy attempt to psychoanalyze him. "Nope."

"Have you ever been inside your neighbor's apartment?"

He was about to say no but changed his mind in the off chance that he'd left some trace of himself inside the drummer's apartment.

"Yes, once."

Blondie waited for him to offer more information. Eric obliged.

"We rode together in the elevator one afternoon, and I asked if I could have a go at his drum set."

"Have a go?"

"Yes. I was the drummer in a band during my youth in Australia."

He paused, proud of this fact. The detective looked back at him blankly. *What a buzzkill*, Eric thought.

"Anyway, I asked if he would mind if I had another crack at it since it had been so long, and he said sure."

"And how long ago was this?"

He should probably make it recent. "Two nights ago."

Blondie crossed his arms and Eric had difficulty reading his expression.

"A few of the tenants complained about his drumming to the building's manager, but not you. I would imagine you felt he was pretty inconsiderate though. Living right next to him and all."

He was fishing for information, but Eric didn't take the bait. "I wasn't bothered by it. But I guess I've always had a deep appreciation for the arts." Eric looked at him like he knew he would understand, even though he knew he wouldn't.

"Did you hear anything last night, before the movie?"

"Mmm..." He pretended to think for a moment. "No."

"Nothing?"

160

"Nothing. Sorry I can't be of more help."

Blondie seemed to study him, obviously not believing what Eric had said.

"It would help if you allowed me to search your apartment. Would you consent to that?"

"I'm afraid not without a warrant."

Blondie looked as though he'd expected this.

"It must be hard to trust people after all the terrible things you see on the job," Eric said. "You have a family, detective?"

When he didn't respond, Eric continued. "I imagine it's difficult to switch off from the dead bodies, heinous crimes, and murderers you encounter when you go home and feel obligated to act normal with your family, wife, or girlfriend. Like it's all just another day at the office. That must be wearing."

Eric could see he'd struck a nerve, but not in the way he intended. He had misjudged him.

"Oh, wait. You don't have any of those," Eric corrected.

Now he had gotten under his skin. The detective's eyes narrowed, but he otherwise tried to ignore Eric's observation. Blondie was young, probably not yet thirty. But old enough to have a family, or at least someone to go home to.

"You let the job consume your life, don't you? Well, I guess that makes things easier. No one to have to interact with after some of the grotesque things you must see."

"While I'm here, I may as well inform you that your client, Patricia, and her husband's deaths are being treated as a double homicide. So, don't leave town. I'll probably need to speak with you again soon."

If the young cop was trying to shock him, he failed.

"Anytime. You know where to find me." Eric took a business card off his desk and held it out for the detective. "Here, this has all my contact information."

He hesitated to accept it. "Thanks, but we've got all your information already on record."

He lifted the card higher. "Just in case."

Reluctantly, Blondie took the card and slipped it into his back pocket before turning to leave.

"Thanks for your time, doctor," he said as he opened the office door.

"If you ever need to talk about anything, I'd be happy to fit you in. I think you'd find I'm an excellent listener."

Blondie slammed his door shut.

CHAPTER TWENTY-SIX

Stephenson looked up from his desk when Adams got back to the Homicide Unit later that evening.

Adams took a seat across from his partner. "How'd it go with the doctor?"

Stephenson placed his hands on the back of his head. "He has an alibi for most of the night. He went to the movies, actually two movies in a row. He watched two back-to-back showings of *Fifty Shades Freed* and paid with his credit card. I stopped at the theater on my way back and checked their security footage. He was there."

"Interesting movie choice."

"It gets better. He stops at a bar on the way home, gets drunk, follows a group of women to their car where he jumps onto the hood and hysterically begs them not to leave. According to the arrest report, he kept calling one of them Daisy. He cried out her name the whole ride back to the station."

Adams raised his eyebrows.

"What did the building's security cameras show?" Stephenson asked.

"Not much. There's a camera at the front entrance and three in the parking garage. Twenty-eight of the seventy-five people who entered through the building's front entrance between five and ten last night had to be buzzed in. The rest used their keycard. I asked Robert's friend, Travis, if he recognized any of those twenty-eight visitors, but he said no. The footage isn't the best quality, but I'll run those images through our facial recognition software to see if we get any hits."

"How did Travis get in the building without Robert letting him in?"

"He was let in by a woman leaving for work. She must've presumed he lived in the building. So much for controlled access.

"Anyway, there's only one other resident on Robert's floor other than Dr. Leroy. She's ninety years old and was watching TV in her apartment during Robert's time of death. She didn't see or hear a thing. The entrance to the parking garage is gated. You can only get in with the building's keycard. The parking garage cameras show Dr. Leroy get into his car and leave the garage at 8:10 p.m. and he doesn't come home until seven thirty this morning."

"So, his alibi's solid, but only from 8:10 onwards," Stephenson said. "I'm guessing the doctor probably killed Robert shortly before he left for the movies, but that's going to be difficult to prove unless we can get a more precise time of death. What else did you find at the scene?"

"Not much. I dropped Robert's laptop and cellphone off at TESU to be analyzed."

The Technical Electronic Support Unit was located on the seventh floor next to the Homicide Unit.

"I also sent the drumsticks to the crime lab on my way here from the crime scene. They're backed up as usual, so it'll be a few weeks before we get the official results. So far, there's no match to Dr. Leroy's fingerprints anywhere in the apartment."

"Leroy said he went over and played the drums two nights ago."

It didn't surprise him that Dr. Leroy lied, but it made him wonder why he'd said he'd been in his neighbor's apartment on Sunday night. There must be something that linked him to Robert's crime scene.

"You think the killer played the drums before he killed him?" Adams asked.

"Or after."

Adams leaned forward and rested his elbows on his desk.

"We need to search Dr. Leroy's apartment. I spoke with Judge Tanner about it this afternoon, but she doesn't think we have enough on Leroy for a warrant. Maybe we should ask if he'd let us do the search without one."

Stephenson let out a sigh and leaned back in his chair. "I already tried. He said no."

Adams nodded. "Figures. Robert's building manager said she'd received two complaints about the noise from Robert playing his drums in his apartment. Both from tenants on the floor below who have solid alibis for last night. There were no complaints from his next-door neighbor, Dr. Leroy. I think he preferred to take matters into his own hands. The manager said if she got one more complaint, she would've given Robert notice to evict the apartment."

"I'll check the traffic cams between his apartment and Martin and Patricia's address on Friday night."

"I'll help you," Adams said.

Even though their addresses were less than five miles apart, it took several hours for them to go through every traffic cam footage between Dr. Leroy's and Martin and Patricia's residence the night of their deaths. Stephenson studied the map after looking through the last of the footage. It would've been possible for Dr. Leroy to have avoided all traffic cameras on his way to their house, but it would have required a great deal of premeditation.

"It's kind of strange that a middle-aged man with a clean record would suddenly murder three people within less than a week. Although, it happens, I know. When did he move here from Australia?" Adams asked.

"Twenty years ago. He was twenty-five. I requested a background check from the Australian authorities, but I'm waiting on the report."

"Oh, and I almost forgot," Stephenson added. "Dwayne's two friends saw his arrest on the news and came home early from their snowboarding trip in Canada. They came into the station this afternoon to confirm Dwayne had spent the night at their place the night of Daisy's murder. Only it doesn't change anything. Like Dwayne had said, he didn't get to their house till about midnight, so it leaves plenty of time for him to have killed Daisy. Their statements will be pretty much useless to his defense."

"I agree," Adams said.

Stephenson shut down his laptop and stood from his chair. "Let's call it a night."

CHAPTER TWENTY-SEVEN

Adams was already at his desk when Stephenson got to work the next morning. Stephenson had his coat halfway off when Adams got up from his seat.

"You might want to leave that on," he said. "I came in early this morning, and I stumbled upon something interesting."

"What's that?" Stephenson pulled his rain jacket back over his shoulder.

"I searched for Martin and Patricia's case file using their address, only I typed in 3898 McGilvra instead of East McGilvra Street. Coincidentally, this pulled up two files, 3898 McGilvra *Boulevard* East and 3898 East McGilvra *Street*. The first report is for a break-in that occurred a few blocks from Martin and Patricia's two nights before their deaths. And the addresses are only one word different. Nothing was taken from the home, and, when the mother and daughter surprised the intruder, he fled but hasn't been caught."

"So, did they see his face?"

Adams smiled. "They did. He was wearing a baseball hat, but they describe him as being in his mid-forties, Caucasian with light brown hair, and approximately five ten with a thin build."

"It could be Dr. Leroy."

"Yes, it could. They believe the intruder entered the house through the back door, *and* there's a slight indication the lock was picked. I'm thinking if I got the address wrong, maybe he did too. Anyway, I've already printed off a photomontage that includes Dr. Leroy for them to ID. If we head there now, we could probably question the daughter too, before she goes to school."

"Nice work. Let's go."

They pulled in front of the Madison Park home twenty minutes later. It was in the same neighborhood as Martin and Patricia's house, where the streets were lined with maple trees and the homes aged from the 1920's to new. Stephenson was glad to see two cars were parked in the driveway. The rain had started to come down hard, and he pulled the hood of his jacket over his head as he stepped out of the car.

When they got under the covered front porch, he drew back his hood. Adams rang the doorbell. Moments later, a teenage girl cautiously opened the door only enough to see who was there.

"Can I help you?" she asked.

According to the police report, she was seventeen.

Adams smiled, hoping to put the girl at ease. "Good morning. I'm Detective Adams and this is Detective Stephenson. We have some questions for you and your mother about the break-in you had last week."

She looked back and forth between the two detectives.

"Mom!" She turned back toward the inside of the house. "Some detectives are here to ask about the break-in," she yelled.

"Okay, I'm coming," a woman's voice called from upstairs.

The girl opened the door wide and stepped aside to make room for the detectives.

"Come on in."

"Thank you," Adams said, stepping into the entryway.

Stephenson followed closely behind. The girl used one hand to fling her long dark curls behind her back while she closed the door with the other. A thin middle-aged woman descended the carpeted stairway that led to the entryway, securing an earring as she went. In contrast to her daughter's casual attire, she wore fitted black pants and a red blouse. She stepped carefully in her stilettos.

"Ms. Phillips?"

"Yes. Call me Beth."

Adams repeated their introduction as the woman reached the bottom of the steps.

"Have you caught him?" she asked, looking expectantly at the detectives.

"Not yet," Adams said. "But we're hoping you and your daughter might be able to answer some questions that would help us identify him."

She let out a sigh in her obvious disappointment. "Of course. Would you like to have a seat?"

She motioned toward the sofa in a formal living room to the right of the entryway.

"That'd be great, thank you."

The detectives took a seat on the sofa. The woman sat across from them in an armchair while her daughter started to go upstairs.

"Kaitlyn, come sit down."

Kaitlyn looked put out as she turned back down the steps. "I'm gonna be late for school."

"This is important. It won't take long," Beth said.

The girl let out a loud sigh before plopping herself down next to her mother in an identical armchair. She looked across at the detectives with a pained expression.

"Has anyone ever told you that you look like Chris Pine?" Kaitlyn asked, staring at Stephenson.

"Kaitlyn." Beth looked slightly shocked at her daughter's question.

Adams rolled his eyes. "Trust me, he knows how good he looks. You don't have to tell him. Don't make my life any harder than it already is. He doesn't even work out. It's disgusting."

Although he knew his partner was half-joking, his comments were out of character for him to say in front of their two witnesses. He was normally nothing but professional. Stephenson wondered if Richard's flirting with him was getting to his partner.

"Anyway, we have some photos we'd like both of you to look at and see if any of these men is the man who broke into your house."

Adams pulled the photos out from the inside of his jacket and laid them on the coffee table.

"Okay," Beth said.

Stephenson held his breath while the mother and daughter leaned forward to look closer at the pictures.

They stared at the photos for almost a minute before Beth spoke. Stephenson knew what she was going to say before she said it. There'd been no look of recognition on either of their faces.

"I'm sorry, I don't know. It all happened so fast, and he was wearing a baseball hat so it's hard to tell from the pictures. I can't be sure."

"What about you, Kaitlyn?" Adams asked.

The girl was still staring down at the photos.

"Maybe this one." She pointed down at Dr. Leroy's photo. "But I'm not sure. He looks different without the hat."

It's him, Stephenson thought. "Take your time, Kaitlyn. Is this the man who broke into your house?"

She bit her lip and took another look at his picture then glanced across at all the others. "Maybe. But he also kind of looked like him." She pointed to a man in another photo who had similar features to Dr. Leroy.

Stephenson tried his best to hide his disappointment. They were so close to her making a positive ID of Dr. Leroy.

"Are you sure?"

"Yeah. It could've been either of those two."

"Did you notice if he had an accent? Did he say anything while he was here?"

Beth's eyes lit up. "Yes, he said he was leaving when I came into the entryway. Now that you mention it, I think he might've had an accent. I'm not sure from where though, maybe British? No, it was subtler. Actually, I'm not sure." She rubbed her fingers against either side of her temples. "I'm sorry. I was so panicked that a stranger had broken into our home. That's all I was focused on."

171

"That's okay," Adams said. "Do you remember an accent, Kaitlyn?"

She shrugged. "I didn't notice." She turned to her mother. "Can I go to school now? I'm already late."

Beth nodded.

She jumped out of her chair and grabbed a backpack laying by the stairs.

"Hope you catch him," she said to the detectives before she ran out the door.

Not as much as I do, Stephenson thought.

She had only been gone for a few seconds when the front door flung open again. She leaned her head around the door. "He said *crikey.* I just remembered."

"And are you sure he didn't have an accent?" Stephenson asked.

"Maybe, I don't know. But I remember he said *crikey* when he dropped his phone because I thought it was a weird thing to say. Anyway, I gotta go," she said before disappearing behind the door and pulling it shut behind her.

"I should probably be getting to work," Beth said. "Unless there's anything else?"

Adams looked at Stephenson before he answered. "No, that's all for now. Thanks for your time."

"Sorry we couldn't be more helpful."

She stood from her chair and the detectives followed her to the door.

"I changed the lock on the back door and had a security system installed in the house. Do you think we're in danger of the man coming back?"

"We can't say for sure, but we don't think so." Adams handed her his card before following Stephenson outside. "If you think of anything else, please let us know."

"I will," she said, closing the door behind them.

"He said crikey," Stephenson said once they got in the car. "It had to be Dr. Leroy. We were so close to Kaitlyn identifying him."

He leaned his head back against the headrest while Adams drove.

"I agree, but it still doesn't give us an arrest."

Stephenson looked out the window. The rain had stopped, but it had been enough to leave puddles in the street. His mind went back to Dr. Leroy's arrest report from two nights before.

"Where do you think Daisy was that night when she told Dwayne she was at her sisters? Her parents said they hadn't seen her in weeks."

"I don't know. Why?"

"What if she was with Dr. Leroy?"

Adams seemed to think about this for a moment. "You think there was something going on between them? Her phone records didn't show any contact between them."

They still hadn't found Daisy's phone but were able to get her text and call history through her phone records. Although, having her actual phone would've been more helpful. There were some things, like photos, that couldn't be obtained through phone records.

"True. But he seemed genuinely stricken when we informed him of her death. It was different than the way he reacted when we told him about the death of his neighbor and one of his patients. Like he actually *cared*."

"Yeah, I agree. But he did work with her every day. He could've had more of a personal relationship with her than with his neighbor and Patricia. Plus, if he killed those two, their deaths wouldn't have come as a shock."

"Right."

Stephenson's eyes were drawn to the oppressive gray cloud cover that hung over them as he thought about how they were going to prove the doctor's guilt. Dr. Leroy had killed three people in a matter of days. If they didn't arrest him soon, Stephenson was sure there would be more. He had to be stopped. He had an idea, but his partner wasn't going to like it. He decided not to say anything as they drove back to the Homicide Unit. He needed to talk to Sergeant McKinnon.

CHAPTER TWENTY-EIGHT

Stephenson could see the sergeant was in his office when they got back. He stopped at his desk to quickly check his email before he went to see the sergeant. He'd gotten an email back from the Australian police in New South Wales. The doctor's record was clean.

He forwarded the email to Adams before he closed out of his inbox, all the more intent to carry out his plan. It might be their only chance of catching Dr. Leroy.

"Can I ask you something?"

He looked to see Richards standing at the end of his desk.

"Only if you promise not to ask if anyone's ever told him he looks like Chris Pine," Adams said.

She looked confused. "What?"

"Don't mind him. He's just kidding," Stephenson said.

She smiled. "Okay. Well, since you've taken over my first homicide case, I wanted to know where you guys were at. Did you talk to his neighbor, the doctor?"

"I did."

"And? Is he your guy?"

"I think he killed Robert, yes. Unfortunately, we're still a ways off from proving it."

"Well, I'll let you get back to work then. Just wanted to get an update."

Stephenson watched Adams' eyes follow her as she walked away. He stood and headed for McKinnon's office.

Adams looked up from his desk. "Where are you going in such a hurry?"

"I need to see McKinnon about something."

Adams waited a moment for him to elaborate. "Okay," he said, turning back to his laptop.

Stephenson felt a little guilty about going to the sergeant before telling his partner about his plan, but he didn't want to argue about it. And he felt he had no choice. It was their only option if they wanted to stop the doctor from killing anyone else.

Stephenson tried to gather his thoughts as he approached the sergeant's office. He knew what he was about to ask was against protocol and there was probably no way the sergeant would go for it. But, if anyone would see the need to break standard procedure for the sake of catching a killer, it would be McKinnon.

The glass door to McKinnon's office was closed and Stephenson could see him sitting at his desk behind his computer. He knocked against the glass enough to get the sergeant's attention. McKinnon lifted his head and motioned for him to come in. He took a deep breath as he opened the door.

CHAPTER TWENTY-NINE

Eric rose early on Thursday morning to get some writing in before work. His drunken escapade on Monday night had put him behind on his writing schedule. He took a sip from his freshly brewed black coffee and sat at his desk. He looked out his large window at the city that was still dark. It was so quiet, he felt like he was alone in the world. It was the perfect atmosphere to work his novel.

After Blondie's visit to his office on Tuesday, Eric started to think he might need to take some precautionary measures in the unlikely event they charged him with murder. He was sure he'd been careful and was confident they wouldn't find adequate evidence to arrest him. All they probably had to go on was that he knew all three of the deceased. It was certainly not proof that he killed anyone.

Even so, he needed to prepare for the worst-case scenario. He had stopped by his bank on his way home from the office the day before and withdrawn ten thousand in cash. It was safely stowed in his fireproof box under his bed where he kept his passport and other important documents. Just in case.

He still had two hours before he needed to leave for the office. He ran a Google search of Dwayne Morrison to see if there were any updates on his arrest and when he might go to trial. Eric choked on his coffee as he read the first headline that came up.

He set down his mug and coughed while he reread the headline. Surely, he'd read it wrong. But he hadn't. He clicked on the article and subconsciously shook his head as he read through it. *Unbelievable.* Starsky and Hutch really were as dumb as a box of rocks. Their incompetency was infuriating.

He looked at the time and got up to take a shower. There was no way he could work on his novel now. He needed to go have a word with his inept friends at the Seattle Homicide Unit.

It was just becoming daylight when Eric got to the Police Headquarters. He knew his way around from his visit over the weekend. After convincing the cop at the front desk that he needed to speak with the detectives regarding his secretary's murder, the officer had Eric wait while he called the homicide unit.

"The two detectives you wanted to speak to are both on the phone, but another detective will be down shortly to escort you upstairs," the officer said after making the call.

"Fine." Eric paced back and forth while he waited for the detective to bring him upstairs.

A dark-haired detective stepped off the elevator five minutes later. He introduced himself as Detective Suarez. He used his ID badge to get back into the elevator with Eric and pushed the button for the seventh floor.

"I'll take you to one of our interview rooms where you can wait to speak to Detectives Adams and Stephenson," Suarez said as they got off the elevator and entered the homicide unit.

Ignoring the detective, Eric stormed into the large open room cluttered with desks. There they were sitting across from each other. Dumb and dumber.

"How could you let him go?" he yelled.

They both looked up as Eric marched toward them.

Adams mumbled something under his breath and looked across at his partner. Eric must've heard wrong because it sounded like, *that's what I said*.

"What?" Eric asked.

Suarez caught up to Eric and pulled both of his hands behind his back.

"It's okay," Blondie said, signaling for Suarez to let him go.

Eric felt the detective slowly release his grip from Eric's wrists.

Blondie rested both his elbows on his desk and leaned forward.

"We're working on a theory that the same person who killed Daisy, also killed your client, Patricia Watts, her husband, Martin, and your neighbor, Robert."

While Eric was happy the blond one was not as smart as he thought, he was irritated he couldn't solve something so simple as Daisy's murder. "That's ridiculous."

"Is it?"

"I *know* her boyfriend killed her. She was clearly afraid of him."

"Did she ever tell you specifically that he'd hurt her? Or that she thought he might kill her?"

No, he thought. But he couldn't say that. "Yes."

They seemed to notice his hesitation. "And did you tell her to go to the police?"

This time Eric didn't hesitate. "Well, she only told me last Thursday. I told her she should leave him. Maybe that's what she was trying to do when he killed her."

"Hmm." Blondie folded his arms and sat back in his chair.

From what Eric could tell, he wasn't taking him seriously.

He turned to Marky Mark. "If you had enough evidence to arrest him over the weekend, why in the world would you release him now?"

Marky Mark cleared his throat. "He has an alibi for the time of Daisy's death. It was just confirmed yesterday." Eric noted that he didn't look happy about it.

"That has to be a mistake. I'm telling you he killed Daisy. You've let her killer back out on the street."

"No one seems to know where Daisy was last Thursday night, the night before she was killed. Was she with you?" Blondie asked.

"Why? You think *I* killed her?" He pointed to his chest.

"Did you?"

"Of course not! I—" He stopped short, realizing he was about to say he loved her. He guessed maybe he did, but he couldn't say that to these buffoons. "She was my friend."

Blondie seemed to be taking pleasure from his outburst, which only made him more furious.

"You haven't come across her phone, have you? Maybe she left it in your apartment?" he asked.

"No, I don't have her phone. Maybe if you two were doing your jobs properly you'd have found it by now. Are you still even treating Dwayne as a suspect?"

"His alibi has pretty much ruled him out. He couldn't have been in two places at once."

"Well he couldn't possibly have been wherever he said he was, because I'm certain he killed Daisy."

"Sorry, doctor. I'm afraid, with a confirmed alibi, we have to accept that he's not our guy."

Only the jackass wasn't sorry. Eric might've been imagining it, but he looked like he was trying not to smile. Eric narrowed his eyes at him before turning to Wahlberg. He couldn't read anything from his expression.

"You're wrong. You need to check his alibi again."

"Do you have any other information you're not telling us?" Blondie asked.

"No. Except that Daisy wasn't killed by the same person who murdered Patricia, her husband, and my neighbor. Daisy was killed by Dwayne."

"And who killed Patricia, her husband, and your neighbor?"

He was nearly tempted to confess for the sake of getting Daisy the justice she deserved. Nearly, but not quite. "That's your job to find out, not mine. You two have made a serious mistake," Eric said before he turned and walked out of the homicide unit.

If they weren't going to make Dwayne pay for what he did to Daisy, he'd have to kill him himself.

CHAPTER THIRTY

Stephenson's desk phone rang an hour after Dr. Leroy's visit. He recognized the number from the security desk on the building's first floor.

"Stephenson."

"Hey, it's Drew from security. I've got a couple down here who want to speak with you about their son's murder. They said his name is Robert Benson."

"Tell them I'll be right down."

Stephenson stood from his desk after hanging up. Adams looked up from his computer screen.

"The Bensons are here and want to talk to us about Robert's case."

Adams nodded. "I'll see if the conference room is available."

Stephenson put his hands on his hips and stared at the floor while he waited for the elevator. It was possible the Bensons had some information that could help him solve their son's murder. But, most likely, they had come for answers. Answers he wouldn't be able to give them.

"How can you not know who killed him? He lived in a secure building."

Robert's mother gripped the armrests of her chair. Her eyes searched for answers as she shifted her gaze between Adams and Stephenson.

Scott and Linda Benson looked like different people from the put-together couple Stephenson had met two days earlier. Linda's strawberry-blonde hair was pulled back in a severe ponytail. From the dark circles under their bloodshot eyes, Stephenson doubted they'd had any sleep since he last saw them.

"We're still processing some of the evidence from Robert's crime scene. And we have a person of interest."

"So, why don't you arrest him?" Robert's father asked, taking hold of his wife's hand.

"We don't have enough evidence to arrest anyone at this time," Adams said. "But we're doing everything we can to prove who killed him."

Scott Benson choked back tears. Stephenson slid a box of Kleenex across the conference table.

Linda pressed Stephenson. "Robert's been dead for nearly three days now. I read that if a homicide isn't solved after the first forty-eight hours the odds of solving the case go way down. Does this mean you might never catch his killer?"

Before Stephenson could answer, Scott loudly pulled a tissue from the box.

"It's true that the first forty-eight hours are critical in a homicide investigation, but we can't always make an arrest that quickly. Some cases just take longer to solve. It doesn't mean that we aren't going to solve your son's case."

"There wasn't even a mention of Robert's death in the news today. All they could talk about was that big-shot author who offed his wife before killing himself. It's like the world has forgotten him already. I want to make sure that you won't forget him."

Stephenson chose not to correct her assumptions about Martin and Patricia's deaths.

"We promise. We're doing everything we can to find your son's killer. And we won't forget him," Adams said.

"We'll let you know when we make an arrest. In the meantime, feel free to contact us if you have any questions."

Linda gave a somber nod and the couple stood from their chairs in silence.

"I'll walk you out," Stephenson said.

After escorting the Bensons out of the building, Stephenson rode the elevator back to the seventh floor. He hated not being able to give them closure by proving Dr. Leroy killed their son and arresting him for Robert's murder. The elevator stopped and the doors slid open.

Stephenson took a deep breath before getting off. He could only hope his plan would work. A lot depended on what the doctor would do in response to Dwayne's release.

CHAPTER THIRTY-ONE

Eric was still seething over Dwayne's release when he got home from work that night. He was too upset to start his evening yoga ritual and instead went about madly cleaning his apartment.

Over the years, he'd employed a few different house cleaners, but none of them ever quite matched his standards for cleanliness. He always ended up finding dust around the baseboards or an unwiped surface in the kitchen after they left, forcing him to do his own cleaning anyway. He'd let all of them go after a brief period of disappointment. It was better to simply do it right himself.

He didn't mind cleaning. In a way, he found it an effective stress releaser. Which was exactly what he needed tonight.

The more he thought about it, the more he became convinced Dwayne's release was a trap. Those cops had to know Dwayne was guilty. And they must have enough evidence to prove it or they wouldn't have arrested him in the first place.

Blondie seemed to have it out for him, but he obviously couldn't prove he killed Patricia, her fat husband, and whatever his name was who lived next door. Eric's guess was that they had let Dwayne go and placed him under surveillance in the desperate hope they could catch Eric in the act of killing him. Then, if they intervened in time, they'd rearrest Dwayne when they arrested Eric. *Killing two birds with one stone*, as the saying went.

But that wasn't going to stop Eric from killing him. If they were watching Dwayne, then they were probably watching him too. He'd just have to work around it. Fortunately, Harry and Lloyd weren't that hard to outsmart.

Two hours later, he was on to his final cleaning task: the floors. He didn't have a single strand of carpet in his apartment. Carpet was disgusting, filled with dust and festering bacteria. He plugged in his vacuum and started in the living room.

When he glided it under his couch, something shiny skidded out from the other side. He picked it up and recognized the bedazzled phone cover instantly. It was Daisy's. And it had been here all along.

He tried to turn it on but it was, of course, dead. He grabbed his phone from his desk and searched for the number for the Seattle Homicide Unit. There could be evidence on it that proved Dwayne killed her.

He found the number but paused before selecting it. How would he explain that Daisy's phone had been in his apartment this whole time? What if it made him look guilty, instead of Dwayne? There was possibly nothing on her phone that would incriminate Dwayne anyway. Plus, the detectives had already let Dwayne walk when it was obvious he killed her; that gave Eric little hope that turning in her phone would make any difference. He set his phone back down on the desk instead of making the call. He had a better idea.

A quick Google search told him the cops probably couldn't track Daisy's phone to his place unless he used it to make a call, but he didn't want to risk it. Plus, if Dwayne used a tracking app on her phone, it could alert him to its location the moment Eric turned it on.

He threw on his coat, grabbed his killing gloves and a pack of antibacterial wipes, and went down to his car in the parking garage. He plugged Daisy's phone into the car charger as he drove. He waited until he pulled into Discovery Park to turn it on.

Leaving his engine running, he watched her screen light up and ask for the passcode. *Crikey.* He tried to think of what it would be. *Daisy was a sweet, simple girl.* He typed E-R-I-C. *Incorrect passcode.*

He drummed his fingers against his steering wheel. *Her birthday.* She'd asked for the day off. He tried 0-1-2-4. Her phone unlocked. *Fair dinkum.*

Eric disabled her phone's location settings and went to her text messages from Dwayne. While some of his texts could be construed as controlling, Eric was disappointed not to find anything more incriminating. There were no threats, not even any hostile messages.

He searched for Dwayne's name in her email next. Nothing. He looked out the window into the night. It wasn't as he had hoped, but he could still use it to blackmail Dwayne. He was grateful he hadn't been stupid enough to turn it over to the police. It wouldn't have helped them build a case against Dwayne anyway.

Eric pulled on his gloves and cleaned Daisy's bedazzled cover and screen with one of his antibacterial wipes before stepping out into the vacant parking lot with her phone in hand. After removing the SIM card, he placed her phone on the ground behind his rear tire. He laid the SIM card on top of the phone and got back into the car. He reversed over it, hearing it crunch against the gravel parking lot. He pulled forward before driving over it once more.

He put the car in park and got out to retrieve the smashed phone and SIM card. He could see by the red glow of his tail lights that they were nicely damaged. The phone screen had shattered, and the SIM card was now broken in two. He picked them up and placed them in his cup holder before pulling out of the dark parking lot.

He hopped on Interstate 90 and headed for the nearest bridge to dispose of her phone. Twenty-five minutes later, he slowed to ten under as he crossed the middle of the floating bridge that connected Seattle to prestigious Mercer Island. With his passenger window rolled down, he grasped the phone and SIM card from his cup holder and flung them as hard as he could out the window.

He watched to make sure they made it over the side of the bridge when the blare of a horn on his left pulled him from his concentration. Eric turned his attention to the road and saw he had merged halfway into the adjacent lane. The car beside him moved as far into the shoulder as the bridge would allow to avoid being sideswiped by his BMW. Their vehicles were only inches apart. He jerked his BMW back into his lane as the car beside him sped ahead, laying on their horn another time.

Eric over-corrected and felt his front fender smash into the concrete barrier, which protected his car from going over the edge. He swerved to the left, crossing over into the passing lane once again. Only this time there was no car next to him. He slowly merged back into his lane and let out a deep breath, thinking how close he'd been to a much worse collision. That was the last thing he needed.

He leaned his head back against the headrest and tried to relax. He'd taken care of Daisy's phone and had a sure-fire plan to blackmail Dwayne. He'd work out the details of his murder later. He just hoped his car wasn't too badly damaged.

His blood pressure had nearly returned to baseline when he saw the flashing red and blue lights in his rear-view mirror. *Crikey.* He hoped the squad car would pass him in its pursuit of another vehicle, but his hope disintegrated as the lights drew closer and the wail of a siren filled the quiet void of the night. *Great.*

There was nowhere to pull over on the bridge, so he kept driving with the cop car on his ass until he found a place to stop when they reached Mercer Island. He rolled down his window and waited calmly for the egotistical patrol officer whom he was about to have the pleasure of meeting.

He squinted from the blinding light that shined in his face as the officer approached.

"Been drinking tonight?" she asked.

He wanted to demand she take that obnoxious light out of his face, but he couldn't afford to have any more unnecessary run-ins with the law when he was currently a suspect in multiple homicides.

"No, ma'am."

"You were pretty out of control back there on the bridge. You sure you haven't consumed any alcohol this evening? Or drugs?"

"I'm sure. I looked down briefly to adjust the climate control when I drifted into the other lane. It was a stupid mistake. I'm just glad no one was hurt."

She sighed like she'd heard it all before.

"License and registration."

His eyes tried to adjust to the dark, but he couldn't see a thing when he opened his glove compartment. He turned on the ceiling light and easily found his registration inside his neatly organized dash. He handed it to the officer before pulling his license out of his wallet.

"I'll be back," she said. "You sit tight."

He waited for what felt like an hour for her to return. Had she seen him throw Daisy's phone out the window? He couldn't even be sure the phone had made it all the way to the water. If it *were* recovered from the bridge and somehow made it back to the cops, it would not help his case to get a ticket in the same location as her lost phone. That is, if they were even able to trace it back to her. Both her phone and the SIM were in pretty bad shape.

Being that he was a murder suspect, he wondered if his name would come up with some sort of flag when the officer ran his information. He was probably just being paranoid. He assumed she would, however, see his arrest from a few nights earlier. Luckily, he hadn't had anything to drink tonight.

By the time the officer finally returned with his license and registration, he concluded he had nothing to worry about. He was sure Daisy's phone had landed in the lake. Even if it didn't, it probably wouldn't end up in the cops' hands anyway.

"You willing to take a breath test?"

"Sure."

"I'm going to need you to step out of the vehicle."

Eric did as instructed. She whipped out a mobile Breathalyzer device and held the small, plastic tube in front of his mouth.

"Blow."

He gave one big, long breath into the device until it beeped, and she pulled it out of his mouth. She looked surprised when she checked the results. She handed him back his license and registration.

"I'm going to let you off with a warning, but only because you have a clean driving record. Next time, keep your eyes on the road."

He couldn't believe his good luck. He thought for sure she'd been writing him a ticket. He climbed back inside his BMW, refolded his registration, and packed it away in his glove compartment as she walked back to her patrol car. It was probably his accent, he reasoned. In all the years he'd been here, it still made the American women swoon.

Eric went into work early the next morning, before his annoying new secretary came in. He rummaged through the filing cabinets behind the front desk and found what he was looking for only moments before Nurse Ratched arrived.

"Morning," he said, stepping out from behind her desk.

"Morning." As usual, she eyed him suspiciously. She looked down at the paper he held in his left hand.

He ignored her gaze and retreated into his office. He closed the door behind him and scanned through Daisy's employment application. Just as he had hoped, she'd listed Dwayne as her emergency contact along with his mobile phone number.

He walked outside to his car on his lunch hour and felt sick when he saw the damage he'd done to the passenger side the night before. Not quite as sick as he'd felt when he learned of Dwayne's release, but almost. The perfect black paint job on the front fender was marred with ugly gray scrapes from where he'd hit the guardrail.

He made himself look away before he got in on the driver's side, telling himself it was nothing that couldn't be fixed. He drove to the nearest gas station to buy a burner phone.

Being lunch time, the place was busy. He was fifth in line for the cashier by the time he found a phone. His eyes drifted to the TV that hung on the wall behind the register. Two news reporters, a man and a woman, sat behind a desk and speculated about Martin's death.

"There are still a lot of questions surrounding the death of bestselling author, Martin Watts. While police have confirmed that his wife Patricia's death was a homicide, they are still unable to confirm the manner of Martin Watts' death," the woman said.

"That's right," the man agreed. "Seems they are still trying to determine whether his death might have been a suicide rather than a homicide like his wife. It does raise questions, however, as to why the police haven't been able to determine this yet."

The reporter continued to talk, but Eric tore his eyes away from the screen when he moved to the front of the line. Blondie had said they were treating Martin's death as a homicide. But, according to the news, he still had no clue.

He activated the phone as soon as he got back into his car. He punched in Dwayne's number. He slowly typed out a text using the old-school numbered keys. *I have Daisy's phone and I can prove you killed her.*

He sat in the gas station parking lot and waited for a response. The phone chirped less than a minute later.

Who is this?

He had sparked his attention. *Good.* He'd let him stew over that for a while before he messaged him again. That way, like a big, fat fish chomping on a well-baited hook, he wouldn't be able to resist when he demanded to meet with him in a few days. He pulled out of the gas station and stopped by his bank to withdraw a few thousand more in cash before he headed back to his practice. He had a homemade salad waiting for him.

CHAPTER THIRTY-TWO

"I still can't believe we let that lady-killer back out on the street," Adams said.

"I think you mean woman-killer. A lady-killer is someone who seduces women, not kills them." Stephenson refilled his coffee mug in the homicide unit's small break room on Friday morning.

"Whatever. You know what I meant."

"Relax. We've got surveillance on him twenty-four-seven. He's not going to hurt anyone else and he's not getting away with anything. Hopefully, if all goes to plan, we'll be arresting him *and* the doctor soon. From the way Dr. Leroy reacted to Dwayne's release, I'm guessing he'll try to kill him before the week is over."

"I hope you're right."

Stephenson took a sip of the cheap, bitter brew as Detective Richards walked into the break room.

Adams stepped back from the old coffee maker and motioned toward it with his empty mug. "Ladies first."

"Okay," she said, looking unimpressed by the gesture.

She turned to Stephenson as she poured her coffee. She had just started to speak when Adams interrupted.

"You know, it can be hard starting out without knowing anyone in this place. It's not any easy job. So, if you ever want to pick my brain or need someone to talk to who's had a lot of experience with this job, I'm here."

She turned back to Adams and tucked a strand of blonde hair behind her ear. She paused for a moment before she spoke, as if unsure how to respond. "Thanks," she finally said.

She turned back to face Stephenson. "How long have you been in homicide?"

"Coming up on two years. Once you start getting cases, you learn the job pretty quick."

"I heard you've already solved a pretty high-profile case."

He assumed she was referring to the Seattle Slasher killings, the case he and Rodriguez had worked together. "I guess so. You get your first homicide yet?"

"No, we're still waiting. Thanks to you." She smiled.

"Oh, right. Sorry for taking over your first case."

"Since you did steal my first case out from under me, maybe you could make it up by giving me some advice on the job. One rookie to another." She took a sip from her coffee and grimaced. "This is disgusting."

"Yeah, but it keeps you awake. You'll get used to it after a while."

"I don't know if I'll ever get used to that. I actually have a couple tickets to the Seahawks' playoff game this Saturday and haven't found anyone to go with me yet. My brother's a backup defensive lineman and my dad has season tickets. We normally go together, but he's out of town this weekend. Would you want to go? Maybe we can talk shop in between plays."

Stephenson nearly choked on his coffee. "The playoff game? Are you kidding me? I'd love to go. If you're sure you wouldn't rather take someone else." Stephenson was surprised she wasn't taking one of her friends, since the two of them barely knew each other. But there was no way he would turn down a seat at a home-field playoff game.

"I'm sure." She gave him a slight smile. She started to leave the break room but turned around when she reached the doorway. "Want to meet here and drive together to the game? I'm sure parking will be a nightmare. I'll get your number later so we can plan what time to meet."

Stephenson nodded. "Sounds great."

Once they were alone, Stephenson turned to see Adams staring at him while he leaned against the linoleum counter.

"I hate you," his partner said before stalking out of the room with his empty mug.

Stephenson lifted his coffee but stopped short of putting it to his mouth. For the first time in almost a week, he laughed.

When they got back to their desks, they went to work seeing what they could dig up on Dr. Leroy. Adams was going through his bank account and credit card statements but hadn't found anything of use so far. Because Dr. Leroy was only a suspect at this point, they'd only been able to get a warrant for his periodic statements, not live transactions. The latest account statements they'd received ended before Patricia and Martin were murdered. But you never knew, maybe they'd get lucky and find something useful. Otherwise, they'd have to wait for the next round of statements.

Stephenson tapped his pen against his desk as he once again read through Patricia's records that Dr. Leroy had turned over to them. From the way Martin's treatment of his wife was described, it did seem plausible for him to have killed her.

"What if Dr. Leroy falsified information in Patricia's chart before he gave it to us? I mean, how do we know any of it is true? I get that it's hard to know what goes on behind closed doors, but this description of their relationship doesn't match what their friends and family said. Maybe the doctor changed her records to make it look like Martin was controlling and emotionally abusive to try and substantiate their deaths as a murder-suicide."

"I suppose it's possible. Those medical records were all electronic, right?"

"Yeah. I'll have to contact the software company Dr. Leroy uses and see if there's a way to tell if the records have been altered."

Stephenson's phone vibrated against the top of his desk. He lifted it and saw it was Serena. It was the first time she'd called him since the day he'd planned to propose. He stared at the screen, debating whether to answer it before hitting *Ignore* and setting the phone back down on his desk.

"You need to take that?" Adams asked.

"No."

Adams gave him a knowing look. "Okay."

Despite having some weak moments, he'd refrained from calling her since that horrible day. Now, he was glad he hadn't. He had nothing to say to her and didn't want to hear whatever she wanted to say to him. She could never undo what she'd done.

"Excuse me, detectives."

Sandra, the receptionist for the homicide unit, stood between their desks. Her short auburn hair flipped out on the sides and her bangs were overly-curled to the point of distraction. Stephenson saw she had the same hair in her ID badge photo that was taken over twenty years before.

"Yeah?" Stephenson asked.

"I have a woman on the line who wants to speak with one of you about her brother-in-law, Eric Leroy. She's in Australia but said she saw on the news that his front office assistant was murdered. She says it's important."

"I'll take it," Stephenson said.

"All right. I'll transfer her."

"Thanks," he said before she walked away.

"That's interesting," Adams said. "Wonder what she's got to say."

"We'll find out."

A moment later, his phone rang. He picked up immediately.

"This is Detective Stephenson."

"Hello, my name is Maggie Flemming. I live in Australia, but I saw on the news that a woman was recently murdered who worked for my brother-in-law, Dr. Eric Leroy."

Stephenson recognized her accent immediately. It sounded like Dr. Leroy's, only more distinct.

"Yes, that's correct."

"I read you made an arrest initially but have since let the man go. I think my brother-in-law may have killed her. I wanted to make sure you're investigating him."

"And what makes you think he killed her?"

Adams' head perked up at Stephenson's question.

"Well, her body was never found and he was never arrested, but Eric Leroy killed my sister. I'm sure of it. My parents and I filed a missing person's report twenty years ago, but nothing's ever come of it. I know she's dead and he killed her. He must've disposed of her body, which is why he got away with it. He immigrated to Seattle shortly after."

This was huge...if what she was saying was true. It could mean that despite his clean record, Dr. Leroy had been a killer all along. Although, from the sounds of it, this would not be something easy to prove.

"He's crazy. Never even showed a trace of remorse."

Sounds familiar, he thought. He picked up his pen and pulled a notepad in front of him.

"What was your sister's name?"

"Stella. Stella Leroy. Her missing person's case is technically still open, even though we know they'll never find her."

The sadness in her voice was unmistakable as he jotted down her sister's name.

"Do you know the exact date the missing person's report was filed?"

"December 18, 1997," she said without hesitation.

"And in what city?"

"Nelson Bay, New South Wales."

"I'll look into it. Thank you. Is there anything else you'd like to tell me?"

"Eric's been walking free for over twenty years. He hasn't had to pay a single day for what he's done. Meanwhile, my sister is dead and, without a body, we've never even been able to give her a proper funeral. Nothing will ever bring my sister back, but promise me you'll put him away for good so he'll never be able to hurt anyone again."

"I promise I'll look into your sister's case. And, if Dr. Leroy is responsible for the death of his front office assistant or anyone else, we'll do our best to catch him."

"I hope you do."

"Can I get your contact information in case I need to speak with you again?"

"Sure."

He wrote down her phone number and email address before ending the call.

"Who does she think he killed?" Adams asked as soon as Stephenson got off the phone.

"Her sister."

Stephenson repeated their conversation.

"Wow."

"Yeah. But even if he did kill her, it sounds like it would be nearly impossible to prove. I'll have to request the missing person's report from Australia."

"Let me know when it comes through."

Stephenson got on his computer and checked what time it was in Nelson Bay. It was five thirty in the morning, but he decided to call anyway. Someone should be at the station.

"Nelson Bay police, how can I help you?"

The man sounded as if the call had woken him from a nap.

"Good morning. This is Detective Stephenson from Seattle Homicide. I'm after a copy of a missing person's report that was filed at your station on December 18, 1997. Would you have that on file at your station?"

"Seattle, huh? I've been to Seattle once. Rained the entire week I was there. We should have the report still on file. It'd be a paper case file, so it might take me a little while to find it. What was the name of the missing person?"

"Stella Leroy."

"Oh, yeah. I know that case. It's a bit of a legend around here. Did you know she was a professional surfer?"

"No, I didn't."

"Born and raised here in Nelson Bay. She was becoming pretty famous before she disappeared. I wasn't working here at the time, but it made the national news.

"There were a few theories surrounding her disappearance. One was that a shark took her while she surfed the huge waves during an evening storm. Her family all claimed her husband killed her, but her body was never found. The case is still unsolved. Can I ask why you're interested in that case?"

"Eric Leroy, Stella's husband, is a suspect in some recent murder cases of ours. Her sister called and told me about Stella."

"Crikey. Well, if he did kill her, I hope you get him."

"Me too."

"I'll need you to fax me an official request for that case file, and I'll send it to you as soon as I find it."

"Sure thing," Stephenson said.

"You know, it was all over the news here when it happened. I'm pretty sure Stella's family were interviewed on national TV about their theory that Stella's husband killed her. You could probably find some of it online."

"Thanks, I'll have a look."

"Good luck with the case."

Stephenson was still waiting to receive Stella's case file over an hour later. He thought about what the Australian cop had said about her case being on the national news and ran an online search to see what he could find. A five-minute video clip of Stella's family being interviewed on what looked like a major Australian news station appeared at the top of the results.

Stephenson clicked on the video. The clip was dated May 1998. A couple who looked to be in their fifties sat next to a young woman who Stephenson guessed was Maggie.

"Hey, come check this out," he said to Adams.

Adams got up and came around their desks. He stood behind Stephenson as the video continued to play.

A female reporter sat across from them wearing a dark pantsuit.

"Stella's been missing for over five months now. What makes you sure her husband killed her?"

Stella's mother spoke first. "We'd been trying to convince her to leave him for years. He was incredibly controlling. We worried about how much worse he might treat her behind closed doors when we witnessed how verbally abusive he was when we were around." She paused and dabbed her eyes with a tissue. "A week before she went missing, she had a black eye. That's when we realized things were even worse than we'd thought. She made an excuse that she'd ran into something, but we knew he'd beat her. We begged her to leave him. She said she was thinking about it, but he must've found out and killed her before she could get away."

She began to sob, and Stella's father took the opportunity to speak.

"Stella was last seen at her work on Friday, December 16. The detectives confirmed with the hospital that Eric had mistakenly shown up for a shift that Friday and went home after realizing he wasn't rostered that night. We believe

Stella had taken the opportunity to leave him while he was at work. When he came home early, he probably found her getting ready to leave him and killed her."

"Detectives searched the home she shared with her husband, Eric. They didn't find any blood or evidence of a struggle in the home. They've also never found her body. If he killed her, what do you think he did with her body?" the reporter asked.

Stella's mother looked too emotional to speak.

"Eric has a fishing boat. We believe he took the boat out and dumped her body in the ocean," the father said.

"And where are the police in the investigation? Do you think they'll ever arrest her husband for murder?"

"Without a body, they are treating her case as a missing person's. Unless they find her body or some other hard evidence that she was killed, it's doubtful they'll ever be able to arrest Eric, even though we know he killed her."

"When we tried to contact Eric for an interview, we learned he's left the country and is now living in Seattle. We were surprised he would make such a big move only a few months after his wife's disappearance. Do you see that as further proof of his guilt?"

"Yes," her mother said. "He never showed any emotion about her disappearance. Just said that she'd left him. He didn't even care. It was disturbing to see that he had no remorse whatsoever. He fled to Seattle to start a new life, while we have to live with the fact that we'll never see our daughter again."

The clip ended, and Stephenson turned to Adams.

"Sounds like the same story her sister told me over the phone. After we get Stella's case file from Australia, let's go pay Dr. Leroy a visit."

CHAPTER THIRTY-THREE

Friday afternoon, Eric had an hour free between clients and was using the time to write another chapter in his novel. He was tirelessly typing away on his keyboard when he heard a tap on his door.

"Come in," he said, assuming it was his secretary.

The door opened, but he didn't bother looking up. She probably came in to tell him something dreadfully unimportant that could've waited until the end of the day.

"I figured it would be easier for you if we came here than to ask you to come down to the station."

Hearing Blondie's voice, Eric tore his eyes away from the screen. In his office doorway, there stood Blondie and his less than brilliant partner. Nice of his secretary to give him a heads up. *What now?*

"If you keep coming here, detective, I might have to start charging you. Are there some things you'd like to get off your chest? Your childhood perhaps?"

He frowned as his partner closed the door behind them, and Eric was filled with gratification.

"I just had a very interesting chat with your sister-in-law."

"You mean my *ex*-sister-in-law?" Eric said.

"No, I mean your sister-in-law. Your wife has never been declared dead and you haven't gotten a divorce, right? So, legally, Stella is still your wife."

Eric closed his laptop. "Technically, yes. But she hasn't been my wife since she left me twenty years ago. And why would you be chatting with my sister-in-law?"

"She saw your name in the news connected with our recent murder victims and thought we should be aware of your history."

"My history?"

"She claims her sister didn't just go missing. She says she was murdered."

He paused, apparently expecting him to respond.

When he didn't, Blondie added, "By you."

This news didn't exactly come as a shock. Although, Eric had conceded the reason her sister made those wild accusations all those years ago was due to grief. It had probably been easier for her to believe that he'd killed her sister than to bear the truth: Stella had left them all for a life she deemed better. But he had hoped by now Maggie would've come to her senses.

He himself had considered that something terrible could've happened to Stella. The media had several theories regarding her disappearance, one of them being that she'd been taken by a shark while surfing. It was possible, but not likely. No body parts or surf board had ever been found. *And me, kill Stella?* It was preposterous.

He sighed. "I hope this wasn't the only reason you came to see me. No wonder you two have so many homicides left unsolved if this is the best you can do with your time."

Another frown. "So, you're not even going to deny it?"

"Look, I'm sure hearing her claim I'm a murderer was like music to your ears. I don't know why, but you both seem like you're dying to arrest me for murder. Probably just so you can close your case. If I had killed her, then where is her body? And why wasn't I arrested for her murder all those years ago? Hmm? Did my lovely sister-in-law have any explanation for that?"

"Solving a homicide without a body is extremely difficult, especially in the absence of other physical evidence," Marky Mark said.

It was the first thing he'd said since they'd come into Eric's office. It was also the first thing he'd ever said to him that actually made sense.

"She figures you dumped her sister's body in the ocean from your fishing boat," Blondie said.

"Well, she obviously doesn't remember my boat very well. You'd have to be crazy to take that boat outside the calm waters of the bay. It was much too small to handle the open ocean."

Blondie smirked. "That's funny, because *crazy* was the exact word she used to describe you."

"I'm not the one telling twenty-year-old conspiracy theories to the police."

Blondie cupped his hand and ran his thumb and index along the corners of his mouth, as if feeling for crumbs left over from his lunch. "Sounded a lot more like the truth than a conspiracy theory to me. But what do I know?"

"Apparently not enough to solve your own homicide cases."

His eyes narrowed ever so slightly. "We're actually pretty close to making an arrest in three of our homicides."

Yeah right, he thought.

"Don't leave town, doctor. I suspect we'll be speaking to you again soon."

Marky Mark opened his door and Blondie followed him out.

"Looking forward to it," Eric said before the door shut behind them.

He opened his laptop but, despite his best efforts, couldn't get back into the head space he needed to write his novel. There was no way they were close to arresting him for those murders. They had to be bluffing. But what if they weren't? What if he had somehow made a mistake along the way? He was almost certain he hadn't, but was he certain enough to bet his freedom on it? His life? He'd have to kill Dwayne sooner than he had planned. And start preparing for his escape.

He glanced at the clock on the lower right corner of his screen. Time for his next appointment. *Stupid cops*. They cost him nearly an hour of creative productivity.

"Cancel my last appointment for me. I've got to take care of a few things this afternoon," he said to his secretary on his way out of the office.

"Your next appointment will be here any minute. I think it's a little too late to cancel."

Nobody asked you what you think, he thought. He ignored her retort and continued moving toward the office doors. Remembering this was probably the last time he would ever see her, he turned around.

"And *I think* you should've given me a heads up before letting those two cops waltz into my office unannounced."

"I'm sure they had good reason to see you. Plus, I thought they might've wanted to have the element of surprise."

He stared back at her while he turned the door handle. He wished he was staying in town long enough to be able to kill her next.

"I don't pay you to think. Just to do your damn job." He let the door slam behind him and walked to his car.

He stopped at the bank one last time on his way home to make another withdrawal. Once back at his apartment, he packed a carry-on bag with basic toiletries, a few changes of clothes, his laptop for writing his novel, and twenty-two thousand in cash. He separated the ten thousand that would go through airport security and the other twelve he would use to purchase his ticket and take through on his person.

He turned off his car stereo and drove to the airport in silence. He parked in the short-term parking and dropped off his bag at the baggage storage outside of security before getting back in his car to drive home. He kept the stereo off while he sat in traffic on I-5 and finalized his plan to ensure he killed Dwayne before the weekend was over—and not get caught.

If Eric was under surveillance, and his recent encounter with those two schmuck detectives told him he was, then he couldn't take his own car to kill Dwayne tomorrow. Fortunately, sweet old Margaret across the hall owned a Buick she hardly ever used. He'd seen her come and go in the parking garage. She had her groceries delivered every week and was too old to be driving, but she seemed to still get out and about occasionally.

She would probably have let him borrow it if he asked, but he didn't want to involve her in any of this. Plus, he didn't want her to tell the cops he had borrowed her car, in case they came looking for him before he was safely out of the country.

Eric waited until midnight and listened outside her door a few minutes to make sure the TV was off and no other noise came from inside her apartment. He pulled his trusty lock-picking kit out of his pajama pant pocket and did a quick look around the hall to make sure he was alone.

He, of course, was the only person in the silent hallway. He smiled to himself. Now that he had killed the little drummer boy, there were no tenants left on the floor to be witnesses.

The door unlocked with a click after he worked his magic with the pick. He slowly stepped inside the dark apartment. From what he could tell, the floorplan was the same as his. He'd traded his slippers for socks before coming out of his apartment, and he padded silently through the entryway toward the kitchen. Not that he needed to worry old Margaret would hear him; she was practically deaf in her old age.

Once he had reached the vicinity of the kitchen, he used the light on his phone to look for her purse. He could make out the kitchen counters now, and noticed they were neat and sparse. The way kitchen counter tops should be. But her purse was not sitting atop them like he'd hoped.

Eric drummed his fingers on the tidy kitchen workspace. He was hoping to avoid having to go in her bedroom, but it was looking like he might have no choice. He'd probably give the sweet old lady a cardiac arrest if she awoke to find a man lurking around in her room. But perhaps it was in the living room.

He used his phone to scan the adjacent room. Empty sitting chair, empty coffee table. He moved his light toward the couch and was startled by both the body lying on it and the sound that came out of Margaret. Instinctively, he shut off the light and jumped behind the couch. It sounded somewhere between a hack and cough, followed by a deep clearing of the throat.

He crouched low to the ground, motionless while he listened. He couldn't kill Margaret. If she came toward him, he would overpower her as gently as possible and race out of her apartment. Except that he still needed her car keys.

Margaret went quiet before exhaling deeply. He waited as her heavy breathing changed to a loud, even snore. He stood slowly and turned his phone light back on. He could see the outline of the old woman lying on her back as he slipped past the couch. He moved down the hall into the bedroom and shined his light on the bedside table. There sat her small black leather purse.

Right. She sleeps in the living room but keeps her purse in her bedroom. Go figure. He'd just opened the bag and shined his light inside when Margaret made a horrendous choking sound from the other room. The dreadful noise continued for nearly a minute. He thought how ironic it would be if she died while he was stealing her car keys. But then she sharply cleared her throat and returned to her rhythmic snoring.

Old people, he thought. He went back to searching for her keys. He found them in a side pocket and crept back to his apartment before she made any more death-defying noises.

CHAPTER THIRTY-FOUR

Eric got up early Saturday morning and started the day with an hour of yoga. He needed to be calm. He needed to be centered. He needed to kill Dwayne and then flee the country before his friends at Seattle Homicide realized he had gone.

Before going to bed the night before, he'd texted Dwayne using his burner phone. He told him to meet him at a cafe on Bainbridge Island that Eric sometimes frequented on the weekends. It was in walking distance from the ferry that came across the sound from downtown Seattle. But thanks to good old Margaret next door, he wouldn't be walking.

He told Dwayne to meet him at four o'clock. After a shower and two cups of coffee, he sat down at his desk to work on his novel. He was nearly halfway done. His progress was slower than he'd hoped, but once he killed Dwayne and fled the country, he would have all the time in the world to finish it.

With his laptop packed into his bag at the airport, he was forced to write on his old iPad that he hardly ever used. He felt himself relax after he typed his first three hundred words. The double-spaced page filled with his typed words was food for his soul. He needed to write like he needed to breathe. He'd once told himself he'd stop writing once he published his bestseller, but he knew now that he needed to write to survive.

Two thousand words later, it was nearly time to carry out his plan. He uploaded his new chapter onto the cloud. Satisfied that his work was saved, he turned off the iPad.

He donned his baseball cap before he pulled on his jacket and took one last look around his apartment. Although he'd always despised Seattle's long gray winters, he was struck by an overwhelming sense of nostalgia as he prepared to leave his current home for the last time. He felt the sides of his jacket to ensure he had his cellphone in one pocket and a necktie and burner phone in the other.

"Well, I guess this is good-bye," he said to his apartment.

He grabbed Margaret's keys off the kitchen counter and his iPad from his desk. He couldn't leave it behind in case the cops came to look through his stuff. He'd have to dispose of it on his way to kill Dwayne. He locked the door behind him and headed downstairs to the parking garage.

Sweet old Margaret had even parked her Buick out of view from the security cameras. *Bless her heart.* The Buick ran surprisingly well for how little she used it. He made it to the ferry dock without incident. He slowed the car and rolled down his window when he reached the ticket booth.

"Bainbridge or Bremerton?"

"Bainbridge."

"Just the car and driver?" the woman asked from inside the booth.

"Yes."

"That'll be $18.70."

He handed her a twenty through the window.

"You'll be on the three o'clock boat," she said as she handed him his change.

"Thank you."

He pulled into the row behind other idle cars and turned off the engine. His stomach growled, breaking the silence in the car. He must've forgotten to eat lunch. With twenty-five minutes to spare, he got out and walked down the street to Ivar's.

The wait was short, and he ordered a large clam chowder. The young girl behind the counter handed him a big paper bowl covered with a plastic lid.

"Spoons are to your right," she said.

"Could I also get a bag for this?" he asked.

"A bag?" She furrowed her brow and gave him a look that said, *What kind of weirdo carries his bowl of soup in a bag?*

He didn't find his request that odd.

She handed him a white, medium-sized paper bag with an Ivar's logo on the side.

He watched her brow furrow again as he took off the lid to his soup, tucked the bag under his arm, and ate as he walked back to the ferry.

He got back to the Buick and set his half-eaten bowl of chowder on the armrest, something he would never do in his BMW. He didn't even drink water in it, let alone clam chowder. But he was sure good old Margaret wouldn't mind. The ten-year-old Buick had seen better days. *Or had it?* he wondered.

He reached into the glove compartment and pulled out his iPad. He dropped it inside the Ivar's bag and rolled down the top, closing it in. Holding the bag from the top, he walked over to the nearest rubbish bin and tossed it inside.

The ferry had just arrived. Cars and walk-on passengers had started to disembark. He hurried back to the Buick as a group of seagulls squawked overhead.

After driving onto the ferry, he turned off the car engine but didn't go upstairs to the passenger deck. The car smelled strongly of clam chowder from his near-empty bowl he'd moved over onto the passenger seat. Bored, he streamed music from his phone while he went over his plan to kill Dwayne one more time.

"Zombie" by The Cranberries started to play when they had almost reached the island. He turned up the volume and lost himself in the music. Not in a way that distracted him from what he was about to do. Instead, he became more focused. The chorus came on, and he played air drums against the steering wheel until the end of the song.

The ferry docked right as the song ended. His blood was pumping when he started the Buick's engine. He was more than ready to get Daisy the justice she deserved.

Eric parallel parked across the street from the cafe on Bainbridge Island where he'd told Dwayne to meet him. He was sure he hadn't been followed but was certain the police had round-the-clock surveillance on Dwayne. Eric looked around for an unmarked cop car along the street but didn't spot any. They were here, somewhere. And they would be watching.

He walked a block to the nearest crosswalk and waited for his turn to cross the street. A minute later, he moved through the parking lot of the business next door to the cafe and approached the cafe from the rear. He'd seen some of its workers taking a smoke break out back on one of his previous visits and knew there was a door marked *Employees Only*.

He covered his hand with the end of his jacket before twisting the handle. He slipped inside the door and found himself in the cafe's back kitchen. A red-haired guy making sandwiches looked up from what he was doing.

"Excuse me, sir. This is employees only," he said sternly.

"Oh, I'm sorry." Eric looked around the kitchen. "I was looking for the bathroom. I must've gotten turned around."

"From outside?"

He looked back at the door he'd come through. "Yeah, I'm pretty sure they told me it was outside and through a side door. This was the only door I could find."

He looked unconvinced by Eric's story. Nevertheless, he set down the sandwich and pointed to a door on the other side of the kitchen. "Well, they told you wrong. Go out the door and make a left."

"Thanks."

The man shook his head and went back to making the sandwich.

With the sleeve of his jacket still covering his hand, Eric let himself out of the kitchen and stood in a small, empty hallway at the back of the cafe. He turned to the left and was glad to find the door to the men's room unlocked. He went inside and closed the door behind him. The loo consisted of a single toilet and sink with a door that could lock from the inside. The small, rectangular window above the toilet was exactly as he had remembered. Just big enough for him to escape through. He checked the latch to make sure it opened. It did.

He pulled out the burner phone and texted Dwayne. *You're being watched. Meet me in the men's room.* He left the door unlocked while he waited for Dwayne to join him. The door swung open less than a minute later.

He recognized Dwayne immediately from his picture in the news. He was bigger than Eric had anticipated, however. Dwayne was only an inch or two taller than Eric, but he had the build of an out-of-shape rugby player. This was not going to be his easiest kill.

"Lock the door behind you."

Dwayne did as he was told.

"You have the phone?"

"I need to hear you say it first."

"Say what?"

"That you killed her." *You son of a bitch*, Eric wanted to add. But he needed to maintain the upper hand if he was going to kill him. He couldn't afford for Dwayne to lose his temper.

Eric realized it was already too late.

Dwayne's face reddened as he took a step toward him. "You're the psychologist she worked for."

Eric refrained from correcting him and explaining how lowly a psychologist was compared to a psychiatrist. He took a step back.

"You're the reason she didn't come home that night, aren't you?"

He didn't answer.

"What makes you think you could sleep with my woman? You think because you're a doctor you can do whatever the hell you want?" Dwayne poked the middle of his chest with his pointer finger.

Eric yearned to laugh out loud at the idea of a psychologist being referred to as a doctor. *Maybe we should award that title to chiropractors while we're at it.* But, once again, he refrained.

"Maybe I should kill *you.* After you hand over that bitch's phone." Dwayne held out his palm for Eric to give him Daisy's cell.

He'd had about enough. Time for Dwayney boy to die. "I don't have it with me."

"What? You're lying!" He put a hand below each of Eric's shoulders and shoved him backward. He fell against the sink.

"If anything happens to me, I've made sure the phone will get to the police."

Dwayne's jaw clenched and both of his hands balled into fists at his side. His eyes looked intently into Eric's as he decided whether or not Eric was telling the truth. Dwayne's eyes narrowed. He'd apparently concluded Eric was lying.

Dwayne grinned through yellow teeth. Eric couldn't imagine what Daisy had seen in him.

"Yeah right. Empty your pockets."

Eric regained his posture and smoothed the front of his jacket. "No."

Dwayne's grin disappeared. He rushed forward and pushed Eric's arm against the sink while he used his other hand to try and open Eric's jacket pocket. The only thing in that pocket was his necktie, and Eric couldn't let him take it. Eric made a fist with his free hand and threw a punch into the side of Dwayne's face.

Pain resonated through his knuckles. Dwayne opened his mouth wide and stretched out his jaw. His hand fell away from Eric's pocket as he raised it to his cheek. He snarled and brought both of his hands to Eric's neck. He clamped his grip tightly around Eric's throat. *Just like he'd done to Daisy.*

Dwayne's hands were crushing Eric's trachea, and his entire throat felt as though it were about to shoot out through his mouth. But the thought of Daisy brought him back to focus. She deserved more than justice. She deserved revenge.

Using every ounce of strength he had, Eric brought his hands to Dwayne's face and jarred his thumbs into each of his eye sockets. Dwayne let out a pathetic cry and flung his head back. His grip loosened around Eric's neck and Eric threw another punch into his Adam's apple. Dwayne gagged as his hands fell away.

This was his moment. Eric pulled the tie out of his pocket and wrapped each end around his hands. Dwayne had rebounded from the blow to his windpipe. He saw the tie just before Eric looped it around the back of his neck. He crossed it in front of his throat and pulled it taunt. Dwayne reached up and grabbed the ends of the tie, but it was no use. Eric pulled tighter. They were face-to-face, but, unlike Patricia, this time it didn't bother him.

Dwayne ripped off his hat and hurled his forehead into his. Stunned from the hit, Eric's feet wavered. He fell back onto the bathroom floor, pulling Dwayne's massive weight on top of him. The air escaped his lungs when Dwayne's body landed on him. His grip on the tie had loosened during the fall.

Eric scrambled to retain his hold and managed to pull it tight again across Dwayne's throat. Dwayne's face was only an inch from his and he watched his veins protrude out of his skin from the pressure of the noose. Eric struggled to fill his lungs with air against the crushing force on his chest. For a second, he worried he might suffocate before Dwayne did. But he told himself that was ridiculous. He just needed to concentrate.

Dwayne pushed himself up from the floor and slammed his fist into Eric's left temple. Eric lost his grip on the tie when Dwayne delivered another punch. His knuckles felt like a sledgehammer when they struck his cheekbone. Eric's hands fell to the floor as he lay stunned from the blow.

He felt Dwayne's enormous weight lift off him and knew he had to act fast if he was going to be the one who walked away from this fight. Dwayne got to his knees and raised his fist in the air. Using all his strength and then some, Eric drew back his knee and kicked Dwayne in the gut before his arm came forward for another hit.

He fell backward, and Eric grabbed the tie off the floor. Dwayne turned toward him on his hands and knees as Eric flung the tie around his throat and climbed onto his back. Dwayne brought a hand up to the tie as Eric crossed it behind his neck and pulled with all his might. Dwayne moved onto his knees. He swayed from side to side in a wild motion, trying to loosen the noose around his neck. Eric strained to pull the ends of the tie against his chest.

His arms trembled as Dwayne's movements gradually slowed. The next minute felt more like sixty. Dwayne's body went slack and Eric moved with him, landing atop his back as Dwayne hit the floor. Eric kept the noose tight for another minute longer before he rolled off him and let his arms collapse at his sides. He lay next to him on the bathroom floor, finally able to take in a deep breath.

A sharp knock sounded at the door and Eric lifted his head. It could be the cops who were watching Dwayne. Crikey. Maybe they were suspicious of what was taking him so long. Or maybe they heard something from outside. Were they loud? He had no idea.

He needed to get out of there. He pulled the tie from Dwayne's discolored, swollen neck and tucked it inside his jacket pocket. He rushed to the window and opened the latch when he remembered Dwayne had knocked off his hat. There was another loud knock at the door. He turned and swiped his hat off the ground.

Eric hoisted himself through the window but only managed to make it out halfway. His legs dangled inside the bathroom as he tried unsuccessfully to pull himself through the small opening. There were three sharp bangs on the bathroom door.

"Dwayne! It's Seattle Police. We know you're in there," called a male voice. "You've got five seconds to open this door or we're coming in!"

His pulse quickened. He pressed his palms against the building's exterior but his lower half didn't budge. The bathroom door shook against its frame as a sharp thud resounded from the other side. The cops must've been trying to kick the door in.

Eric grunted as he sucked in his stomach and pushed against the outer wall one last time. Astoundingly, his lower body slid through the window frame and he fell to the ground. He'd no sooner landed on the pavement when he heard the door to the bathroom bust open. He crawled past the edge of the window before he got to his feet.

"Call an ambulance!" He heard the male voice yell from inside.

It's much too late for that, Eric thought with a smile before he broke into a run.

CHAPTER THIRTY-FIVE

Richards told him during their walk to CenturyLink Field that they'd have pretty good seats. When Stephenson saw where they were sitting, he realized she'd lied. Their seats were incredible, only ten rows up from the fifty-yard line. You could hardly do any better.

They were nearly an hour early, but the stadium was already filling with fans sporting blue and green from head to toe. Many had their faces painted.

"Not bad, huh?" she said as they sat down.

Stephenson grinned. "Yeah, not bad. I think you might've downplayed how good these seats are. Just a little."

"Well, I'm glad I could impress you. All the players get a few tickets for family and friends, but the seats are way up the top. My dad has had season tickets for years, so we have a close-up view when my brother plays."

"I'm definitely impressed. You said your dad was out of town this weekend?"

She nodded. "Yeah, on business. He'll still be watching, but he was pretty bummed he couldn't be here."

"I bet. I'm gonna grab a beer before the game, you want one?"

"Sure." She rubbed her gloved hands together to warm them.

"I'll be right back."

Twenty minutes later, he walked down the steps back to their seats with a beer in each hand and marveled at how he'd gotten so lucky.

Richards turned when he got to their row and reached out for her beer. "Thanks." She took a sip from the nearly overflowing cup.

He'd been taken aback by how stunning she looked when they met at the station. Her makeup accentuated her high cheekbones and full lips. Her hair was always pulled back when he'd seen her at work, but today it framed her face and fell almost to her waist.

They chatted comfortably as the stadium continued to fill. The noise from the fans grew louder the closer it came for the game to start, and they eventually had to yell to hear one another.

They stood and cheered as the Seahawks ran onto the field. The energy from the crowd was electric.

"Which one's your brother?"

"The one in the pink shoes." She pointed to him on the field. "Most of the players only wear them in October for breast cancer awareness month, but because we lost my mom to breast cancer, he wears them every game."

"I'm so sorry," he said.

"Thanks. She's been gone nearly five years now, but I still think about her every day." She took a sip from her beer. "Anyway, it's his first year on the team, so he hasn't had a lot of playing time. Hopefully we'll get to see him out there today."

The scores were tight from the beginning and the two teams were tied at halftime. Richards' brother came out and played for most of the third quarter, and they were both too intent on watching to engage in much small talk. At one point, he felt her hand brush against his. She smiled when he looked over at her.

The score was just as close in the second half as it had been in the first. At the end of the fourth quarter, they went into overtime. They watched, frozen in anticipation, as a coin was flipped to see which team got the ball first. The opposing team won the toss and the Seahawks kicked off again.

In the first play, the other team's quarterback threw a long pass to their receiver. Stephenson held his breath while he watched to see if the pass would be complete. The Seahawks' star defensive back read the pass the whole way and intercepted the ball deep in their own territory. He and Richards screamed with joy as they watched him run it all the way back for a touchdown. The roar of the Seattle crowd was deafening as Richards threw her arms around his neck and he returned her embrace. It was an exhilarating end to one of the most intense games he had ever watched. Their embrace lasted a little longer than it needed to, but neither one was ready to let go right away.

Celebratory fans began to leave their seats, and they followed the slow-moving crowd toward the exit. Their arms touched as they climbed the stairs amid the mass of people leaving the stadium. Stephenson couldn't deny he liked the feel of her close to him.

"My brother invited us to an after-party for family and friends here at the stadium. The players won't be there for a little bit, but we can head down there now. Would you mind if we stopped by before we go?"

"Are you kidding me? Of course I wouldn't mind. That'd be awesome. I'll try not to embarrass you by acting starstruck in front of some of the greatest NFL players in the world."

She laughed. "You better not. Especially not in front of my brother. He already thinks he's hot stuff as it is."

It took them awhile to move through the crowded stadium. Stephenson's phone rang as they reached the entrance to the party. It was Adams. He probably wanted to talk about the game and give him a hard time for going with Richards.

"Sorry," Stephenson said. "It's Adams. I'll tell him I'll call him later."

"No problem." She stopped in front of the door and waited for him to take the call.

"Hey. I hate to rub it in, but we're about to go say hi to Richards' brother at the team's after-party, so I'll give you a call back in a bit."

"We have a problem." Adams' tone was serious. It sounded like he was driving. "Dwayne's dead."

"What?"

The door in front of them opened, and Stephenson recognized the team's star tight end, who emerged into the hall. He said hello to Richards while Stephenson turned away to talk to Adams.

"How did that happen?"

"He was at a cafe on Bainbridge Island. He got up to use the bathroom and the two officers assigned on his surveillance got distracted by the end of the Seahawks game that was playing on TV at the cafe. He'd been gone for about ten minutes before one of them went to check on him and found him on the floor of the bathroom. Strangled. They did CPR but it was too late.

"The bathroom's window was open. They said it was big enough for someone Dr. Leroy's size to squeeze through. They never saw him, but one of the cooks said a man fitting his description came into the kitchen from the back alley saying he was looking for the bathroom right before the time Dwayne was killed. They're canvasing the area for him now."

Stephenson rubbed his head. This was bad. He couldn't believe Dwayne was killed by Dr. Leroy while he'd been under police surveillance. McKinnon was going to be pissed. The sergeant did him a favor by allowing him to release Dwayne in the hope of being able to arrest Dr. Leroy. And he'd trusted him to carry out his plan. Dwayne shouldn't have been in any danger of the doctor getting to him without the surveillance team knowing.

"Did they show the cook a photo of Dr. Leroy?"

"They did, but he wasn't able to give a positive ID. Said he was wearing a hat and he didn't get a good enough look at his face."

"Do they have any surveillance video?"

"None. It's a small, locally-owned cafe."

"How could Leroy have *possibly* killed Dwayne and escaped unnoticed when he was under our surveillance?"

Richards walked over to where he stood and raised her eyebrows. He realized he was yelling.

"Those officers will have to answer for that," said Adams.

And so will I, thought Stephenson.

"The cafe is within walking distance to the downtown Seattle ferry. It's just left for the city. It's possible Dr. Leroy is on it. I'm on my way to the ferry dock now. Can you meet me?" Adams asked.

The stadium was only a short walk from the ferry. "I'm on my way. I'll be there in fifteen minutes."

"I've already requested to have a couple patrol officers to assist with the search. We'll start by searching the vehicles as they get off the ferry, and I'll have them hold the walk-on passengers for you to check when you get there."

"Okay, see you there."

"What was that about?" Richards asked as Stephenson zipped his phone back into his coat pocket.

"Dwayne's dead and it looks like Dr. Leroy killed him. I have to go."

"I thought Dwayne was under twenty-four-hour surveillance so you could catch the doctor in the act? Before he killed him, I mean."

"He was. I'll explain later. Sorry."

"It's fine. Go."

"Thanks for an amazing day. Tell your brother congratulations," he said as he backed down the hall.

"I will."

He saw her wave before he reached the exit at the end of the hall. He picked up his pace. *What a horrible end to such a perfect afternoon.*

CHAPTER THIRTY-SIX

When Eric got back to the street, he could see the Seattle ferry docked at the bottom of the hill. They'd almost finished loading cars for its journey back to the city, but if he hurried he could make it as a walk-on passenger. He walked as briskly as he could without drawing attention to himself. The wind came in strong off the water, blowing the rain into his face as he went. He put his hand on top of his head to keep his hat from flying away.

His blood was pumping when he reached the gangway. The last car had just been loaded onto the ferry as Eric jogged toward the boat. Thankfully, he didn't have to stop to buy a ticket. Walk-on passengers only had to pay when getting on in Seattle. Out of breath, he made it to the ferry right before a ferry worker closed the gate behind him.

"You just made it," he said.

Ignoring his comment, Eric let out a sigh of relief and casually strolled onto the upper deck. He went inside and glanced around at the tables near the windows, which were already mostly filled. Still flooded with adrenaline, he decided to go back outside despite the storm. The door flung back from the force of the wind when he opened it.

He pulled his hood over his head as he felt the rain blow sideways against his face. The boat dipped down and then up again as he made his way to the edge of the stern.

A small group of preteens were leaning over the edge of the railing on the other side. They were trying to be bad-asses, but in reality just being idiots. A few of them were lifting their legs off the ground as they leaned forward onto the railing, seeing who could lean over the farthest without falling.

Eric turned away and grabbed hold of the railing. He looked at the rough water below. The whitecaps on the choppy water seemed to remind him of something in his distant past, the details of which he couldn't come to remember. The ferry picked up speed as more and more water separated them from the island.

A seagull struggled to hover above the boat, getting tossed about by gusts of wind. Eric turned around at the sound of kids screaming. He watched the middle-schoolers fall back onto the deck as ocean spray came over the side. It was apparently more than they could handle, and they took off as a group toward the doors that led inside.

Alone on the ferry deck, he took out his phone. After removing the SIM card from the back, he tossed them both into the Sound. He watched them disappear into the gray-blue water almost instantly.

He stayed outside despite the weather, admiring the evergreen-covered island as it faded from his view. All these years he'd hated the dreariness of Seattle. He hardly even allowed himself to enjoy its summers, knowing they would be over all too soon. He seemed to be appreciating its beauty for the first time, now that he might never see it again.

He leaned against the railing, filled with a sense of righteous indignation. Now that Dwayne was dead, he could start his new life over in peace. Even if he'd been wrong to kill Patricia, her husband, and his twit of a neighbor, surely he'd redeemed himself through the act of removing such a disgusting human being like Dwayne from this earth.

It had been a risk to kill him while he was under surveillance. It also delayed his escape out of the country. He could already be on a plane, browsing the in-flight movie selection on his way to a new life. But he knew it had been the right choice. It had been worth it to ensure that worthless scumbag never took another breath.

Maybe Daisy would have come with him if she'd been alive. What a life they could've had.

He looked out at the sea and thought about Blondie accusing him of killing his wife. It was absurd. Stella's family was obviously still as crazy as ever. And Stephenson had been dumb enough to believe them. *He* was the one they should feel sorry for. *She was the one who left me.*

He felt an uneasiness well up inside him and he tried to think of something else. The taste of salt in his mouth and the stormy sea below gave him a sudden sense of déjà vu.

Eric was a fourth-year medical student and arrived at the teaching hospital for his night shift in the emergency room. It was the start of summer, and he'd watched a colony of flying foxes soar overhead during the drive. When he got there, however, he realized he had looked at the schedule wrong. He wasn't due back at the hospital until the following night.

Even though the hospital was an hour south of where they lived, he was happy to go home and spend the rest of the evening with Stella. Throughout the drive, he made plans in his head of how he and Stella might enjoy his unexpected night off. He pictured them cuddling on the couch while they watched a movie or sharing a bottle of wine on the back porch while they gazed at the stars and listened to the ocean waves crash on the beach. In both scenarios, of course, they ended up in bed, making love well into the night.

But he couldn't have been more wrong.

When he got to the small home he and Stella shared in Anna Bay, he unlocked the front door and called out to his wife. Seeing she wasn't in the kitchen, he called out to her again and continued to their master bedroom. He stopped in the doorway to their room.

"Stella?"

A suitcase lay open on the bed, piled high with clothes. Stella stared at him with her emerald eyes. Her mouth gaped open, obviously frazzled by his presence. More than frazzled. She looked terrified.

"What are you doing?" Eric asked.

She took a deep breath and slammed the suitcase closed. "I'm sorry, Eric. I didn't want it to be this way. It's not exactly what it looks like. I think we need some time apart. I'm going to stay with my parents."

"You're leaving me?"

"I just think we need to take a break."

He took a step toward her. Her eyes widened, and she moved back.

"Why? Did your parents talk you into this?"

"No, this has nothing to do with my parents. You know why. You're starting to scare me with your mood swings and your temper. After you hit me the other night, I don't think it's safe for me to be here anymore."

Now she had insulted him. "Hit you? That was an accident!"

He watched her demeanor change, and she no longer looked afraid. She was angry.

"It wasn't an accident and you know it!" she yelled. She moved forward, bringing her face within an inch of his. "And I'm not going to stick around and let that happen again."

There was a look in her eyes he had never seen before: hatred. She leaned over and zipped the suitcase shut. She started to pull it off the bed, and Eric realized he couldn't let her go. She would probably never come back. He loved her too much to lose her.

He didn't mean for it to end the way it did. She was just so...stubborn. He grabbed the suitcase and pulled it out of her hands.

"No. You're not leaving. I'm your husband. Your home is with me. You're not going anywhere."

He was trying to be understanding, but that's when she pushed him over the edge.

"Oh, yeah? What are you going to do? Hit me again?"

She had never used that tone of voice with him, and Eric knew there was no way he was going to win this argument with words. She grabbed his arm and tried to tear it away from the suitcase.

"You can't make me stay. I'm leaving and there's nothing you can do about it. Let me go or I'll call my parents to come get me!"

She pushed him away, and that's when he lost it. He grabbed her by the throat with both hands and shoved her against the wall. She kicked and thrashed her arms at him before trying to pry his hands away from her neck. This only made him squeeze harder. She slowly stopped fighting him, but, because of his rage, Eric held tight for another few minutes.

When he finally let go, she fell to the floor and Eric knew she was dead. He hadn't meant to kill her. She just wouldn't listen.

When his emotions calmed, it became clear he needed to get rid of her body. He paced their bedroom floor, trying to think of where he could leave her so no one would find her. Then he heard the sound of the waves pounding against the sand. *What better than the ocean?*

Lightning flashed outside their window. Eric remembered hearing on the radio that a severe thunderstorm was predicted for the night. He couldn't risk leaving her body at their house any longer. If her parents had been expecting her, they might come looking for her when she didn't show. He would have to brave the storm.

He and Stella owned a small fishing boat they mainly used inside the bay. The water could be rough outside the headlands, and it made Stella nervous to venture into the open waters on anything but a flat calm day. He looked down at her body on the hardwood floor. *Sorry, Stella. Tonight we are going to have to risk it.*

He couldn't just throw her overboard. He needed to make sure she would never wash up on shore. He pulled out all the frozen meat from their freezer and went into the garage to grab some rope. He used a knife to cut a hole in the middle of every steak and chicken breast. He strung them all onto the rope and tied it three times around her waist. He made sure the knot would hold before carrying her body to the garage. Even now, he was amazed at his quick thinking.

Eric threw her into the boat before running back inside to find his four heaviest dumbbells. He brought them into the garage, grabbed another long piece of rope, and hopped into the boat alongside his wife. He cut the rope into four pieces and tied each dumbbell to one of her limbs. Fortunately, he had a tarp in the garage and used it to cover her body. He placed the dumbbells on top of its edges to hold it down.

After hitching the boat to the back of his car, he drove fifteen minutes to the boat launch at Little Beach. Eric was happy to see the parking lot was empty and he was the only one there. It was silly to think he wouldn't be. No one else was desperate enough to be launching their boat at ten o'clock at night in the middle of a storm.

It was raining by the time he pulled the boat away from the pier. The roaring thunder and lightning flashes became more frequent as he pushed the throttle forward and steered toward the headlands. The water was choppy inside the bay, and Eric knew it would be much worse once he got outside the port. The visibility was terrible, even with his outer lights on. Somehow, he managed to pass safely through the headlands into the open ocean.

The boat rocked up and down on their way to the outer waters as he rode over the waves coming in with the tide. He checked to make sure Stella was still in the boat. He couldn't see a thing through the blur of the rain as he powered farther out. There were islands staggered throughout these waters, and he could only hope he didn't run into any of their limestone shores.

The area also had an outer reef that was popular with scuba divers, so he kept cruising until the ocean depth reached 150 meters. Eric pulled back on the throttle and put the boat into neutral. A wave crashed into the boat as he turned to grab Stella. He fell forward, his foot slipping on the wet tarp under his feet. His armpits landed on the side of the boat, which dipped into the rough sea from the weight of his body. His arms and top of his head went into the water, and, for a moment, Eric thought he was a goner.

He reached back and clasped one of his hands around the side of the boat. As it tilted upward from the force of another wave, Eric threw himself backward on top of Stella's body. He lay on the tarp and caught his breath while the boat thrashed around in the wild sea.

One by one, he slid each dumbbell that was tied to Stella's arms and legs off the top of the tarp. He grabbed her arms and pulled them over the side of the boat first. The boat rocked so violently he had to be careful not to get too close to the edge or he would go with her. Eric sat down and grabbed her waist on either side. He pushed her top half overboard, but her legs were still in the vessel, weighted down by his heavy dumbbells.

Thankful Stella hadn't been very big, he lifted her calves up and over the side. The dumbbells clunked against the side of the boat as she sank beneath the surface. Eric felt a rise in emotion when she disappeared into the deep, but he forced himself to stay calm. Now he had to get home.

With the aid of his compass and an incredible amount of luck, he succeeded in getting back inside the headlands of Port Stephens safe and sound with minimal damage to his boat. Eric would've felt like a hero if he hadn't just disposed of his wife's body.

When he got home, there was no sign of his in-laws. Stella must have not told them she was leaving him tonight. Eric knew they were partly to blame for her trying to leave him. They'd been planting the seed inside her head for years.

He parked the boat in the garage and went inside to take a warm shower. When he crawled into their empty bed, he tried not to think about the fact she was gone.

Eric went back to the hospital the next night as usual. He didn't want to appear suspicious by calling in sick, plus it helped take his mind off things.

A couple of Stella's friends came by their house over the next few days wanting to know where she was. He told them she'd left him and had gone to stay with her parents. When Stella's parents and sister heard this, they were furious. They accused him of all kinds of horrible things and said they were filing a missing person's report with the local police. He told them to go right ahead, but they were wasting their time. If she wasn't staying with them like she'd said, she obviously didn't want to be found. But they were adamant he had done something to her and knew where she was.

As time went on, her family became convinced Eric had killed her, and they tried to sell the police on this as well. They even went on national television and shared their story. Through tear-soaked eyes, they pleaded with Eric to confess what he had done to their daughter. But he never did. And the police never had enough evidence to arrest him. What was it Marky Mark had said? *It's extremely difficult to solve a homicide without a body.*

CHAPTER THIRTY-SEVEN

Eric moved to the front of the ferry as they got closer to Seattle. It didn't take long to see he had a problem. He'd underestimated the local law enforcement. A squad car and an unmarked vehicle were parked on either side of the ramp at the ferry dock. Two uniformed officers stood between the vehicles, ready to inspect every car as it got off the boat. The unmarked car likely belonged to Beavis and Butthead, who were probably waiting for him inside the walk-on passenger terminal.

Eric hurried back inside and down the nearest stairwell before most of the passengers returned to their cars. Once on the lower car deck, he moved toward the back of the boat. Fortunately, the setting sun would work to his advantage. He braced himself for what he had to do as the foamy water came into view.

He stopped when he reached the chain that had been pulled across the rear of the last car. A ferry worker stood at one end of the chain, waiting to remove the blocks from tires of the cars last in line once they docked. *Crikey*. It wouldn't exactly help his escape to jump off right in front of this bloke. He eyed Eric curiously while Eric planned his next move.

"You all right, sir?"

"Fine, thanks," Eric replied as he turned toward the stairwell. It was full of passengers coming down to get back into their cars as he made his way up. Hopefully, that would mean there would be no witnesses on the rear upper deck. Keeping his head down, Eric bumped shoulders with more than one as he ascended the stairs two at a time.

Once upstairs, he dodged through more passengers heading back down to their vehicles. When he got close to the rear deck, he could see it was empty. *Good.* He was accosted by wind and rain when he opened the door and stepped outside. He grabbed hold of the railing and looked over the edge at the choppy waves that had grown darker with the setting sun. He realized the weather he was enduring on the upper deck was nothing compared to what he was about to do.

Eric took a quick look around to make sure no one was watching, glad he'd had the foresight to wear black. Seeing no one, he climbed over the railing, took a deep breath, and dove into the deep.

It took everything in him to not inhale from the shock of the cold the second he became submerged in the Sound. The rumbling of the ferry engine filled his senses and sent a vibration through his body. Eric forced himself to take a few strokes underwater before coming up for air. There was already good distance between him and the ferry.

He hyperventilated and forced himself to keep moving through the frigid water toward the shore. A wave came over his face and he inadvertently drank in salt water. He swam to the left as the ferry veered right. Eric focused on a pier down away from the ferry dock. At least he didn't have to worry about sharks in these waters like he would in Sydney, but he'd happily take his chances with them now to be free from this hypothermia.

Eric swam as fast as he could for the next few minutes but was dismayed to see the pier didn't look any closer. His body seemed to be slowing down. He may have underestimated the distance to the shore. Despite being out of breath, he concentrated on making one stroke after another, hoping his slow, continual progress would get him to the pier before his body shut down completely from the cold.

CHAPTER THIRTY-EIGHT

"He's not here," Stephenson said after the last walk-on passenger had disembarked the ferry.

He had tried calling the doctor's cell on his way to the ferry, but, not surprisingly, the doctor's phone was off. He held his phone to his ear and peered over the railing at Adams who stood in the waiting bay below.

"I just checked the last car to leave the ferry. He wasn't in any of the vehicles. And none of the passengers recognized him from his driver's license photo."

"Same here," Stephenson said. "Let's see if any of the crew spotted him." He flashed his badge to the ferry worker on the upper deck and stepped onto the boat. "I'm on the ferry. I want to do a search of the inside in case he's hiding somewhere on the ship."

They got off the ferry and walked through the terminal after their search of the boat yielded nothing. None of the crew had recognized the doctor from his photo either. However, one of the workers did report seeing a man dressed in black and a black baseball cap acting strangely near the back of the boat shortly before they docked. Although the worker was unable to ID him from the doctor's license photo, the vague description he gave to the detectives sounded like it could've been Dr. Leroy.

"You think it was him?" Adams asked.

"It'd be my best guess. Since we didn't see anyone who matched that description leave the ferry, he could've jumped off before the boat docked."

"You want to notify the Coast Guard?"

Stephenson shook his head. "No. It's dark out and the ferry's been docked for an hour. If he's still in the water, he'd be unconscious from hypothermia and likely drowned by now. But he could've made it to shore, and our priority is the safety of the public." Stephenson wished they could put out a bulletin with Dr. Leroy's photo to the local police. However, since no witnesses could ID Dr. Leroy from his driver's license photo, they had insufficient grounds to bring him in. "Let's send one of our sketch artists over to meet with the cook from the café. Maybe the artist can get more details out of him. Then, let's use the composite to put out a bulletin to Seattle PD."

"You know," Adams said as Stephenson pulled out his phone, "I hate to say *I told you so* but we should've never let Dwayne out of custody to use as bait for Dr. Leroy. It would've made a lot more sense if we could've justified putting the doctor under surveillance too."

Stephenson shot a sideways glance at his partner. "That's exactly why we needed Dwayne. We needed his release to provoke the doctor, which it obviously did. Only we should have him in custody right now and Dwayne should be alive. If those two surveillance officers had paid a little more attention to Dwayne and a little less to the Seahawk game, none of this would've happened."

"Maybe. I'm just glad it's your ass on the line and not mine. This is all you and Sergeant McKinnon. I never wanted to release that dirtbag."

"Yeah, well you can let me worry about that. For now, let's find the doctor."

CHAPTER THIRTY-NINE

Exhausted, Eric finally made it to the end of the pier. It had nearly grown dark in the time it took him to reach it, and he could only hope he'd managed to cross the distance unnoticed. He looked at the pillar that held up the end of pier. The pier stood about two meters above the water, and there was no way he'd be able to climb the barnacle and algae-covered post to the top.

He spotted a ladder about ten meters ahead. It hung down from the side of the pier and almost reached the water. It took every bit of willpower he had left to swim toward it. It felt like an eternity until he reached it. Triumphantly, he encircled his hand around one of the rusted, metal bars and slowly pulled himself onto the pier.

Eric collapsed on the wooden structure and looked over at the ferry landing. His body shivered uncontrollably as he took in slow, shallow breaths. The two police vehicles were still there, stopping every car as it drove off the boat. Hopefully, that meant Eric had escaped the ferry unnoticed.

When his breathing returned to normal, he stood up. He trembled from the cold and walked down the empty pier toward the city. He needed to get out of here, away from downtown. He needed to get to the airport. But first, he needed some dry clothes.

Eric felt for the burner phone in his pocket and realized it probably no longer worked after his swim. Nevertheless, he held up the wet device and attempted to turn it on. Nothing.

As he neared the street, a man and woman holding hands under a shared umbrella stopped and stared at him. Eric's shoes squished with each step from the water inside. Sopping wet, he smiled at the gawking couple.

"Good evening," Eric said with a nod of his head.

The woman's mouth fell open and she continued to stare. Eric broke their gaze and turned left onto the sidewalk.

"Good evening," he heard the man say.

Eric shoved the useless phone back into his pocket and ducked inside the first gift shop he saw. An old man sat behind the register reading a novel.

"Hello," the man said, not bothering to look up from his book.

Eric headed straight for a rack of hooded sweatshirts with a picture of the space needle on the front. He grabbed a pair of matching sweatpants on his way to the dressing room. His lips were purple when he saw his reflection in the dressing room mirror. His left cheekbone had already started to bruise in the shape of Dwayne's fist.

He threw off his wet clothes and retrieved his burner phone and wallet from his jacket pocket. He felt warmer almost immediately after putting on the dry sweats. He stepped back into his wet shoes. Eric took the extra minute to fold his clothes into a neat pile in the corner of the dressing room.

The old man looked up from his book when Eric approached the register. He carefully bookmarked his page before setting the book aside. Eric rolled his eyes when he spotted the author's name on the cover. *Martin Watts.* Martin was so overrated, it was maddening.

"I'll take this sweatshirt and sweatpants," Eric said.

"Couldn't wait to wear them, huh?"

"It's a wet one out there today. My clothes got soaked by the rain." Eric pulled a saturated hundred-dollar bill out of his wallet and laid it on the counter.

The man gawked at the bill before looking up at Eric.

"You drop your wallet in the Sound?" He took in Eric's appearance for the first time since he'd entered the store. "From the color of your lips, you look like you jumped in after it."

"Like I said, it's coming down hard out there. Keep the change," Eric said before walking out of the store.

Eric stopped at the nearest bus stop only a block away. It was time to get off the street.

The bus arrived after only a few minutes. He rode it to Pioneer Square, where he got off and jumped on the light rail that would take him all the way to the airport. Eric took the last seat in the carriage, not bothering to get up for the old man with a cane who got on at the next stop.

Eric leaned his head against the window for the rest of the way. He continued to warm up from his swim and felt himself relax when they reached the airport. He was going to make it. A few more hours and he'd be on a plane out of the country, ready to start his new life.

He picked up his bag from the luggage storage kiosk, thankful for his preemptive planning of a change of clothes and cash. He found a bathroom outside security and changed into jeans and a t-shirt. He left twelve thousand in cash in his carry-on bag. Two thousand for the airline ticket and ten thousand to declare through customs. He hid the other ten thousand on his person. He carefully placed five thousand inside the bottom of each of his socks before getting in line for the ticket counter at Air Canada.

It felt strange to be fleeing the country he had once fled to. It was right after Stella's parents went on TV that he moved to America. Even though he was never arrested for Stella's murder, people in their small town started to look at him differently. Especially after her family went on TV.

His parents eventually sided with Stella's family. He was crushed to learn they too believed he had killed her. Even though he had. During his shifts at the hospital he would get the question, *Hey, aren't you that bloke who was on TV for killing his wife?*

He even felt like an unwelcome outsider at his local grocery store. It began to wear on him. He didn't want to live with a stigma like that for the rest of his life. The final blow had been when his parents told him they never wanted to see him again. It was then that he knew he needed a fresh start. Being born a dual-citizen made America an easy choice.

"Can I help you, sir?"

The voice of the ticket agent brought him out of his thoughts, and he realized he was standing at the front of the line for the ticket counter.

"Um, yes. I need to buy a ticket for the next flight available to Australia. Sydney, preferably, but I'll go to Melbourne or Brisbane if you can get me there today."

"Okay, let me see what I have available for tonight." Her long, acrylic nails tapped loudly on the keyboard. "I can get you on the red-eye flight to Sydney out of Vancouver. I've got seats on the seven o'clock flight to Vancouver, which will put you there in plenty of time. It'll be 2200 dollars."

He let out a sigh of relief at his good luck.

"Great, I'll pay cash."

He set the money on the counter and waited to see if she found this unusual. She took the money and counted it out without blinking an eye, and he realized he was being paranoid. After all, she didn't know he'd killed anyone.

"Could I have your passport and I'll check you in?"

"Sure." He placed his passport on the counter.

A minute later, she handed it back to him along with his tickets. He flashed her a grateful smile.

"Thank you," he said as he picked up his bag. She'd just made his day.

He got to the front of the line at security and realized there was a problem with his plan. He watched as most travelers were made to walk through the full-body scanner. He placed his shoes and bag on the conveyer belt of the x-ray machine, aware of the stacks of cash under his feet. Surely, they would see the cash if he went through the scanner.

He held his breath as the woman in front of him was told to go through the full-body scanner. The TSA agent held up his hand for Eric to wait. *How could I have been so stupid?*

The woman exited the scanner and the agent motioned for Eric to come forward. Eric took slow steps toward the scanner, fearing his escape was about to come to a bitter end.

"Sir, this way," the agent barked.

Eric stopped and saw the man was pointing to the metal detector.

"Come on through," he said impatiently.

Eric's jaw fell open. He turned away from the scanner and went through the metal detector as instructed.

"Thank you. Have a good flight."

Eric smiled at the agent before retrieving his bag from the x-ray machine. "I will."

Although he made it through security without a problem, he felt slightly nervous as he walked to his gate. He couldn't shake the feeling his escape was too good to be true.

CHAPTER FORTY

Adams hung up with the surveillance officer who'd found Dwayne's body that afternoon.

"They've searched the area surrounding the café, but there's no sign of the doctor or anyone else fitting his description."

"Let's stop by the homicide unit and grab that photo montage we used for the break-in at Madison Park before we go to the crime scene. I want to give the cook another chance to ID him."

"They're in the process of checking the Bainbridge Island ferry holding cameras, but so far they haven't found any trace of the doctor's car being on the island today. The officers found text messages on Dwayne's cell from someone who claimed to have Daisy's phone with evidence that Dwayne killed her. The texts threatened to turn her phone into the police unless Dwayne met them today at that cafe on the island. The texts weren't from Dr. Leroy's number, but they're sending Dwayne's phone over to TESU to be analyzed."

"Dr. Leroy knew we didn't find Daisy's phone. We never released that to the media."

"They also found part of a broken-off zipper on the ground outside the window of the bathroom. We should have the fingerprint analysis back in a few hours."

They rode together to the doctor's apartment. The sky was dark and lights had come on around the city. The traffic moved slowly from the Seahawks game. They needed to get to Dwayne's crime scene, especially since they had a witness who could possibly ID the doctor. But Dwayne's body was already being transferred to the Seattle Medical Examiner's Office, and first they wanted to find Dr. Leroy.

His car was in the parking garage when they got to his building. Stephenson guessed he probably walked to the ferry to kill Dwayne.

There was no answer when they knocked on his apartment door. Stephenson tried the doorknob. It was locked.

"We need to get in there. We might find Daisy's phone. The doctor could even be hiding out in the apartment."

Adams pulled out his phone. "I'll see if I can get a warrant in case we find anything incriminating in there."

"See if you can get one for his car, too, while you're at it."

Adams nodded.

Stephenson had put the building manager's number in his phone when they came to Robert's crime scene. He dialed her number while Adams made the call to the judge. Fortunately, she was on site and brought up a key to the doctor's apartment before Adams got off the phone.

"Thank you," Stephenson said as she handed him the key. "We'll bring it back down to you when we're done."

"You're going to search his apartment then?"

"Yes."

She bit her lip. "Has he done something wrong? Did he kill Robert?"

"We're in the process of investigating that."

She lingered uncomfortably for a moment, as if wanting to ask more but not sure of what to say. "Okay. I'll be downstairs when you're done with the key."

She walked slowly back to the elevator as Adams ended the call and walked back toward him.

"We've got it. Let's go."

He looked back at the building manager as she stepped into the elevator.

"You already got the key?"

"Yeah. I didn't see the point in waiting till you got off the phone."

Stephenson unlocked the door and announced themselves as they cautiously entered the apartment.

"Dr. Leroy? It's Detectives Stephenson and Adams from Seattle Homicide. You home?"

The apartment was silent.

The unit was meticulously neat, just as it had been when they came to inform the doctor of his front office assistant's death. Too neat, Stephenson thought. No one he knew kept their place *that* perfect. *A sign of a sick mind*, he thought.

"I'll check the bedroom."

"All right. I'll start out here," Adams said, pulling a pair of gloves out of his coat pocket.

"Dr. Leroy?" Stephenson called again when he reached the bedroom door.

He donned his own gloves before reaching through the doorway and flicking on the light. The bed was made and the nightstands on either side of the bed were bare apart from a lamp. The floors were spotless.

He opened the double doors to the doctor's closet. It was filled with perfectly organized clothes. He entered the en suite bathroom and noticed the shower was empty. No shampoo, no soap, nothing. This struck him as odd, even for a neat freak like Dr. Leroy. He went through the bathroom cabinets and found they too were nearly empty. There was no toothbrush, toothpaste, deodorant, razors, shampoo, or soap. Despite the closet being full of clothes, he feared the doctor had already skipped town.

While they could monitor his airline travel and entry into other countries, they couldn't stop him. Not without a warrant for his arrest. And they still didn't have enough evidence to get one.

"I found something," he heard Adams call from the other room.

Stephenson stepped out into the living room and found Adams holding up a small black leather case.

"Found a lock picking kit in the top drawer of his desk. It was sitting next to a pair of black leather gloves." He pointed down to the opened drawer. "I already took photos of them in the drawer." He pulled two plastic evidence bags out of one of his pockets and bagged the items.

"Can you smell paint thinner on the gloves?" Stephenson asked.

Adams pulled them out of the bag and lifted them to his nose. "It's faint, but I think so." He pushed them back into the evidence bag. "We still don't have results back on Robert's drumsticks, but I'll make some calls when we get back to homicide and see if they can speed it up. Hopefully we'll get results as soon as tomorrow."

Stephenson told him about the lack of toiletries in the doctor's bathroom.

"You think he's going to try and disappear?"

"Maybe. But wherever he goes, we'll find him. Even if we can't stop him from leaving the state or the country until we have an arrest warrant, we can at least monitor his travel until we get one. When we get back to the homicide unit, I'll work on getting a warrant we can serve to the airlines." Stephenson pulled his phone out his pocket. "In the meantime, I'll call my contact at the Port of Seattle and ask him to notify us if Dr. Leroy shows up on any flight manifests out of SeaTac."

They searched the doctor's apartment for another hour before heading back to the homicide unit. Adams made the necessary phone calls to speed up the lab analysis of Dr. Leroy's gloves while Stephenson filled out the paperwork for their warrant to monitor the airline manifests.

With Adams still on the phone, Stephenson retrieved the photo montage for their witness at the café. Other than the gloves and lock picking kit, they didn't find anything else in Dr. Leroy's apartment to help with their investigation. Stephenson found a fireproof box under the doctor's bed with the key left in it, but the box was empty. He guessed it was where the doctor would've kept his passport, and he now worried he might be planning to leave the country, not just the state.

There was no computer or laptop and they didn't find Daisy's phone. Until they got the lab analysis back on the doctor's gloves and Robert's drumsticks, they needed more evidence to arrest him.

Stephenson logged into his email when he returned to his desk and saw he had a new message from his contact at the Port of Seattle. He swore under his breath when the doctor's name came up on his screen in an international passenger manifest.

"What is it?" Adams asked as he hung up his desk phone.

"Dr. Leroy is on a flight to Vancouver, B.C. It took off ten minutes ago. He's booked on a connecting flight from there to Sydney, Australia."

"Well, that makes things a bit more complicated."

Stephenson gritted his teeth as he stared at his screen. He was beyond frustrated they didn't have enough on the doctor to arrest him before he fled the country. Now, when they finally got what they needed to arrest him, they'd have to go through the process of extradition.

"Yeah, just a bit."

It was late when Stephenson got home. He retrieved a beer from the fridge on his way to the couch, glad he'd remembered to put some in there that morning. After the day he'd had, he needed one.

He collapsed on the couch and dialed Richards. It was after ten, but he figured she'd still be awake. She answered on the second ring.

"Hi. You arrest Dwayne's killer already?"

He felt himself relax at the sound of her voice. "I wish. But no. I wanted to thank you for taking me to the game today. I had a great time."

"You're welcome. I had a good time too. Plus, it didn't hurt that we won."

"I'm sorry I had to leave so quick."

"That's okay. You only missed meeting my brother. Oh, and Russell Wilson. It was the first time I'd met him. He was super nice. Came over and talked with us for like ten minutes."

"That makes me feel a lot better about rushing out."

Hearing her laugh on the other end of the call, he smiled.

"Did you get back to your car okay?"

"Yeah, my brother gave me a ride back to the station. I'm leaving his place now. He had a small party at his house. Have you eaten anything tonight?"

It was the first time he'd thought about food since he'd left the stadium. Now that she mentioned it, he realized he was starving.

"No, we were too busy to think about food."

"I'm actually at Northgate, isn't that close to where you live? Want me to bring over some take out?"

"That sounds great, but you don't have to do that." He glanced at his work laptop sitting on his coffee table. "Plus, I've got some work to do tonight, so I probably wouldn't be that great of company."

"I don't mind. Maybe I could help you."

"I'd love that, but only if you're sure that's how you want to spend your Saturday night."

"I'm sure."

Twenty minutes later he heard a knock at his door. He got up and opened the door to let her in. She looked as beautiful as she had earlier that day, maybe even more so.

"Mexican okay?" She held up a large paper bag.

"Perfect. Come on in."

She followed him into the living room and took a seat next to him on the couch. He was already halfway through his burrito by the time she took her first bite.

"Good thing I bought you two," she said, watching him inhale the second half of his burrito.

"Thank you." He wiped his hands on a paper napkin. "I didn't realize how hungry I was."

"So where are you at on Dwayne's murder case?"

"A cook at the café saw a man matching Dr. Leroy's description in the kitchen right before Dwayne was found dead. Unfortunately, he was wearing a baseball hat, so the cook was unable to positively ID him in a photo montage."

He sighed and pulled another burrito out of the bag, irritated that Dr. Leroy's average looks and baseball cap had kept him from being positively ID'd twice in their investigation.

"We found threatening text messages on Dwayne's cell from someone saying they had Daisy's phone and could prove Dwayne killed her. They told him to meet them at the cafe where he was killed. Problem is, the texts were sent from an untraceable burner phone. There was no other communication between him and Dr. Leroy.

"We visited the crime scene, but there wasn't much to see. We did, however, get a partial fingerprint match to Dr. Leroy from a piece of a zipper that was found outside the bathroom's window, which is how we think he fled the scene."

"That's great! I mean, that's huge isn't it? Does that give you enough for his arrest?"

He shook his head as he swallowed the last bite of his second burrito. He crumpled its paper wrapper before tossing it back inside the empty take-out bag.

"No. Well, we might've been able to justify an arrest warrant with that, but we could've used more to strengthen our case."

She leaned back against the couch while he went on.

"But Dr. Leroy is now on a flight to Australia. Since we didn't get the fingerprint analysis back until after he'd left the country, there was nothing we could do to stop him."

Her eyes grew wide. "So, what? You'll have to extradite him?"

He nodded. "Yes, when we have enough evidence. The partial on the zipper might've been enough for a warrant while he was still in the country, but it may not be enough to make a case for extradition, which will be a drawn-out, complicated process. But I'm going to do whatever's necessary to bring him back and charge him with murder."

"I'm sure you will."

Their eyes met. He wanted to lean over and kiss her but wondered if maybe it was too soon. Instead, he cleared his throat and told her about the call he got from Dr. Leroy's sister-in-law.

"Wow. So, you think he killed his wife and has gotten away with it for twenty years?"

"Personally, yes. But I don't think we'll ever be able to prove it. Unless he confesses."

"Well, he must think you have something on him if he's fleeing to Australia. Maybe it means he screwed up somehow."

The same thought had already crossed his mind. "I hope so."

He looked into her blue eyes and was suddenly overcome by how stunning she was. He wondered if he was boring her with all the details of his case, but she didn't seem bored. She looked intrigued.

"I hope I'm not ruining your Saturday night with all this shop talk," he said.

She smiled, and he felt his heart rate quicken.

"Not at all. It's fascinating. Plus, I'm enjoying being with you."

"Me too."

"I actually had a bit of a crush on you when we were at the police academy."

That would've been six years ago, but he didn't remember her being at the academy when he was there. He was sure he would've remembered her.

"You were in my class?"

"Well, no. I was in the class below yours, but I used to see you around at the training center. I never worked up the nerve to introduce myself."

"I wish you would have."

His urge to kiss her grew even stronger. He might've imagined it, but she seemed to be sitting closer to him on the couch than she had a minute ago. He leaned forward slowly, bringing his mouth to hers. Her lips moved against his as she returned his kiss.

Her fingers intertwined with his. They reclined on the couch and continued to talk between kisses. After walking her to her car an hour later, he didn't think about Dr. Leroy again for the rest of the night.

CHAPTER FORTY-ONE

Eric boarded both flights without a problem. He had a window seat on the leg to Sydney, and he leaned forward to take in the view of his homeland as they descended.

Rugged sandstone cliffs dropped into the bright sapphire water along the outer shores of Sydney's coastline. The view of Sydney Harbour was breathtaking as they flew over the Opera House and Harbour Bridge. He suddenly realized how much he had missed this beautiful, diverse country.

After clearing customs without a hitch, Eric relaxed even more. He stepped outside into the warm, morning air. He drew in a deep breath as he squinted in the bright sunlight. Seeing the palm trees that lined the street immediately lifted his spirits.

He knew without a doubt he hadn't left Australia because he wanted to. He'd left because he felt like there was no other option. He pulled out the sunglasses he'd bought in the airport gift shop while killing time in Vancouver.

After nearly twenty years, it was good to be home.

CHAPTER FORTY-TWO

On Monday morning, Stephenson sat next to Sergeant McKinnon and looked across at Lieutenant Greyson, who frowned from behind his large desk. The wall behind him was covered with plaques and certificates of what looked to be every achievement and award the lieutenant had ever been given. They confirmed to Stephenson that Greyson had always been more interested in ass-kissing and moving his way up the department's ladder than he had ever been in solving crimes.

Stephenson had felt like a kid getting called into the principal's office by the way the lieutenant had summoned them into his office. Greyson seemed to enjoy exercising his authority, which made their meeting all the more painful. Stephenson couldn't help but notice the lieutenant's hair was significantly thinner than the last time he saw him.

"So, let me get this straight. You released Dwayne Morrison, a known killer, for the purpose of using him as bait to catch a supposed serial killer who you couldn't justify putting under surveillance."

"Well, actually—"

McKinnon raised his left hand in front of Stephenson's chest, signaling he'd do the talking.

"Not as bait. We released him and placed him under twenty-four-hour police surveillance in the hope of using any communication or interaction he had with Dr. Leroy as something we could use to prove Dr. Leroy was responsible for a string of recent murders. If the doctor threatened Dwayne, or the officers felt Dwayne was in danger at any point, they were ordered to intervene and arrest the doctor."

"So, as I said, you released him and used him as bait. You not only risked his life but also posed a risk to the community by letting a killer back on the streets."

Stephenson heard McKinnon let out a sigh. As he looked back and forth between his two superiors, he thought they couldn't have been more different. Not only in appearance, but also in personality. Even sitting down, one could see that Greyson was small in stature. His pale complexion gave him a washed-out look, especially in the middle of winter. And he was all about upholding policies and procedures. A man who lived for the rule book.

McKinnon was a couple inches taller than himself. Stephenson guessed he was about six three. And, much to Greyson's disapproval, McKinnon felt that in extreme circumstances rules sometimes needed to be bent, if not broken, to get the job done.

"Being under round-the-clock surveillance, Dwayne should never have been in any danger nor been allowed to harm anyone else. Prior to his release, we also had received a confirmation of Dwayne's alibi for the time around Daisy's death. Without a more precise time of death for Daisy Colbert, we couldn't be certain Dwayne was her killer."

Stephenson knew McKinnon was stretching the truth a bit but hoped it would pacify the lieutenant. Since they only had an approximate time of death for Daisy, it was *possible* she was killed right after Dwayne got to his friends' house. But his alibi also left plenty of time for him to kill her within the window of her time of death, so it wouldn't have given them cause to release him.

The lieutenant stared back and forth between them as if deciding what to do next.

McKinnon took the opportunity to continue in their defense. "We aren't responsible for the actions, or lack thereof, of the two officers who were watching Dwayne at the time of his death. Plus, he wasn't in police custody when he was killed. We didn't owe him any protection. Their job was to see what we could learn from any interaction Dwayne had with the doctor."

This seemed to appease the lieutenant, at least for the moment. He turned his focus to Stephenson.

"And where are you in the investigation of Dwayne's death and your recent strangulation cases, including Martin and Patricia Watts?"

"Our prime suspect is Dr. Eric Leroy, but we're still working on compiling enough evidence for his arrest."

He didn't add that they would be closing Daisy's case by attributing her death to Dwayne. Or that the doctor was now in Australia and they'd have to extradite him once they could make a strong enough case. McKinnon sat silently next to him, and Stephenson was thankful he didn't bring up either of those things either.

They found Daisy's fingerprints in the passenger side of the doctor's BMW when they processed his car over the weekend. It made Stephenson wonder what sort of relationship the two of them had, even though there was no record of any calls or texts made between them. If Dwayne had suspected there was something going on between them, his jealousy could've been part of his motive for killing her.

Greyson leaned over and pulled that morning's edition of *The Seattle Times* from his desk drawer. "I take it you've seen this?"

Stephenson tried not to cringe when he read the front-page headline. Adams had told him there was an article but not the extent of what it had said.

MURDER-SUICIDE OR KILLER WALKING FREE? COPS STILL HAVE NO ANSWERS IN DEATH OF MARTIN WATTS AND WIFE PATRICIA

"We're very close to getting an arrest warrant for Eric Leroy."

Greyson tossed the paper onto his desk. "I want to see those cases solved. And soon."

Like I don't? Stephenson thought. "Yes, sir," he said.

McKinnon stood, taking the cue they'd been dismissed and Stephenson followed suit. Stephenson shut the door to Greyson's office behind him.

"Thanks for having my back in there," he said.

"You're welcome. Just find a way to bring the doctor back and put him away for good."

"I will."

The sergeant gave him a firm pat on the back before heading to his office. Stephenson walked back to his desk and tried to believe his own words.

He checked his email when he sat down and saw he had a new message from Patricia's health insurance company.

Before he'd left on Friday, he called the software company Dr. Leroy used for his medical records. They confirmed Patricia's medical documents had, in fact, been edited by Dr. Leroy a few days before she was killed. However, when they tried to look up the previous versions of her records in their system, they found they'd all been deleted by Dr. Leroy.

He'd contacted her insurance company before his meeting with the lieutenant to request a list of other doctors she'd seen in the past couple years. He hoped maybe one of them had been sent her records from Dr. Leroy and he could compare them to the file the doctor had given them.

He scanned through the list of specialist doctors and stopped when he read she'd seen another psychiatrist three months earlier. That'd be his best bet for receiving a copy of her records from Dr. Leroy's office. He saw their address was in Madison Park, not far from where Patricia had lived. He dialed the number and spoke briefly with the receptionist.

She looked up Patricia in their database and verified she'd been seen once by their office three months before. She said their psychiatrist had agreed to cover for Dr. Leroy by seeing his patients while he was on vacation. She confirmed they'd received Patricia's entire file from Dr. Leroy at the time of her visit. It was exactly what he'd hoped for. He stressed the importance of them receiving her file and promised to fax over a warrant within a couple of hours.

It was late afternoon when Patricia's medical records came over their fax machine. Her file was lengthy. Stephenson and Adams worked together for over an hour comparing the file to what Dr. Leroy had given them.

Stephenson set down his highlighter when he reached the last page. "He completely falsified all the verbally abusive and controlling behaviors of Patricia's husband."

"Yeah, looks like she complained about him a lot, but there's nothing in this file that would suggest he was any sort of danger to her. Dr. Leroy obviously wanted us to think Martin killed his wife. Falsifying her medical records should give us enough to start his extradition process. Plus, we have his prints on the zipper from Dwayne's crime scene."

Stephenson picked up his highlighter and tapped it against the desk. "It's a start, but the medical records aren't enough to prove he killed Martin and Patricia. I think we need to find more before we request his extradition. With double jeopardy, we only have one shot to get him convicted of Dwayne's murder. I want to bring him back on solid murder charges, not just this."

"Blake?"

He turned and was shocked to see Serena. Unlike the last time he'd seen her, her hair was dry and she wore a tight black skirt that stopped above her knees and a button up shirt.

"What are you doing here? Who brought you up?" he asked.

"Suarez. I told him it was really important that I speak to you. I got off work early, and I figured you'd still be here."

Her demeanor was serious, and Stephenson wondered what she'd possibly want to speak to him about. He couldn't imagine she'd come all the way here to say sorry for cheating on him. He had no desire to speak to her again; there was nothing to say.

Adams looked nearly as shocked to see her as Stephenson did. He glanced back and forth between the two of them, waiting for his partner's response.

"Okay. Go ahead." Stephenson leaned back in his chair. "But make it quick, because I need to get back to work."

She looked over at Adams before turning back to him. "Could we go somewhere private for a few minutes?"

Stephenson debated for a moment before answering. "Fine. We can talk in the break room." He reluctantly got out of his chair. "I won't be long," he said to Adams as he led the way to the small room down the hall from the large, open area where they worked.

He stepped aside and motioned for Serena to enter first. He followed behind, leaving the door open behind him. She turned to face him. He crossed his arms and waited for her to speak.

"So, how are you?" she asked.

The look of concern on her face was almost laughable. *Seriously?* he thought.

"I'm fine. I hope that's not what you came all the way down here to ask me."

She took a step toward him and looked up with her big brown eyes, now brimmed with tears. "I wanted to say that I'm sorry. I'm *so* sorry. I made a huge mistake."

A tear spilled onto her cheek, but Stephenson made no effort to comfort her. If she wanted sympathy, she'd come to the wrong person.

"I don't know what I was thinking. Things seemed to be getting so serious between us I guess I... got scared, you know?"

"No, I don't."

She put her hand on his arm. "I want you to know I'm not seeing Shawn anymore."

"I don't care."

Another tear slid down her face. "I was wrong. It was stupid, and I hope someday you can forgive me. I love you, Blake."

Before he could pull away she reached her hand behind his neck and put her mouth to his. The familiar feel of her lips against his left him frozen in shock.

"Guess who got their first homicide? Oh—sorry."

He tore his mouth away from Serena's at the sound of Richards' startled voice in the doorway. Their eyes met for only a second before she turned away down the hall. He swore and pulled Serena's hand away from his neck.

"Tess, wait!"

He hurried after her down the hall.

"That wasn't what it looked like," he said as he closed the distance between them.

He could see the hurt in her eyes when she whipped around to face him.

"It looked like you were making out with your ex-girlfriend. Or is she even your ex?"

"There's nothing going on between us. I—"

She put her hand in the air to silence him. "I have to go. We're about to leave for the crime scene. I was just coming to tell you I'd gotten my first case."

She turned and marched back toward her desk. He started to follow her, then realized they were in a room filled with other detectives working their cases. Not exactly the time or place for him to try and explain what she just saw.

"You ready?" her partner asked, putting on his coat.

She glanced back in Stephenson's direction. "Yeah. Let's go."

He watched them leave before he returned to his desk. Even though he'd only known Tess a short time, the thought of losing her made him feel sick. He was about to sit down when Serena appeared at the end of the hallway. It was obvious she'd been crying. Her eyes were red and her dark eye makeup was now smudged underneath them.

It was embarrassing for her to come to his workplace and act like this. He took a deep breath and tried to suppress his anger toward her before he went to where she stood.

"You need to leave, *now*," he said in a lowered voice. "It's completely inappropriate for you to be coming here like this."

She nodded and started to leave. Stephenson let out a sigh of relief when she didn't cause more of a scene. She turned when she was only a few feet away and he held his breath for what she might say in front of his coworkers.

"Call me if you ever want to talk. I miss you."

"Goodbye, Serena."

He went back to his desk without looking back. He ran his hand through his hair after sitting down.

"Sorry, man. Richards came over and asked where you were, and I told her you were in the break room and you'd be back in a minute. I thought she'd wait here for you to come back. When she headed back there, I wasn't sure how to explain you were talking privately with Serena."

"It's okay. It's not your fault."

"She didn't look too happy when she came back down the hall. Everything okay between you two?"

"No. She walked in on Serena trying to stick her tongue down my throat."

"Yikes."

"Yeah."

"Well, I'm sure you can explain to her what really happened."

"I don't know. I hope so. But I'm sure what she saw didn't look good."

Stephenson waited until the end of the day to try talking to Richards again. When he saw her pack up her laptop, he followed her out of the homicide unit and down the stairwell.

"Tess, wait!"

His footsteps echoed in the stairway as he hurried after her.

She was three flights down before she paused on the landing half a flight below him and looked up. Her expression was both weary and annoyed.

"There is *nothing* going on between me and Serena. I know what it looked like, but believe me—"

"Stop. I don't want to hear it."

He stopped two stairs up from where she stood. "It's not what you think."

"It's best if we just keep things professional between us, okay? Getting involved with someone at work was obviously a bad idea. I need to focus on the job for right now."

He longed to move closer to her but could see she needed her space.

"There's nothing you can say to change my mind. It's better this way. I'll see you tomorrow," she said before continuing down the stairs.

He slumped down onto the steps when he heard the door open and shut at the bottom of the stairwell.

CHAPTER FORTY-THREE

Eric took the train from the airport to Newcastle and caught a bus from there to Nelson Bay. He would've hired a car, but the rental companies required too much personal information. Like a driver's license. It was information he couldn't afford to give.

The fact that he'd made it all the way to Sydney was a great sign. The cops must've not had enough evidence to arrest him. If that remained the case, they wouldn't have enough evidence to extradite him.

They might've not even realized he had gone yet. Eric knew they'd eventually figure out he fled to Australia, but he clung to the hope they wouldn't be able to do anything about it. He didn't want to take any unnecessary chances.

He rented a one-bedroom unit downtown, close to the beach. He paid cash for one week. In the meantime, he'd look for something more permanent. The weather was glorious in Nelson Bay in February. He awoke early to the bright morning sun and the sound of kookaburras laughing in the trees outside his window. He spent the morning at the beach, where he sat on the white sand and basked in summer sun. When he felt overheated, he waded into the clear blue water and watched as juvenile whiting swam past his legs.

After stopping for gelato at the marina on his way back to the apartment, he worked on his novel for the rest of the afternoon. In the evening, before sunset, he headed back down to the marina and walked along the break wall. It was alive with people this time of year. The area was home to over twenty inland and coastal beaches, making it a popular holiday destination, especially in summer.

There was a mix of both locals and tourists, fisherman, couples holding hands, and a few young families. Pelicans hovered on the rocks near the fishermen, waiting for handouts. Dolphins often surfaced along the wall during their evening feed.

Eric climbed down the rocks and admired the small reef fish swimming in the shallow waters. His father used to take him fishing along this break wall as a kid. He remembered seeing the occasional penguin swim by in the winter and sea turtles in the summer. Growing up, this magical place had seemed ordinary to him. Well, maybe not ordinary. He knew it was a great place to live, but it had also seemed normal. It was the only home he had ever known. He promised himself he would never take this paradise for granted again. After dusk, he went back to his unit and wrote late into the night.

He wrote tirelessly during that first week back in Australia. Being home gave him a new energy and he felt free to unleash his unfiltered creative genius. He even wrote a scene where he recreated Stella's murder. He figured since she was already dead, some good might as well come out of it. By the time Eric moved into his new apartment where he intended to stay as a long-term tenant, his manuscript was complete. He had a bit of editing to do, but the end was in sight.

He'd found an ad for a furnished granny flat close to downtown that was for rent by owner. It was a one-bedroom, standalone unit situated at the rear of the larger home's property. He contacted the owners, a retired couple looking to bring in a little extra cash. They hit it off right away. When he offered to pay for three months up front, they were happy to let him move in the next day.

In another week he had completely edited his manuscript. He emailed it to a dozen top literary agents in New York. Now all he could do was wait.

Eric kept up his same routine, minus the writing. He didn't stop writing intentionally, he just didn't have any ideas yet for the next novel. He walked everywhere. He even found a scenic bushwalk that ran through the natural habitat behind his granny flat. He jogged it in the early morning on days he felt especially ambitious, before the summer heat became too intense.

This town brought back so many memories for him. As he strolled down the quaint downtown enjoying his gelato, he felt like he was reliving the past.

Eric walked past his parents' house not far from the town center. He had checked the phone listings to see if they still lived there. It was the house he had grown up in. His heart ached for the family he no longer knew as he stood in the street in front of the house. He could see that his mum still kept the yard in exceptional condition. She had always taken great pride in her garden. The hedges were trimmed to symmetrical perfection, the front lawn a lush green despite the hot weather, and there wasn't a single weed in sight.

He longed to knock on the front door and tell them he was home. He fantasized about them throwing their arms around him, their eyes glistening with tears of joy. In this fantasy, they would tell him how much they'd missed him and how happy they were that their only son was finally home.

Eric snapped back to reality, knowing that would never happen. They had made themselves clear: he was dead to them. Nearly twenty years later, the words still stung.

He pushed his sunglasses farther up the brim of his nose and blinked back his tears. He took one last look at the house before turning around and heading back to his granny flat.

Eric checked his email fanatically over the next few days. Six of the literary agents had replied to him with rejection letters, one had requested his full manuscript for review, and five had yet to respond. He clung to the hope that the agent to whom he'd sent his book would fall in love with his writing and offer him representation. It nearly killed him having to wait for her decision.

He was at the local grocery store one morning picking out a perfectly ripe avocado for that night's dinner when he caught a woman, a little older than himself, staring at him from across the produce table. She was not just staring but gawking at him with a look of horror, as if he were a zombie looking for a fresh human to devour in the middle of a supermarket.

She continued staring, the whites of her eyes growing bigger by the second. It dawned on him that she didn't think he was a zombie. She thought he was the man who'd killed her sister.

She hadn't aged well. The smooth face he remembered was now marked with deep lines. She'd also gained a good sixty pounds since the last time Eric saw her. But there was no mistaking who she was. He was standing less than a meter away from Maggie, Stella's older sister.

When Maggie's shock faded, a look of anger washed over her face. She dropped the tomato she was holding and pointed her finger toward his face.

"You! You killed my sister!"

He pulled down the brim of his straw hat as he watched her become even more enraged.

"How dare you come back here!"

She was screaming now. People around them stared. A mother put her arm around her small child and pulled him away from the scene.

"I'm afraid you must have me confused with someone else," Eric said.

Her dark brown eyes seemed to pierce through him, as though she could read his thoughts.

"Don't lie to me. I know exactly who you are. You killed Stella! You killed her!"

She was shaking with anger. Her finger remained pointed at his face.

Eric set down his avocado and put both of his hands in the air.

"It's all right. I'll just go."

He left his cart and backed away.

"It will never be all right. Stella's dead!"

Now she was sobbing.

Eric turned around to face a store clerk who stared at him with a gaping mouth.

"It's okay," he said to the young man.

Eric felt surprisingly unaffected by the encounter with Stella's sister as he walked back to his place in the morning sun. It was crazy to think he wouldn't run into one of her family members sooner or later; Nelson Bay was just too small. But he hadn't considered what would happen if he did.

She couldn't prove anything, so he knew he didn't have to worry. He supposed it was possible, however, that she would let his friends at Seattle Homicide know where he was. But he doubted those detectives would be able to do anything about it. He figured if they had enough evidence to extradite him, they would have found him already.

CHAPTER FORTY-FOUR

Stephenson awoke to darkness at the sound of his alarm. He moaned, seeing the time on his phone. Four thirty. He shut off his alarm, rubbed his eyes, and got out of bed. He walked to the kitchen and was glad to see that his coffee maker had already brewed a full pot of coffee.

It had been more than two weeks since the doctor had escaped to Australia. They were tracking the IP address of the doctor's laptop and could see he was staying in Nelson Bay, New South Wales. A few days after Dwayne's murder, Dr. Leroy's ninety-year-old neighbor had reported her Buick stolen. They'd found the car parked across the street from the cafe where Dwayne was killed with the doctor's fingerprints all over the steering wheel and driver's side door. His prints were also on a plastic spoon from a half-eaten bowl of chowder left on the passenger seat. They'd started the process for his extradition from Australia but were waiting for all the paperwork to go through.

Right now, they were only able to charge him with falsifying Patricia's medical records and the murder of Dwayne Morrison. But, it was enough to bring him back into the country. Stephenson was trying to find a way to prove he killed Martin, Patricia, and Robert. It drove Stephenson mad to think the doctor was lying on a sunny beach when he should be serving time for his crimes, but that would change soon enough. Although, he was beginning to worry they might never have enough to charge him with the three other murders.

It had been weeks since he'd gone for a run before work. His ankle was still sore from the plane incident, but he needed to clear his head. After downing a cup of coffee, Stephenson got dressed and wrapped his ankle to avoid further injury. He stopped in his entry way to put on his running shoes when he realized they weren't there. He opened his small coat closet, but they weren't in there either.

He thought of the last time he'd worn them and remembered where they were. He swore as he went back to his bedroom to get his phone. He sat on the side of his bed and hesitated before sending the text. *It would be easier to buy new shoes.* Except, he loved those shoes. *Screw Serena,* he thought. He wasn't going to let her stand between him and his favorite shoes.

He sent the text and was surprised when she responded immediately despite the early hour. *I'll be home tonight between 4:30 and 5. You can come over then.*

He typed a quick reply. I'll probably still be working. Can I come over later?

Her response came as quick as the first. Sorry, I'll be showing homes for the rest of the night.

He rubbed the back of his head while he thought of what to do. He doubted she would be showing homes for *the rest of the night* and was probably just being difficult because of what happened between them at the station. It meant he would have to leave work to go to her house during rush hour before turning around to go back to station. *Fine,* he typed. He tossed his phone onto his bed before getting into the shower.

Noticing the time, Stephenson stood from his desk and threw on his coat.

Having hours of work still to do on their case, Adams looked inquisitively at him from across their desks.

"I'll be back. I just have something personal to take care of."

Adams waited for more details before responding. "Okay."

"I'll be back in just over an hour."

Stephenson rang the doorbell at Serena's home in Shoreline. With traffic, it had taken him forty-five minutes to get to her house.

The door swung open. Serena was dressed to the hilt in a form-fitting black dress and platform heels. She greeted him with a straight face.

"Come in," she said.

Stephenson shook his head. "That's okay. I have to get back to work. Would you mind getting my shoes? I thought I left them by the door anyway." He looked around at the bare floor of her entry way.

"I think they got moved," she said. "Sorry, I haven't had time to look for them. I just got home. I have to leave soon, so why don't you just come in?"

"Fine."

She held the door as he came inside.

"Would you mind taking off your coat? It's soaked from the rain, and I don't want you to drip all over my floors."

He pursed his lips. "I'm not going to drip on your floors. And I'm not staying. I just need my shoes."

A buzzer sounded from her kitchen.

"I need to check on dinner. Why don't you take a look upstairs? I think that's where I saw them last." She turned before scurrying down the hall in her tight dress and four-inch heels.

"You never cook."

"And seriously, can you take off your coat before you go up there?" she called from the kitchen.

"Sure," he muttered. He shook it off and hung it on the bottom of the banister before going upstairs.

He entered her bedroom and found his shoes on top of her perfectly made bed.

"What the—" He swiped them off her comforter and turned for the door. "Whatever."

He heard his phone ring from inside his jacket pocket when he stepped into the hall.

"Hello?" he heard Serena say.

There's no way she would answer my phone. He hurried to the top of the stairwell. His jaw dropped at the sight of her standing over his coat, holding his phone to her ear.

"What the hell are you doing?"

He flew down the steps.

"Yes, he's right here. Just a moment."

Stephenson ripped the phone from Serena's hand.

"This is Detective Stephenson."

"Umm, hi. It's Tess. I just wanted to run something by you about a case I'm working on, but you're obviously busy. I'll ask Adams."

He glared at Serena who gave him a look of wide-eyed innocence.

"No, I'm not busy. Go ahead." The phone was silent. "Are you still there?" More silence.

Stephenson checked his screen. *Call ended.*

He brought the phone to his side. His eyes narrowed at his ex-girlfriend.

"What is wrong with you?"

"Nothing's wrong with me! And you don't have to yell."

"I'm not yelling."

She raised her eyebrows and gave him a look that said, *Yes, you are.* "I figured you wouldn't want to miss a call that could be important. Sorry for trying to help you."

He opened his mouth to respond when Shawn walked in through her front door. Shawn looked as shocked to see Stephenson as he did to see Shawn.

"So, that's why you're cooking," he said to Serena.

"Blake, I know this looks bad. But you made it very clear that you didn't want to get back together."

"And you made it very clear that you'd stopped seeing Shawn."

"I did." She put her hand on his arm. "But after what you said at the homicide unit, I thought I'd give Shawn another chance."

He pulled away and threw his coat over his arm. "You're unbelievable."

He moved to the doorway, coming face-to-face with Shawn. He looked dumbfounded by Stephenson's presence. Stephenson got halfway out the door before he turned around. Serena remained still at the base of the stairs.

"I hope you ate before you came," he said to Shawn.

"Why?"

"You'll see." He stepped outside into the heavy rain and walked to his car without looking back.

CHAPTER FORTY-FIVE

Adams was on the phone for nearly ten minutes after Stephenson got back to his desk. He looked across at his partner with excitement after he hung up.

"Who was that?" Stephenson asked.

"A literary agent in New York. Apparently, our friend Dr. Leroy has written a novel. He's titled it *Inspired By Murder*. He sent the manuscript to this agent, and when she Googled him, she saw his name had come up in connection with some recent murders in the news. She started reading his manuscript and says the murders in the novel are all strangulations and have striking similarities to the murders in the Seattle news articles. She's forwarding me the email from him with his full manuscript."

"That's kind of bizarre. But I'll take whatever we can get. How come we haven't already seen that email?"

"We can't view his email activity live, and he only sent it a couple days ago. We'll be getting a report tomorrow for his email activity over the last forty-eight hours."

"Forward it to me when you get it," Stephenson said. Let's hope it's something we can use."

Stephenson started reading from the beginning and Adams from the middle so they could get through the manuscript as quickly as possible. They remained at their desks as their cohorts from the morning shift all went home for the day and were replaced by the afternoon squad.

Stephenson looked across at his partner after he finished chapter eleven of the doctor's manuscript.

"I think he peed on the floor," he said.

"What?" Adams' forehead creased between his eyebrows as he glanced up from his computer.

"At Martin and Patricia's. I think he peed on the floor. It's something he wrote in chapter eleven. CSI took a sample of Patricia's blood from the bathroom floor, right?"

"Yeah."

Stephenson picked up his desk phone. "I'll call CSI and have them test it for Dr. Leroy's DNA. The bacteria in the urine has probably degraded the DNA by now, but if it's been refrigerated, we might still be able to get his DNA from it. It's worth a shot."

A few minutes later, he hung up with the forensic technician who'd agreed to test Patricia's blood sample for the presence of the doctor's urine. Now all they could do was wait for the results.

He went back to reading the doctor's novel. He finished reading the first half at nearly the same time as Adams got to the end.

"That asshole put us in the book."

"I know." Adams grinned. "You think I look like Mark Wahlberg?"

"No."

Stephenson watched his partner's grin fade. "Really? Because I could see how you'd be mistaken for Debbie Harry."

Adams contained a laugh, seeing the unamused look on his partner's face.

"He was obviously recreating murder scenes from his own kills," Stephenson said. "There were details about Martin, Patricia, and Robert's murders in the first half of the book that would've been impossible for the doctor to know unless he killed them. It explains a lot, especially how he killed Martin and Patricia."

"Yeah, it's the same in the second half. He's clearly recounting Dwayne's death. The killer buys a burner phone on his lunch break from a gas station close to his work. I'll work on getting the security footage from the gas stations near Dr. Leroy's practice the week before Dwayne's death. There's also a chapter where a man strangles his wife and dumps her body in the ocean out of his small fishing boat. I wonder if that's what he did to Stella."

Stephenson sat back in his chair, growing more impatient every hour the doctor was still at large.

Later that afternoon, Stephenson and Adams began the slow process of going through the surveillance footage from the four gas stations closest to Dr. Leroy's office.

"Have you patched things up with Richards yet?"

Stephenson shook his head. "I couldn't convince her there was nothing going on between me and Serena. I guess it seemed hard to believe after what she saw in the break room. Anyway, she's made it clear she doesn't want anything more than a professional relationship with me."

"Well, give her some time. I'm sure she'll eventually see you were telling the truth."

He went back to work on his laptop and Stephenson tried to do the same but found he couldn't concentrate. And not because of the whole Serena-Tess situation. Something had been bothering him, and, after reading the doctor's novel, it was nagging at him even more.

"Do you still have all the traffic cam footage from around Discovery Park the night of Daisy's murder?" he asked Adams sitting across from him at his desk.

"Yeah, why?"

"We need to look through it again. I think we may have missed something."

CHAPTER FORTY-SIX

Stephenson and Adams had been knocking on doors for over an hour at Dwayne and Daisy's Lynnwood apartment building. They'd split up to make the most of their time. They had waited until five thirty to go to the apartment complex, hoping that most of residents would be home from work. So far, none of the neighbors recognized Dr. Leroy from his driver's license photo. The temperature had dropped after the sun went down, and Stephenson was starting to think this was a waste of time as he knocked on a second-story apartment door.

A skinny, thirtysomething guy wearing a dress shirt and slacks opened the door.

"Good evening," Stephenson said. "I'm Detective Stephenson from the Seattle Homicide Unit. I'm investigating the death of Daisy Colbert. She was a resident of this apartment building. I'd like to ask you some questions about what you remember about the night of January 19, and if you saw anything suspicious."

Like most of the other residents he'd talked to, the man looked surprised by the news and slightly uncomfortable at being questioned by the police.

"Okay, sure," he said.

Stephenson held up the picture of Dr. Leroy on the well-lit porch. "Have you ever seen this man?"

His eyes narrowed as he studied the picture. "Yeah," he said. "He was here a few weeks ago."

Stephenson raised his eyebrows. "Are you sure?"

He nodded. "I remember because it was snowing when I saw him on my way to my mailbox."

"And what time was this?"

The man rubbed the back of his head with his hand. "A little after ten I think. I'd just gotten my mail and was walking back to my apartment when he pulled up in a BMW. I noticed it was a nice car. Then, he hurried toward one of the ground floor apartments and bumped into me hard enough that I dropped my mail. He didn't even have the decency to say sorry."

"Do you remember what color his BMW was?"

He thought for moment. "Like a blueish-gray."

"And did you see what apartment he went in to?"

"I'm not sure if he went inside, but I watched him bang on the door until a blonde woman opened it. Then I came back to my apartment. I don't remember the unit number, but I can show you which one it was if you want."

"Yes, that'd be great."

Stephenson waited for the man to get his coat before they descended the stairs and walked across the apartment complex. Stephenson spotted Adams walking along the sidewalk. He motioned for his partner to join them.

The man stopped in front of Daisy's apartment and pointed to her front door. "That's the one."

CHAPTER FORTY-SEVEN

It was a few days after seeing Maggie at the grocery store when Eric got an email from the literary agent who'd requested his full manuscript. He hovered his cursor over her name in his inbox, holding his breath until he got up the nerve to open her email. Being that she'd had his manuscript for less than a week, her email could only mean one of two things: either she hated it and stopped reading right away, or she loved it so much she couldn't put it down.

Eric clicked on the email and braced himself for the news he was about to receive as her response filled the screen.

Dear Eric,

Thank you for sending me your full manuscript of Inspired By Murder. As a whole, I really enjoyed your story. I think with a few minor revisions I would be able to sell your novel to a major publishing house and would like to offer you representation as a literary agent. Please respond by signing the attached contract if you wish to accept this offer and we can get started on making the necessary revisions to get your novel ready to sell.

Sincerely,
Elizabeth Stone

Eric stood from his chair and raised his arms above his head as if he'd just crossed the finish line after a marathon. It was the news he'd been waiting for. He was over the moon.

He unplugged his laptop and rushed outside. He crossed the lawn and knocked on his elderly landlords' back door. They were kind enough to let him use their printer and scanner so he could get his signed contract back to the agent as soon as possible.

Even though it was now evening in New York, his agent replied immediately saying she received his contract. She added that she was confident she could sell his book to a major publishing house within the next couple of months.

Finally, the world would receive his gift. He'd always known his creative genius was likened to the great Stephen King, but it still felt surreal.

To celebrate, that night he treated himself to a three-course dinner at the most expensive waterfront restaurant in Nelson Bay. He couldn't remember food ever tasting so good. He sat outside at the busy restaurant overlooking the bay. The surface of the water was perfectly still. He finished off a bottle of wine as he watched a paddle boarder glide across the calm sea. A pod of dolphins surfaced near the shore as the sun began to set. It was a night completely opposite to the one all those years ago when he'd taken Stella's body out to its final resting place.

He enjoyed the view until it grew dark. When he got up to leave, a pretty, dark-haired woman sitting alone at a table caught his eye. He guessed she was in her early-thirties. Although she wasn't exactly his type, he felt an instant attraction to her. Their eyes met as he walked by her table and he stopped next to the empty chair across from her.

"Beautiful night, isn't it?"

"Yes, it is." She gave him a pleasant smile. "Are you here on holidays?"

"No, I've just moved back here. I grew up in Nelson Bay but spent the last twenty years in America."

Her blue eyes grew wide with fascination. "I've always wanted to do something like that."

"Do you live here?"

She nodded. "I'm from Sydney, but my family used to holiday here when I was a kid. I took a job here about five years ago. It's a beautiful place, but it can be a little too quiet. Especially in winter."

"Do you mind?" He pointed to the chair across from her.

"No, go ahead."

He pulled the chair back away the table and took a seat. "You miss the city?"

She looked into his eyes before shaking her head. "No, but I think I'm just bored with my mundane life. I'm ready for an adventure." She smiled. "Maybe I should go live in America for twenty years."

"It's exciting to move to a new country, but after a while, you start to miss home."

She played with the stem of her empty wine glass. "How long have you been back?"

"A couple weeks."

"And did you move with your family?"

"No, it's just me."

From the twinkle in her eyes, it seemed that was the answer she was hoping for.

"I'm Talia, by the way."

"I'm Eric."

"So, what do you do for work?"

"I'm a psychiatrist."

She laughed. "Oh, so are you psychoanalyzing me right now?"

He grinned. "No, I'm actually trying to get up the nerve to ask you back to my place for another drink."

She turned serious. "Oh. I probably shouldn't. I've just had two weeks off, but I have to be at work early tomorrow."

"I live only a few blocks from here. How about just one drink?"

"I live just a few blocks away too." She bit her lip before giving him a half smile. "Okay, let's go."

He put his arm on the small of her back and led her out of the bar. They made small talk on the short walk back to his place. They strolled slowly along the water, enjoying the calm evening air.

He flicked on the lights when they got to his granny flat. As usual, his place was meticulously clean. She looked around the small space before setting her purse down on his kitchen table.

"This is nice," she said.

"Thanks. Can I get you a glass of wine?"

"Sure."

"White or red?"

"White, thank you. Mind if I use your bathroom?" she asked as he pulled a glass out of his kitchen cabinet.

"Not at all. It's there on the left." He pointed to the far corner of the room.

She went into the bathroom as he poured her a large glass. He set it down next to her purse. Her wallet protruded out the top of her bag, and, out of curiosity, he picked it up. When he pulled it out, he inadvertently removed a square, black leather object that fell to the floor with a thud. His jaw dropped when he bent down, seeing that it was a Nelson Bay Police ID badge. Was she an undercover cop sent to spy on him? No wonder she'd been so eager to come back with him to his place.

Hearing the toilet flush, he stuffed her wallet and badge back into her purse before he rushed to his bedroom closet. He hurriedly pulled the shoelace out of his running shoe and slid it into his shorts' pocket. He returned to the main living area the same time Nancy Drew emerged from the loo. With his most charming smile, he handed her the large glass of wine. He'd be a gentleman and let her finish it before he choked the living daylights out of her.

Eric walked back from the beach the next morning and stopped in at his landlords' place to borrow *The Port Stephens Examiner*, as was his routine every Wednesday. The husband invited Eric in for a cup of tea and he obliged. Now that his manuscript was finished, he had all the time in the world. He led Eric to a small sitting room at the front of the house while his wife went into the kitchen to put the kettle on. His landlord sat in a worn-out armchair and motioned for Eric to take a seat on a two-seater lounge.

They had started to chat about the weather when they heard a loud rap against the front door. The old man excused himself before he got up to answer it. When he did, Eric immediately recognized Blondie's horrible American accent. He cocked his head to see him for his own eyes.

He was almost as shocked as if Stella had been standing on the doorstep. The detective was the last person on earth Eric wanted to see. His blond hair looked almost white in the Australian sunlight. A grim-faced U.S. Marshall stood behind him.

Blondie looked pleased with himself at the sight of Eric. That was not a good sign. *This can't be happening*, Eric thought. Not when he had just landed an agent and was on the brink of a publishing contract. He wanted to kill him.

Stephenson flashed his badge to Eric's landlord and ordered for him to step aside. He sauntered into the sitting room, the U.S. Marshall following behind along with a meaty Australian officer. He looked down at Eric with a look of smug gratification.

"You've come quite a long way just to tell me you finally figured out who killed Daisy," Eric said. "Let me guess, he's already dead."

"I did figure out who killed Daisy. But I'm afraid he's not dead. In fact, I'm looking at him right now."

Eric scoffed at his accusation. "You've got your facts wrong, and I hope the Seattle PD didn't pay you to fly halfway around the world based on that misinformation."

"It's not misinformation, and I actually paid for my flight myself. I wanted to see the look on your face when I arrest you for murder. Plus, I've always wanted to come to Australia. So, it was a win-win."

"Arrest me for murder?" There was no way Blondie had enough on him to arrest him. "And where's your partner?"

"He didn't think you were worth the airfare." Blondie shrugged his shoulders. "Can't say I blame him. I enjoyed your book by the way."

"My book?"

"Yes, *Inspired By Murder*. Not bad for a work of fiction. Problem is, it's not really fiction is it? You killed Stella, Patricia, Martin, Robert, and Dwayne and made them fictional characters in your book. You carried out their murders in the *exact* same way on paper as you had in real life. You killed Daisy too, but I'm not sure why you chose to leave her out of your novel."

"You haven't read my book."

"Oh, but I have. Elizabeth Stone sent it to me." He took off his sunglasses and folded them into his shirt pocket. "I'm afraid she didn't get a chance to read your full manuscript. After she saw your connection to the recent murders in the news that shared a striking resemblance to the killings in your book, she got concerned and forwarded your manuscript to my partner. But, if it makes you feel better, we quite enjoyed it.

"Anyway, in addition to the evidence we'd already compiled, we used the details from your book to find your DNA at Martin and Patricia's crime scenes and security footage of you buying the burner phone you used to text Dwayne. We'd already found your fingerprints at his crime scene and your neighbor's stolen car parked across the street from the cafe with your prints inside. We also have footage of you driving to Discovery Park where you dumped Daisy's body. When we examined the trunk of your car more closely, we found fibers that matched the sweater Daisy wore when she died. We also found small amounts of acetone and mineral spirits on your gloves matching the paint thinner you used to wipe off Robert's drumsticks after you killed him. Altogether, it's practically a confession."

His landlord's wife came into the sitting room holding two steaming mugs. She looked startled at the sight of the officers. Her wide eyes gawked between them and Eric. Stephenson ignored her presence and continued.

"We were tracking your IP address and confirmed your Australian address from the contact info you sent to Elizabeth. I also got a call from your sister-in-law saying she ran into you at her local grocery store.

Sorry that you actually don't have a literary agent. But, congratulations, you are under arrest for the murders of Martin and Patricia Watts, Daisy Colbert, Robert Benson, and Dwayne Morrison and are being extradited to the United States."

When the wife bent over the side table to Eric's right to set down his tea, Eric took the opportunity for a way out. He stood and pulled her into a choke hold. She let out a weak cry. Stephenson drew his firearm and Eric made sure her body shielded his own from the officers. Her husband looked on in silent horror from the front doorway.

"Let her go!" Blondie ordered, his gun aimed at Eric's head.

Eric tucked his head behind hers and squeezed his arm tighter around her neck. He backed into the kitchen, dragging her resistant weight with him. The U.S. Marshall also drew his weapon and aimed it at Eric. Stephenson moved with them into the kitchen, followed by the U.S. Marshall.

Eric swiped a butcher knife from the knife block on the counter. The woman began to sob as he held it to her throat.

"Drop the knife, Eric! I don't want to kill you, but I will if I have to." Blondie kept his gun fixed at Eric's head.

But he couldn't kill him. Not with the woman's head blocking Dr. Leroy's. There was no way he could get a clean shot. With the knife pressed to her throat, Eric retreated to the door behind him that led to the backyard.

"It's over—there's nowhere to go. Don't make me shoot you."

The woman's sobs grew louder, and Eric could hardly hear himself think.

"Shut up!" he yelled into her ear.

Eric quickly considered his options. He didn't have many. He decided it wouldn't do him any good to kill her. Instead, he shoved her toward Blondie's aimed gun and ran out the door. He jumped over the back-porch steps, his feet landing hard on the lawn.

He looked beyond the yard to the undeveloped bush. That's where he would have to make his run for it. He sprinted across the lawn. He'd only made it halfway when he spotted the Australian officer out the corner of his eye. The officer came at him at full speed. Eric pushed to widen the distance between them.

He heard Blondie jump off the deck and make a what sounded like a rough landing onto the grass. He knew he wouldn't be far behind. Luckily, Eric was in good shape from all his recent exercise.

He reached the bush trail and forced himself to run faster. Eric knew he had the advantage now since the bush was familiar to him. He maneuvered easily through the dips and curves of the terrain. He could hear the heavy footsteps of the officers on his tail but managed to keep the distance between them until the trail came to an end.

Eric ran to the open field and couldn't believe his good luck. The scenic flight helicopter that was usually parked in the field during his morning runs was in mid-takeoff, only a foot off the ground. He dashed toward it at lightning speed.

Eric ran against the wind force created by its rotor blades. Knife in hand, he grasped the door handle before it lifted out of his reach and leapt onto the landing skid. He slid the door open before he threw himself into the empty seat next to the pilot. The pilot looked so startled when he turned to him, Eric was afraid he might lose control of the chopper. In his desperation for a safe escape, Eric thrust the knife against his throat like he'd done to his landlord.

The rhythmic pulsation from the spinning blades overhead muted the screams from the couple in the backseat.

Eric brought his face closer to the pilot's. "Go!" he yelled.

The pilot broke Eric's stare to look out the windshield as he lifted the lever in his left hand. Keeping the knife against his throat, Eric let out a sigh and leaned back in his seat as the pilot did what he was told.

Eric felt two hands clamp around his left ankle that dangled out the side of the helicopter. He grabbed the inside of the open doorframe to stable himself and carefully leaned his head over the side. They were nearly ten feet off the ground. Blondie hung in the air, all his weight suspended from Eric's lower leg. *What a showoff.*

Eric pressed his hand against the wall of the helicopter and fought to stay inside the aircraft while he shook his foot as violently as he could against Blondie's weight. One of the detective's hands fell away from Eric's leg. Blondie grabbed onto the landing skid before reaching back for his leg. Eric looked frantically for his seatbelt but couldn't risk taking the knife away from the pilot's throat or his hand away from the doorframe to buckle it.

The Australian officer stood in the field looking up at them. Blondie hollered something to him that Eric couldn't make out through the noise from the rotor blades.

His foot was numb from Blondie's tight grip around his ankle. Eric watched Stephenson shake his legs above the officer's head.

"We need more weight!" he heard Blondie yell.

Eric watched in horror as the hefty officer jumped and grabbed onto one of Stephenson's legs with both arms. Eric pulled his head inside the helicopter as it dipped to the side.

Eric spotted the pilot's elbow a second before it slammed into his temple. He lost his grip on the doorframe and fell toward the open door. He was searching for something to grab hold of when the pilot shoved his torso. Eric toppled out of the aircraft. His hand skimmed Blondie's pant leg on the way to the ground.

He landed flat on his back against the grass, air leaving his lungs upon impact. He had a déjà vu of landing at the bottom of Patricia's staircase next to Martin's still-warm corpse. Only instead of a chandelier crashing down on him, he was almost crushed by Blondie and his Australian sidekick. Fortunately, both landed a few feet away.

Despite the pain from the fall, Eric got to his feet as fast as he could. He dashed toward the motorway across from the field. He'd only made it a few steps when he was tackled from the side. They went down hard before skidding to a stop on the lawn.

Eric felt a knee dig into his back as he tried to get up. The officer wrenched Eric's hands behind him and placed them in handcuffs. Eric recognized Blondie's legs come to a stop in front of him on the lawn. Eric could see his smug look of satisfaction had returned when the Australian officer pulled him to his feet.

They were eye to eye and, for a moment, neither of them spoke.

"Let's go," Blondie finally said, grabbing him by the arm.

Eric felt like crying as he read him his Miranda rights. *No literary agent? How could that be?* It wasn't fair. He was destined to be a bestselling author. As Blondie led him through the bush trail, Eric decided he wasn't going to spend the rest of his life in an American prison. They might even give him the death penalty. Australia had done away with capital punishment a long time ago. Plus, this was his home. He'd wasted twenty years living in America, and there was no way he was going to let Blondie take him back now.

"I have to confess something," Eric said.

Stephenson stopped in the middle of the trail. "What?"

"I killed someone."

"You killed several someones. We can stop at the Nelson Bay Police Department if you want to tell me what happened."

"No. I killed a cop. Last night."

CHAPTER FORTY-EIGHT

Stephenson moved in front of Eric and looked him in the eyes.

"What did you say?"

On their way to arrest Eric, the Nelson Bay detective had told Stephenson that one of his colleagues hadn't shown up for work that morning and they hadn't been able to get ahold of her.

"Her name was Talia," Eric said without emotion.

The detective who'd come to help them arrest Eric grabbed Eric's shoulder from behind and swung him around.

"You're lying!"

Stephenson watched the detective's face turn red with anger.

"I buried her in the bush right over there." He pointed to a clearing about ten feet from the trail.

The detective ran toward the clearing and used his hands to dig through the recently disturbed native grass. Stephenson left Eric with the U.S. Marshall and ran after the Australian detective. The U.S. Marshall grabbed Eric by the arm and pulled him toward the clearing.

"Stop! We need to wait for the forensic team. You might disturb the evidence if she's actually buried here," Stephenson said.

"She might still be alive!" he yelled and continued to dig through the sandy ground with his hands.

Stephenson put his hand on the front of the large detective's shoulder. "She won't be alive if what Eric said is true. Don't risk contaminating her crime scene if he's telling the truth."

"A little to the left," Eric said when he and U.S. Marshall approached the site.

The detective shook Stephenson's hand away and, per Eric's instructions, clawed into the soil to the left of where he'd been digging. Stephenson felt a knot form in his stomach as he watched him dig an even deeper hole with his bare hands. An image of his late partner's dead body ran through his head. No matter how much he tried, it was something he could never erase. Even though Rodriguez had been gone over a year, the memory of finding her the morning after she'd been killed was fresh in his mind.

"Talia!"

The detective's shout brought Stephenson out of his thoughts. A pale, cyanotic hand lay exposed in the dirt at the bottom of the two-foot hole.

"I'll call it in," the U.S. Marshall said, pulling out his phone as the detective worked frantically to unearth her body.

"I know this is hard, but I think we should wait for forensics," Stephenson said, knowing she was beyond saving.

Ignoring Stephenson, the detective removed enough dirt to expose her face. Recognizing her dead face, he sank back on his heels and brought the back of his hand to his mouth.

"It's her," he choked.

Stephenson looked down solemnly at the woman's face, enraged by her death and the memory of Rodriguez.

"You son of a bitch!" he heard the detective yell.

Stephenson turned to Eric, who wore a slight smirk as he overlooked the scene. The detective jumped to his feet and charged him. The U.S. Marshall quickly stepped in between them. Stephenson rushed toward the detective and gave him a shove in the opposite direction of Eric and the U.S. Marshall who blocked him. Although Dr. Leroy would've deserved it, Stephenson and the U.S. Marshall struggled to block the infuriated detective from delivering any blows.

"I'm afraid this is going to halt his extradition to America," the U.S. Marshall said to Stephenson once the Australian detective had calmed down. "The Australian government won't release him until after he goes to trial. If he's convicted, we won't be able to extradite until he's completed his sentence here in Australia."

"New South Wales has a mandatory life sentence without parole for killing a cop," the Australian detective added.

"But no death penalty." Eric flashed a disgusting smile at Stephenson.

Stephenson knew he wouldn't have faced it anyway. The Australian government had requested the death penalty not be used in Eric's sentencing upon extradition, and Washington State had agreed to those terms. But he was too repulsed to offer any rebuttal to the sadistic doctor.

The four of them remained in the clearing by Talia's dead body and waited in silence for the forensic team to arrive.

CHAPTER FORTY-NINE

An hour later, Stephenson and the U.S. Marshall led Eric to the front of the house where their borrowed squad car waited to take Eric to the Nelson Bay Police Station. The Australian detective had stayed behind to continue processing the scene with the forensic team. A handful of journalists stood by their vehicle when they approached. Their cameras flashed as they captured Eric being led to the car in handcuffs. When they got closer, the reporters all shouted questions at once.

"Is it true you killed your wife in Nelson Bay twenty years ago?"

"How many people have you murdered?"

"What do you want to say to Stella Flemming's family?"

"Does your family know you're here?"

"That's enough," Blondie said. "Give us some space."

He pushed him into the car and buckled his seatbelt. The press continued to spout questions and take pictures from outside. Eric sank back into his seat. He couldn't believe he'd been duped by some idiot cop into thinking that he had gotten an agent. It was an even bigger blow than getting arrested.

Eric took one last look at his hometown through the backseat window as they drove through Nelson Bay's town center. They passed a bookstore that displayed a bestselling hardcover in its front window and his heart ached. That should've been his book.

Then it dawned on him. He was an international fugitive. A media sensation. He felt a smile surface when the car pulled out onto the gumtree-lined motor way, knowing the headlines of his arrest would ensure his book a number one spot on the *New York Times* bestseller list.

Eric remained lost in thought for the rest of the short drive. Later that afternoon, he sat alone in an interview room at the Nelson Bay Police Department. He couldn't believe they were arresting him for Daisy's murder on top of all the others. He knew Blondie and Marky Mark weren't exactly Seattle homicide's best and brightest. At least not Marky Mark. But even a child could've figured out that Dwayne killed Daisy. Eric shuddered at the thought of beautiful Daisy ever being with such a lowlife.

Maybe he should've handed her phone over to them instead of destroying it. He didn't think he was in jeopardy of being arrested for a murder he had nothing to do with. He'd do the time for the murders he was guilty of, but he refused to go down for something he didn't do.

If only he had gone to her address that night after she left his practice for the last time. Maybe he could've rescued her from that pathetic loser. He suddenly had a strange recollection that he'd tried. On his way home from killing Patricia. She was alone, Dwayne wasn't even there. But she refused to come with him. She actually chose Dwayne over him.

She told him she'd only stayed the night at his apartment because she didn't want to go home to Dwayne. It had nothing to do with Eric. She told him she was leaving Dwayne, but that didn't mean she'd be desperate enough to jump into another relationship with someone his age. *His age*. That's when he lost it.

An image of his secretary's final moments came to his mind. She'd looked so peaceful when he finally pulled his hands away from her delicate neck. So peaceful, it had almost made him feel as though she were still alive.

EPILOGUE

Stephenson pulled a beer out of the fridge, wishing he had someone to celebrate with. It was Friday night, and he'd only been back from Australia for twenty-four hours. Adams was out of town for the weekend. He had tried explaining to Tess again before he left for Australia that there was nothing going on between him and Serena, but she was adamant she wanted to be nothing more than coworkers.

Dr. Leroy had given his full confession to the Nelson Bay Police for the murder of Talia Palamo. The doctor was being held at Cessnock Correctional Centre, a large maximum-security prison an hour inland of Nelson Bay, while he waited to go to trial for her murder. He would probably never be tried for the murders of Stella, Martin, Patricia, Robert, Daisy, and Dwayne, but at least their families would have the reassurance he was no longer living as a free man. Although, Stephenson felt he'd let them down by not bringing the doctor back to be convicted for the killings of their loved ones.

The only good thing about the trip was that the pursuit had served as a distraction from the emptiness he felt from losing Richards so soon after falling for her. Even though he'd only known her a short while, he felt they had an instant connection, as if he'd known her a lot longer. Now that it was over, she kept finding a way back into his thoughts.

He took a swig of his beer as he walked into his living room. He was about to turn on the TV, for lack of anything better to do, when he heard a soft knock at his door. He opened it to find Tess standing on his front porch in the pouring rain.

"Mind if I come in?" she asked.

He opened the door wider. "Of course not."

She stepped inside and pulled down the fur-lined hood of her down jacket, exposing her long, blonde hair. There was an awkward silence between them. Stephenson wondered if he should invite her into the living room to sit down. She spoke before he could ask.

"I just wanted to say I'm sorry I didn't believe you when you told me there was nothing going on between you and Serena."

"What made you change your mind that I was telling the truth?"

"Adams. While you were in Australia, he told me the whole story. How you caught her cheating on you and then what happened that day she came to see you at the precinct. He also said you want nothing to do with her and are head over heels for me. Is that true?"

Adams never ceased to surprise him. Despite their differences at times, his partner always had his back. "Yes, it's true."

A slight smile surfaced on her lips, and he moved toward her.

"Why don't we start over? Maybe I take you to dinner over the weekend?"

"That sounds nice. How about after you watch the Super Bowl with me?"

"You have tickets?" he asked, taking a small step back.

She let out a laugh. "Sorry, no. My brother is having a Super Bowl party, even though they didn't make it. A bunch of his teammates will be there. Want to come?"

"Love to."

He moved toward her and placed a hand gently on either side of her face. He felt her hand on the lower part of his back, pulling him closer. Their lips met, and he didn't think about Dr. Leroy again for the rest of the night.

WANT MORE?

Get your FREE bonus content and deleted scenes, including an ALTERNATE ENDING to INSPIRED BY MURDER at AUDREYJCOLE.COM/sign-up

Detectives Blake Stephenson and Tess Richards return in the next Emerald City Thriller

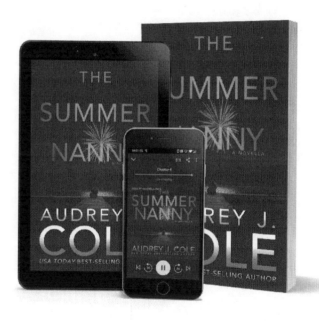

It was the perfect summer job— until it turned into her worst nightmare

Also By AUDREY J. COLE

EMERALD CITY THRILLERS

THE RECIPIENT

INSPIRED BY MURDER

THE SUMMER NANNY: A NOVELLA

VIABLE HOSTAGE

FATAL DECEPTION

STANDALONES

THE PILOT'S DAUGHTER

THE FINAL HUNT

ONLY ONE LIE (DECEMBER 2022)

ABOUT THE AUTHOR

Audrey J. Cole is a registered nurse and a writer of thrillers set in Seattle. After living in Australia for the last five years, Audrey has returned to the Pacific Northwest where she resides with her husband and two children.

Connect with Audrey:

f facebook.com/AudreyJCole

BB bookbub.com/authors/Audrey-J-Cole

instagram.com/AudreyJCole/

You can also visit her website:

www.AUDREYJCOLE.com